EVERY DAY I BALL
(Young Adult Version)

BY MICHAEL SANDERS

"Pleasure without conscience
Knowledge without character
Life can change with a single drop."

Every Day I Ball (Young Adult Version) © 2013

ISBN: 978-0-692-45376-6

Published by:

"Pleasure without conscience
Knowledge without character
Life can change with a single drop."

This book is dedicated to my two daughters Michaela Sacha Sanders (Babygirl) & Maliyah Renae Sanders (Cupcake)

"Pleasure without conscience
Knowledge without character
Life can change with a single drop."

''Pleasure without conscience
Knowledge without character
Life can change with a single drop.''

To Daniel Bernstein

6/29/15

I thank GOD for your belief and Vision for my Son GOD has truly put you on your path for so many reasons. Keep being you

Najee Rasheed

#MIZZWERK

"Pleasure without conscience
Knowledge without character
Life can change with a single drop."

Patience is Everything

Dedication

It is finally done, but the trilogy is yet to come. I want to thank God for making this all happen. My family-Mom, Dad, my brother, Jamie, my beautiful daughters mother, Letrice Warren, Tyler and Whirlee. My mentor, the mighty Joe Young Jr. Special thanks to Deanna Hassan for her smarts and creativity on the editing and teacher's guide. Your knowledge is a weapon. Thanks also to other editors Gretchen Ruiz, Agron Belica, Rich Alden, Katrina Zickwolf, graphic designer Kyle Young-good looking...

"Pleasure without conscience
Knowledge without character
Life can change with a single drop."

ABOUT THE AUTHOR

Michael Sanders is CEO and founder of the company *EDIB Immortality*; a revolutionary company designed to allow individuals to have the ability to work hard forever for their stay here on Earth. We strive to provide a positive alternative and hardworking attitude so individuals can build self-confidence and self-esteem while becoming more well-rounded and highly skilled as they are working towards success.

Michael enjoyed an international career of pro basketball for ten years. Now he wants to share the gifts and ideas with those who aim for the limitless, also choose to work hard, want to become the best at their craft and are fearless to see where their skills will take them.

"Pleasure without conscience
Knowledge without character
Life can change with a single drop."

My level:

This goes out to the woman
who helped me reach my level,
it's the little things that count.
She knows who she is.

"Pleasure without conscience
Knowledge without character
Life can change with a single drop."

EVERY DAY I BALL

Prologue

It was just like any other day for these two 10 year old best friends, Mizzier Sanders and Myshawn Greene. They got together to partake in what could be considered their daily ritual; hop out of bed and head to the park to hang around on the monkey bars or just chill on the swings. However, the turn of events that day forever changed their lives.

The little league coach looked at the two kids standing on the sidelines, hoping he would even the odds if one of them agreed to play. Mizz and Razah had been there for quite some time watching the other kids playing football. Both looked like they could handle themselves on the field.

"Son, you wanna play?"

"Sure," Razah spoke up first, "but I never played before, 'cept in the projects. So, I'm not very good."

"No matter, we only need one and that means you."

"Man, I'm gonna go watch the guys play some b-ball," Mizz said as he turned and headed across the street. He stood behind the chain link fence and watched as one of the players drained a three to end the game.

"Hey, you wanna play?" asked one of the guys who had been waiting on the sidelines to get next.

Mizz looked around and pointed at himself, "Who, me?"

"Yeah, you. Come on."

Hearing the screams from the football field, Mizz chilled while his teammates hustled back to play some D. He looked over and saw Razah killing, juking, catching and

"Pleasure without conscience
Knowledge without character
Life can change with a single drop."

scoring touchdowns. The other little kids and even the coaches were cheering Razah on, watching in disbelief as Razah looked like a pro that had been playing all his life. 'Word, what the?' one of them muttered to himself.

"Where did you get this?" the other one asked.

"He just walked up and I asked him if he wanted to play."

Action on the court was like a carbon copy of what was happening on the football field; Mizz was crossing dudes and dropping dimes all over the court as if he were a little "The Answer," Allen Iverson.

"This kid is serious!" One of the players shook his head as he watched.

"How old are you?"

"Ten."

In the Spotlight

"Thanks for tuning in, this is _Sportscenter_ and I'm your host, Sage Steele. Today's _Sportscenter_ Spotlight is on Mizzier Sanders and Myshawn Greene, two home boys from Waterbury, Connecticut who are two huge names in the world of high school sports. Mizzier, better known as Mizzary or Mizz and Myshawn, also known as Razah, for his sharp style and clean moves on the field, are both the number one ranked players in their respective high school sports. Mizzary is Sacred Heart High School's point guard, ranked first in his class academically and is president of the National Honor Society. Razah is Sacred Heart's running back, ranked second in his class and is vice-president of the National Honor Society. They are both fifteen-year-old sophomores and, as you would expect, they are the most popular duo; not only in their city and state, but also in the

"Pleasure without conscience
Knowledge without character
Life can change with a single drop."

nation.

These two kids have the whole package, including the game and the brains, and are both being heavily recruited by big-time universities. As sophomores, some analysts say they could both go pro right now and not only play, but also be effective and do work. They haven't seen the likes of these student-athletes in these two sports in decades. In basketball, as the likes of Lebron James, Mizzary is America's new phenom. Razah on the other hand, has athleticism and lateral movement that we haven't seen since the likes of Walter Payton and Barry Sanders. He's like Michael Jackson with a football! Academically, they both have the ACT and SAT scores to qualify for college eligibility.

In their spare time, these two remarkable young men co-teach an ACT/SAT course. I hear Mizzier is a genius with an IQ of 168. These two boys are a force with which to be reckoned! The best part is that they are the best of friends and neighbors. Wow, what a great story! Folks, if that doesn't inspire you, get someone to check your pulse, because you're not breathing! This is Sage Steele reporting from _Sportscenter_. "

Business as Usual

Mizzier's alarm buzzed, waking him to thoughts about what the new school year will bring. He stretched and rolled out of bed, kissed his chain, tapped his chest twice, looked up and said a little prayer; a ritual that he developed while in grade school and one that he has followed religiously since. Good ball players have their little superstitions and this was his.

Surrounded by posters of Allen Iverson, Michael

"Pleasure without conscience
Knowledge without character
Life can change with a single drop."

Jordan, a few bikini models, clothes on the floor, shoes scattered and school books lying around, his room looked pretty typical for a fifteen year old and not what you would expect for a rising star genius athlete.

"Yo Mizz, you ready?" shouted Razah from the fence outside of Mizz's window.

"Yeah, be right down," Mizz replied.

Today was the first day of school after a hot and crazy summer. Only sophomores, Mizz and Razah were being scouted by schools across the country and those schools across were eager to speak to them. As they made their way, Mizz could see Razah wanted to share details about his adventures from last night.

"Yo Mizz, what's good? That chick was crazy last night," Razah said with a smile on his face.

"Yo, you had a good time?" Mizz wanted details.

"Oh yeah B, she was cool," Razah was smiling.

"Word, you mad nutty," Mizz said with a slight smirk. Changing the subject, he asked, "Anyways, how's your mom doin'?"

"Same ol' same ol' you feel me?" Razah answered in a somber tone revealing just a little of the pain he was feeling inside from his home situation.

As they continued toward school, used crack bottles snapped under their feet while the daytime fiends stepped out from their dark corners to see if they could persuade the duo into giving them a few dollars. Mizz and Razah crossed the street to avoid the hassle, and couldn't help but look back to take one last look at all the hood stars that had rolled out of bed nice and early to catch the school crowd. After all, every dealer knows that if you get to them early, you have a customer for life. No matter how short that life

"Pleasure without conscience
Knowledge without character
Life can change with a single drop."

was, they would still pay to play. No strangers to the game, Mizz and Razah ran into their good friend Leak hustling on the corner. Leak was a former teammate of Mizz's in Little League who dropped out of school to hustle.

"Yo Leak, what up dude? You stay getting money B? I wish I could get down wit' that, G." Mizz said as he half-hugged, half-bumped Leak.

Following Mizz's lead, Razah spoke up. "Yeah Leak, man. I saw that new whip you got. It's dope."

"You cats playin' them sports and you dudes is mad smart. That school stuff wasn't for me. I saw you two clowns on _Sportscenter_ last night. You two really reppin' the hood, you feel me?" Leak said.

"I feel you G." Mizz responded. "We tryin' but we got no paper, no whip for the chicks. Nothin'." Mizz and Razah rubbed their fingers together as if they were counting money.

"Well here you go, a lil' somethin'. It'll hold you down for a minute," Leak smiled knowing that staying on their good side may pay off for him some day.

"Word! Leak, good look. A hundred for both of us? That's what's up," said Mizz excitedly.

"You two want a ride to school?" Leak asked the boys.

"Nah, we good." Mizz said knowing Leak didn't have a driver's license. "Stay up Leak, holla back," Mizz and Razah turned to continue on to school.

"No doubt. Remember, stay focused." reminded Leak.

"No doubt," Mizz and Razah answered back.

Continuing on toward school they passed burned-out cars and boarded-up abandoned buildings where

"Pleasure without conscience
Knowledge without character
Life can change with a single drop."

apartments were used as crack houses. It was a scene that these two had known their entire lives and they were determined to make it distant memory.

Mizz breathed hard as the smell of urine and vomit filled his nostrils. "We gotta get money. My Mom just got laid off and my Pops ain't doin' nothin' either. We just barely makin' ends meet. I gotta think of somethin'."

"Yo, I been thinkin' the same thing for the past month. Mizz, somethin' gotta give fo' real," Razah said as he walked by a man lying face down in the gutter.

Mizz thought a moment and then said, "Yo, you know we can get money from these colleges that's recruiting us, but you know the game though. We gonna be obligated to these dudes. I'm not tryin' to send mixed signals."

"Yeah, and it's illegal anyway. Even these people 'round our block, especially Leak, would hit us off," Razah said.

"That's different, he fam," Mizz replied.

"True, true, whateva though," agreed Razah.

"Yeah, whateva," Mizz replied as his mind drifted off.

As they approached Sacred Heart High School, groups of kids gathered outside smoking and taking their last hits before the morning bell. Mizz and Razah learned to avoid the before school crowds and made their way towards a side entrance. After all, they had a rep they needed to maintain and they learned the further away they were from the everyday nonsense, the closer they got to their goals.

As they passed a bulletin board with advanced classes offered for the school year, Mizz tapped the list and

"Pleasure without conscience
Knowledge without character
Life can change with a single drop."

said, "Let's go see the guidance counselor and register for these classes. Since we both in the Honor Society, let's ask Mr. Holmes to give us college classes."

"Mizz, I'm feelin' your 'G' right now. Maybe out of these classes, somethin' will pop off to give us ideas on how to get some money," commented Razah.

"Razah. That's what I'm talkin' 'bout," Mizz agreed.

"That's why you my dude," Razah said as he pushed Mizz ahead of him.

"Come on, let's change up this street mentality and let's get corporate. You know how we do," Mizz explained.

"Yes sir," Razah said pretending to straighten a tie. With about fifteen minutes before their first class, they made their way to the guidance counselor's office. After the _Sportscenter_ piece last night, Mizz and Razah were now looked upon as true celebrities. Friends and teachers stopped them in the hall to share their thoughts, tell them congratulations and offer other meaningless words that they hoped would keep them in the boys' thoughts when they went pro. It was cynical to think that way, but that's how people are, and that will never change.

"Come in boys," Mr. Holmes called out from behind his desk as he spotted Mizz and Razah standing at his door. "Hey guys, how was your summer? I see that these colleges are really after you two, heavily."

"Yes sir, they are most definitely trying to get our attention," Mizz responded.

"We need to stay focused on our goals and we believe everything will fall into place," Myshawn added.

"Well, you fellas have the grades, so it is all up to you. Anyway, what can I do for you two?" asked the

"Pleasure without conscience
Knowledge without character
Life can change with a single drop."

counselor.

"Well, Mr. Holmes, we want to take some college courses. We're up for the challenge," Mizzier said with confidence that was well beyond his fifteen years.

"We love making adjustments and this is a new endeavor we'd like to conquer," Myshawn said with equal confidence.

"Wow, you guys continue to impress me every day. No problem. Here is the list of classes. Just choose what's up your alley and we will take it from there. Look it over and get back to me next week with your decisions."

"We really appreciate you, Mr. Holmes," they said as they smiled and left the office.

It was five minutes before their first class of their sophomore year. Little did they know at the time how much this year would impact the rest of their lives.

Mizz looked at Razah, "We need to get on this paper chase."

"No doubt Mizz, I'll see you later. We'll get up after school. I've got football practice, so I'll meet you at your crib 'bout eight," Razah said.

"No doubt," Mizz said. They bumped fists and headed their separate ways.

The day dragged for Razah as he thought about what he and Mizz talked about that morning. He needed money and so did Mizz, but how would they get it? He knew they could call in favors from the recruiters, but that could come back to bite them. They could hustle, but how much could that get them? Nah, he thought, it had to be something big and fast. Razah knew he wasn't the thinker, but he was sure that Mizz would come up with something. The last bell of the day rang and Razah headed for football

"Pleasure without conscience
Knowledge without character
Life can change with a single drop."

practice.

At football practice, Coach Caine called Razah over for a little recruiting chat. "So, what do you think, Myshawn? Are you leaning towards any specific colleges yet?" the coach asked.

"Which schools should I be talking to?" Razah was curious the coach's opinion on schools.

"Well, just to name a few conferences – the ACC, PAC 10, Big 10, Big 12 and the SEC," coach said with a smile.

"So, what you sayin'? I can go anywhere I want?" Razah was somewhat surprised. He was confident of his skills on the field but didn't realize so many others felt that way.

"That's what I'm sayin'. Anywhere you want," the coach was enjoying telling Razah this news.

As Razah walked out of the locker room after practice, he thought about the possibilities that were in front of him. Soon, those thoughts were replaced by images of hot cars, hot chicks and more and more loot. Sadly, all of that would have to wait at least three years, if not more, depending on how his college career went. 'Nah,' he thought to himself, 'Bump that, 'I ain't waiting that long. I guess it's time to go see what's really good wit Mizz's plan."

Mizz looked at his black G-shock watch. It was just a little after eight and Razah would be there shortly. He still couldn't believe how far the two of them had come and still had no paper to show for it. Bread was the goal and they had to figure out a way to get some. After looking at the school schedule and jotting down some ideas for the two of them to go over, Mizz stood up and walked over to

"Pleasure without conscience
Knowledge without character
Life can change with a single drop."

the window. He saw Razah at the door and motioned for him to come on up.

"What's good?" greeted Razah.

"I got a plan fo' real. I been checkin' out these classes for us dude. If everything goes according to plan, we be paid," Mizz said excitedly.

"You know I'm good wit' everything. What's poppin'?" Razah had been waiting for this all day.

"Some of the research I been doin' is crazy, but this is ill. Well, after talkin' to Mr. Holmes, he said we can get a jump on stuff. So, here are the classes – Organic Chemistry and Bio Chemistry are two just to get started," Mizz stated sure of himself.

"Worrrrddddd u serious dude!!! Sounds illmatic? Are you sure we can handle these classes?" questioned Razah.

"This is some high power stuff, feel me?" Mizz answered.

"I can see. How did you come up wit' this crazy stuff, G?" asked Razah.

"Just readin' this, word up, I'm feeling your G. Remember the internship I did at the pharmacy, this summer? Pharmaceutical Compounding is how you make a drug into a tablet," Mizz said.

"Drugs?" a concerned look washing over Razah's face.

"Yeah, but this ain't heroine, crack cocaine, weed or the usual death wish. This combination is more potent, completely legal and the way we gonna freak it is crazy," Mizz said with confidence.

"Word?" questioned Razah.

"Word, we gonna make it into a piece of candy,"

"Pleasure without conscience
Knowledge without character
Life can change with a single drop."

Mizz said while smiling.

"Candy? Huh? ," Razah asked while he nodded his head wanting to hear more.

"Word. Now we gotta figure how we gonna get the money for the machinery to make it. That's what's botherin' me," Mizz's brow was furrowed with thought.

"I'll get a plan." Now it was Razah's turn, "I got you."

"What?" Mizz asked.

"I trust you, now you trust me," Razah said, his wheels already turning, inspired by Mizz's plan.

"No doubt. I trust you, do your thing," Mizz stated.

"A'ight Mizz. I'm out. I'll have a plan in the next day or two." Razah said encouragingly.

Razah's Reasons

The walk to school seemed a little bit different to Mizz as he and Razah discussed their future. They could smell the paper in the air as they headed into school and went straight to Mr. Holmes's office.

"Hey boys," Mr. Holmes greeted them.

"We have our classes," Mizz and Razah said with just a slight cockiness in their voices.

"Okay, let me see what you have. Geez! Wow! These classes are extremely difficult. You guys ready for this?" the counselor questioned.

"Of course we are," they looked at each other and then back at Mr. Holmes.

"Well, if it was anyone else, I'd say no way, but you guys can pull this off," Mr. Holmes said as he updated their classes in the computer system. He retrieved the printouts, handed them their new class schedules and shook their

"Pleasure without conscience
Knowledge without character
Life can change with a single drop."

hands.

"Good luck, boys," Mr. Holmes said as the boys turned and left his office, smiling and thinking about what lay ahead for them. School seemed to be the last thing on their minds as they anticipated the photo shoot with ESPN magazine that was set for them at the end of the day.

At last, the final bell rang and classes were dismissed. They made their way to the school's gym where the photographers had already set up their equipment and were waiting for the dynamic duo to arrive. The photo shoot started with still shots of Mizz on his home court. After about half an hour of lighting the gym up like a Christmas tree, they moved over to the football field to grab some frames of Razah in action. Another half-hour passed and the camera crew moved the shoot to the front of the school where they took shots of both Mizz and Razah together for the cover.

When the shoot was over, Mizz walked with Razah back to the football field where practice had already started. "You come up wit' the plan?" Mizz asked.

"And you know this man!" Razah responded enthusiastically.

"No doubt? Cool, we can talk later." Mizz said.

"I'll come over your crib after practice." Razah said putting on his helmet. They bumped fists and headed their separate ways.

Later on that night, Razah made his way to Mizz's crib. To his surprise, Mizz's mom answered the door.

"Hey nappy head, how you doing?" she greeted him warmly with a wink.

"I been good. How's everything with you?" he asked politely with a smile.

"Pleasure without conscience
Knowledge without character
Life can change with a single drop."

"It's going," she said with a distressed look upon her kind face. Once considered a beautiful woman, the years of hardship had taken their toll. "I'll go get Mizz," she said as she headed toward Mizz's room.

Razah had been inside Mizz's crib a million times before but tonight things looked a little different. They weren't different in a physical sense, but his perspective was just different. The same old checkered couch was in its spot. The same stains were on the living room rug and the same cream-colored paint was still peeling in the same places. Tonight, all of these things began to feel like future memories that Razah and Mizz would recall when talking about what life used to be like. Razah's mind jumped back to the present as Mizz entered the room.

"What's good? Let's take a walk. I don't wanna talk in the house," Mizz whispered.

"I feel you," Razah responded as he opened the front door and walked out into the still warm night air.

"Holla at me. What you come up wit'?" Mizz asked as they made their way down the street.

"A heist," Razah replied nonchalantly.

"What?!" Mizz wasn't sure he had heard his friend correctly.

"You heard me bro, a heist!" Razah said sounding excited.

"Wow! You dumb nutty," Mizz responded as if Razah was crazy. "How do you expect us to pull that off? I mean, what do we know about stuff like that?"

"Have faith in me Mizz, like I have faith in you," Razah said.

"No doubt, I do. I just woulda never thought that we'd be talking 'bout this type of thing," commented Mizz,

"Pleasure without conscience
Knowledge without character
Life can change with a single drop."

sounding concerned and shaking his head still, not believing what he was hearing.

Changing the subject, Razah asked, "I feel you, but for real, how is it on the home front?"

"It ain't good. Just barely makin' ends meet. You feel me? How 'bout you?" Mizz asked.

"Same. Why you think I'm always comin' over your crib, B? It's bad, Mizz," Razah answered sadly with a frown on his face.

"One thing left to do. Let's get this money," encouraged Mizz.

"No doubt," Razah said as they dapped each other up and went their separate ways for the night.

The walk home from Mizz's house was short but Razah had already started to put together more details of his plan. They knew the right people in the right places to make it work. It had to work, because they needed money and they couldn't wait for their skills to pay the bills. No, they had to take matters into their own hands and create their own destiny.

Neither one were able to sleep that night as they paced around their rooms, each thinking about the next step of the plan.

"Dang!" Razah said to himself staring up at the ceiling, as if calling on some extra help. 'I need to come with a plan of attack and a team of wolves, not goons, for this,' Razah thought to himself as he climbed into bed.

"Pfft!" Mizz said as he walked around still trying to get his head around what his friend had planned. "I need to get money. Now Pops ain't workin' an' Moms be trippin'. Man, I really need to get on my G, fo' real," Mizz mumbled to himself as he got into bed and turned out the

"Pleasure without conscience
Knowledge without character
Life can change with a single drop."

light for the night.

The next morning Razah sensed something weird about the house as he awoke. There was no noise, no sound, no yelling, nothing. He rolled out of bed and went to his little brother's room to find him still sleeping. Mikey had just turned seven and thought of Razah as his hero, even had pictures of his big brother from last year's championship game hanging over his bed. Razah looked at him, closed his door, and then went down the hall to his mother's room to find her bed was empty.

'What the...?' Razah thought to himself as he heard the sounds of his little brother waking up.

"Where's mommy?" Mikey stood there in his Sponge Bob pajamas looking to Razah for an answer, any answer.

"Not sure, lemme see if there's a note. Get ready for school, okay?" Razah instructed trying to hide his concern.

"Okay," Mikey turned around and went back to his room.

Razah looked around the house and didn't find a note or anything to indicate where his mother had gone. He went back to his brother's room. Not wanting to worry his little brother, Razah just said, "I'm gonna get dressed and walk you to the bus stop, so just be ready little man."

Fifteen minutes later Razah and Mikey were ready to leave. As Razah opened the door, he was startled to see his Mom fumbling with her keys. More startling was her attire. She was wearing a short skirt, low-cut top, leather jacket and heels. Her hair and makeup looked like a movie star.

"Where you been?" Razah said in an almost demanding tone, hands shaking in disbelief.

"Pleasure without conscience
Knowledge without character
Life can change with a single drop."

"Grocery shopping," she said, avoiding eye contact and acting as though it wasn't unusual to look like that for such a mundane chore. "Now don't ask no more questions and take your brother to the bus," she snapped back. She changed her face and said, "Have a good day, Mikey. Love you." Mikey smiled.

Razah and Mikey walked in silence to the bus stop. Razah had his suspicions on where his Mom had been. As he watched Mikey get onto the bus, he hoped that his suspicions were wrong. Razah turned and started toward Mizz's house to see if they might be able to chat before they headed to school.

Mizz looked as tired as Razah felt. "So I couldn't sleep at all last night," Mizz said, still half asleep.

"Me neither. Guess what though?" Razah needed to talk about this morning.

"What up?" asked Mizz.

"My Moms didn't come home last night. This morning, when I opened the door to take Mikey to the bus stop, she was standing there wit' a bag of groceries. Get this though, she was dressed like she was at the club all night," Razah said shaking his head trying to forget the scene from just a few minutes ago.

"Ewhhh! Cousin," Mizz reacted as if Razah had just slapped him in the face.

"Word," replied Razah solemnly.

"You think..." Mizz's voice drifted off not really wanting to complete the thought.

"I don't know, I don't know. It don't look good and I know we need to get money," Razah was shocked he was thinking about his Mom in such a way.

Feeling that Razah needed a change of subject,

"Pleasure without conscience
Knowledge without character
Life can change with a single drop."

Mizz asked, "The plan, the plan, what's really good?"

Relieved that Mizz had changed the subject, Razah's face lit up as he thought about the plan he was working on. "I'm almost there. I was plottin' last night, comin' up wit' ideas," he said.

"Me too. Real talk, me too," Mizz shared.

"I was thinkin'," Razah rubbed his face thoughtfully, "We won't need goons, but we'll need wolves. Straight family, I need to talk to Leak."

"Leak, yeah, he's fam. He'll be down for anything. He always hungry for action. Plus he is a G and I trust him," Mizz agreed.

Razah's diversion was short-lived. He heard Mizz's voice but this morning's image of his Mom reappeared in his mind. "Pfft, life is crazy, Bro," Razah said with a heavy sigh.

Mizz looked at his friend, unsure of what to say to ease his pain. They walked in silence for a block.

"I got a game today. You goin'?" Razah asked.

"Of course, I'm goin'," Mizz said as if shocked that Razah even had to ask.

"I was wonderin' if my Moms is goin'? If not, can you bring Mikey for me?"

"Whateva' Bro, I got you."

"It's supposed to be on ESPN. Mad scouts are supposed to be there. That's what coach said, but, I don't care, real talk. I'm on this paper chase," Razah admitted.

"I'll be there. We on the grind now," Mizz agreed.

They arrived at school and headed to their separate classes. Neither of them could concentrate on any of the teachers' words that day. All they could think about was green. Even the upcoming game didn't keep Razah from

"Pleasure without conscience
Knowledge without character
Life can change with a single drop."

working on the plan and how they were going to score. Mizz just kept going over and over in his mind the formula that was going to make them stars.

Razah stretched and went through his pre-game ritual in the locker room. Even with the game just minutes away, he couldn't shake the memory of his mom standing on the porch looking like…'Pfft! That was some crazy stuff this morning. Dang!' He thought to himself. He sat down on one of the benches, covered his face and tried to shift his focus back to the game. Coach Caine walked over to him and told him he wanted to see Razah in his office.

"Are you ready? I'm just giving you a heads up. No pressure or anything, but this game will be televised on ESPN as a high school game of the week, so every major Division 1 scout will have the opportunity to check out the game. I'm saying this even though I know you have an unofficial visit to USC in a couple days."

"Coach, I'm good. Pressure busts pipes and I don't feel pressure. Y'know I'm a wolf, Coach. Anyways, I got other things on my mind. To be honest, this game is the least of my worries."

"What do you mean?" Coach asked cautiously, trying not to reveal the concern that he was starting to feel.

"Ah, Coach," Razah said with a half-hearted reassuring grin, "this is what I do, feel me Coach. This game is minor to me. I play this game to forget what's happenin' in the real world out there. Always have, an' always will. Looks like you stressin' more than me," Razah added with a wink.

"I'm just making sure you're ready son," Coach Caine said placing a reassuring hand on Razah's shoulder pad.

"Pleasure without conscience
Knowledge without character
Life can change with a single drop."

"I'm good and Coach," Razah paused, "thanks." Razah turned and walked toward the tunnel that led out to the field where thousands of people were waiting to see the much talked about sensation. The sensation, who at the moment, couldn't care less.

With just seconds before kickoff, Razah stood on the field and looked around trying to locate his Mom, Mikey or Mizz. Mizz saw him and stretched his arms out to get Razah's attention. Razah smiled as Mizz bumped his chest twice to let him know that it was game time. Razah did the same and saluted his little brother who was standing next to Mizz. Mikey returned the salute just as the kickoff came. The ball sailed through the air all the way back to the one-yard line, where Razah caught it and took off like a rocket.

"Run, run!" Mizz shouted as Razah spun and dodged tackle after tackle and ran back the opening kickoff for a touchdown. Razah stood in the end zone looking at his little brother who was holding up a sign that read, "**IT'S TIME TO BE ILL!!!**" In that moment, that one brief moment, Razah forgot about the morning, the money, the 'hood. He forgot about everything and played as he was born to play. At the end of the game, the stats said it all. He had rushed for over 273 yards, 100 yards receiving out of the backfield and scored four touchdowns, and which led his team to victory. The ESPN analysts ran out of accolades to describe his performance. The crowd continued cheering long after the game ended. As Razah came off the field, his coaches were silent, awed by the performance they had just witnessed.

Coach Caine, wearing a big smile, put his arm around Razah and said, "I should never have been

"Pleasure without conscience
Knowledge without character
Life can change with a single drop."

concerned after our pregame chat. Wow! Your game was great tonight. I'm sure the scouts are going crazy. Geez, my phone will be ringing off the hook this week."

"Thanks Coach," Razah said in a somewhat somber tone.

"You ok? You had a great game. What seems to be the problem?" asked the concerned coach.

"Nothin' Coach, I'm good," reassured Razah.

"You sure?" asked the coach, who wasn't convinced.

"Of course, Coach, I'm just chillin'," Razah said as he headed to the locker room.

After he showered and dressed, he walked out of the locker room to face a mix of local and national media reporters who were waiting to interview the high school phenomenon. Amazingly, all the lights, all the cameras and all the hype couldn't drag Razah's mind away from the plan that had begun to take even more shape while he played the game of his young life. After the interviews, he was exhausted and was happy to see Mizz and Mikey waiting for him.

"Dang, Razah!!! You was givin' it to them cats," Mizz said bumping chests with Razah.

"Yeah brother, they couldn't see you," Mikey said expressing some of the pride he was feeling being a super star's brother.

"Moms ain't come, huh?" Razah asked somewhat discouraged, already knowing the answer.

"Nah, she had to work late," Mikey said, knowing how that hurt his big brother.

"Oh well, it's all good," Razah sighed and then straightened up a little.

"Pleasure without conscience
Knowledge without character
Life can change with a single drop."

"It's all good. She'll be at the next one," Mizz said hoping to ease a little of his friend's pain.

"Except for a few times, the whole game, all I thought about was gettin' money ma' G," Razah said.

"Word? You a nutty dude. You wasn't focused?" Mizz asked in shock.

"Psst, focused on money!!! Mizz, I play great ball in my sleep. Feel me, I was lookin' in the stands, saw how hyped the crowd was. I wanted to get my Jay-Z and P-Diddy on but then I remembered I ain't got no bread," Razah rubbed his fingers together.

Mizz laughed, "You a fool. I would hate to see you when you focused 'cuz it was ugly. I was like, Razah he dumb nasty."

"Thanks cuzo," smiled Razah.

"Did you come up wit' the rest of the plan yet?" Mizz asked.

"Jus' have a few more details to fix," Razah stopped and looked at Mizz and added, "It gotta be perfection, ya dig?"

"That mess wit' my Moms is trippin' me out," blurted Razah suddenly changing subjects.

Mizz placed a reassuring hand on his friend's shoulder, "It's nothin', stop buggin'. We gonna make it right."

"You right Mizz, it's just my moms. Feel me?" Razah snapped, sounding annoyed.

"No doubt Bro, I feel your pain. But, stay focused on what we doin'." Mizz quickly replied trying to smooth over the awkward moment.

"Fo' sho," replied Razah as they reached his house. Realizing the time, Mizz started his goodbye, "Great game.

"Pleasure without conscience
Knowledge without character
Life can change with a single drop."

Peace out." Mizz bumped fists with Razah and headed toward home.

"No doubt," Razah replied. Looking down at his little brother, he whispered, "Mikey, tell Mizz 'later'."

"Later Mizz," Mikey screamed as Mizz crossed the street.

"Later, lil' man," Mizz responded to Mikey.

Once they got home, Razah and Mikey opened the door only to find all the lights off and seemingly no one home. "Mom, you home?" Razah called into the darkness. There was no reply. Razah felt a little sick to his stomach thinking about where she might be. Not wanting to give Mikey any cause to worry and figuring he might be hungry, Razah suggested that they go up the block and grab some pizza. As they approached the pizza shop, they saw a black Porsche Cayenne Turbo with black tints parked on the corner.

"Mikey, that car is hot," Razah said thinking someday he'd have a whip like this.

"I like it," Mikey replied.

"I will get one of these, just you watch," Razah predicted.

As they were about to enter the pizza shop, the owner of the Porsche exited the shop. He was dressed in a black leather trench coat that went all the way down to his purple crocodile leather shoes. On his fingers were large gold gem-encrusted rings. Around his neck was a collection of thick gold chains, each sporting a heavy looking medallion. To be friendly, he smiled at Razah, revealing his abnormally white teeth. Then a look of recognition lit up his face, "Hey, ain't you that superstar high school running back I saw on _Sportscenter_? You nice,"

"Pleasure without conscience
Knowledge without character
Life can change with a single drop."

he said as a sincere compliment.

"Thank you but not like this whip. Dang B, now *this* is hard. What you do man?" Razah asked while staring at the car.

"I own my own business. One of my employees is comin' out right now. I'll let you meet her. Then you can find out what I do," the businessman replied.

"Cool, no doubt," Razah said as the door to the pizza shop opened behind them.

"Hey babe, meet the next Barry Sanders," The man said as Razah and Mikey turned around.

There was a brief moment of silence before anyone spoke. "M-m-mom...what's good? W-w-what are you doin'?" Razah asked shaking his head and stuttering from shock.

"Mom? What the? This your son? What, you got a son?" The man said almost stuttering himself.

"Mom, what are you doin'?" Razah asked again, this time shaking a little bit, "Are you serious?"

"What are you and Mikey doin' outside at this hour?" His mom replied, dodging the questions.

"We just came from my game and Mikey was hungry."

"Two kids?!? That's crazy. I'm out," The man started to head towards the driver's side of the luxury SUV.

"Wait, Stefan, wait for me, I'm still going with you," Razah's mom said to her boss. To Razah she glared and said. "Razah, I will see you at home."

"What's good? You straight?" The man asked as he looked at Razah and then at her.

She nodded her head turning her eyes away from her boys. Stefan came back to the passenger's side and

"Pleasure without conscience
Knowledge without character
Life can change with a single drop."

took her hand as he opened the car door for her. She got in, and as he walked around to the other side, he peered at the boys, almost a look of disbelief on his face. As he was climbing in, he nodded to the boys, then slammed the door. The Porsche's engine roared to life and quickly bolted from the boys' sight.

"Oh my God, I wonder what mom was doin' wit' that clown." Razah said out loud to himself. "YO, this is it. I'm gonna get this money. This is whack. I swear enough is enough!" Razah declared as he clenched his teeth and narrowed his eyes. They walked into the pizza shop and ordered a pepperoni to go. Both of them stood in silence as they waited for their pizza. Razah was surprised at Mikey's silence and he wondered what his little brother was thinking. Razah wouldn't know what to say if Mikey started asking questions, so they didn't discuss their Mother the rest of the night.

Sitting at home later, with Mikey sleeping soundly, Razah's mom finally walked in the door.

She turned toward Razah and spoke, "Son,   come here, please."

"Yes mom?" he said as he got up to approach her.

"What do you think I was doin' with that guy?" she asked.

Razah's eyes quickly moved from her gaze. "Honestly ma, I don't wanna know," Razah said hoping the conversation would go no further.

"All right son," she wasn't going to push it.

"Mom, I did well tonight at the game but I'm tired," Razah got up and walked toward the stairs. "See you in the morning." He paused then caringly added, "Goodnight, I love you ma."

"Pleasure without conscience
Knowledge without character
Life can change with a single drop."

"All right son. Goodnight baby, I love you," she replied.

As Razah walked up the stairs, he didn't see his mom sit down on the couch and put her face into her hands. She also was playing her favorite album The Legacy Project by Hameed. She played this album when she wanted to relax and clear her mind. Razah didn't hear her as she began sobbing. She didn't see him sit on the edge of his bed and put his face in his hands. Nor did she hear him start to cry. He needed that paper, not just for the ladies, the cars, and for the plan. No, he needed that paper so he and his loved ones could survive. He closed his eyes and eventually drifted off to sleep.

The Wiz

Razah couldn't sleep again that night. He kept thinking about his mom, that dude Stefan, the plan and what he had to do to get away from all of this mess. He got out of bed and looked up to the ceiling as if praying to get the answer he needed. Then it hit him, exactly what needed to be done to pull the heist off without any problems. He tapped his chest twice, saluted toward the ceiling as if thanking whoever might be on the other side and went back to bed.

The next morning, he got dressed in a hurry and practically ran out the door so he didn't have to see or talk to his mom. Moments later, he stood outside of Mizz's house and knocked. Mizz looked out his window and told Razah to come on up.

"Guess what?" Razah said as he met Mizz in the

"Pleasure without conscience
Knowledge without character
Life can change with a single drop."

hall.

"What's good ma' dude?" questioned Mizz.

"Saw Ma dukes wit' this fake pimp last night in a Porsche truck," Razah informed his best friend.

"Say word. Black on black my G?" Mizz didn't know what else to say.

"Yeah," Razah replied.

"Ewwwh," Mizz shook his head. "So, what happened cuz'?"

"When Moms came home, I was like 'I don't wanna know nothing.' But Mizz, I do know we gotta get this money," Razah gestured with his fingers rubbing together.

"We will, we will," Mizz reassuredly said.

"Few more days and the plans should be straight. Just a few more days, right?" Razah confirmed, almost excitedly.

"Yo, we got that meeting today," Mizz reminded Razah.

"What meeting?" Razah asked.

"National Honor Society," Mizz reminded him, surprised that Razah had forgotten.

"Right, Mr. President, yeah, I forgot," Razah laughed.

"That's right Mr. Vice President, fool," said Mizz getting all-presidential, "I'm like Obama out here. You feel me?" They laughed and headed to school.

Today's meeting was just an informal get together to introduce Mizz, Razah and the other officers to the newcomers and to outline some of their plans for the upcoming year. After classes, the group got together. Mizz and Razah mingled with everyone until the secretary called the meeting to order. Both Mizz and Razah were

"Pleasure without conscience
Knowledge without character
Life can change with a single drop."

going to briefly address the group.   The secretary introduced Razah so he could speak first.

"Thank you," Razah said to the gracious applause. "I hope everyone had a nice summer. For those of you that don't know me, my name is Myshawn Greene. I am your class vice-president and I'm happy to see all of you. I look forward to working with you this academic year. I'm not one for long speeches but let me share my daily philosophy with you. I strive to be successful in my daily endeavors. I hope you can benefit from those words as well. And now, it's my pleasure to introduce to you, our class President, Mizzier Sanders," Razah turned and gestured toward Mizz.

Mizz nodded and smiled to Razah as he approached the podium, "Thank you, Vice-President Myshawn, for that introduction. Good afternoon. It's a pleasure to see old and new friends alike. I have a few things to outline as our goals for this year. Let's get down to business, shall we? First, let's acknowledge those that have gone on and are achieving great accomplishments in college and in the real world. Let's follow in their footsteps and use their positive influences as inspiration. Hard work and a clean slate will get us to where we have to go and we will succeed." Mizz stood straight as the audience applauded indicating their agreement with his words. He turned, looked at Razah and smiled.

Unlike Razah, Mizz was more comfortable speaking in front of large groups. His ease was evident as he outlined the plans and goals for the year to the group. The first meeting was a success as Mizz concluded his speech to enthusiastic applause. After the meeting, Razah had football practice. They had agreed to meet at Mizz's afterward.

"Pleasure without conscience
Knowledge without character
Life can change with a single drop."

After practice, Razah sat in the locker room. Coach Caine walked up and addressed his star player, "Hey Razah, good practice, son. You have an unofficial visit to USC coming up. What do you think of USC?"

"I've always liked USC, especially when Reggie Bush was there. He was my dude," replied Razah.

"It's a good school. I think it's smart for you to go there unofficially," Coach continued, "it'll give you some experience and an idea of what you can expect from the different schools looking to recruit you."

"Yeah Coach, it works out well cuz' I have family there. I lucked out 'cuz the school's flying me out there for the National Honor Society conference. So I figure, why not kill two birds with one stone, right? Go to USC unofficially so I don't use up one of my five visits," Razah said tapping his temple with his index finger as if indicating his intelligence.

"You gotta be the luckiest and most blessed kid I know," said Coach Caine sincerely.

"Thanks Coach, I think I am too," responded Razah. "Sorry Coach, I gotta get going but good talk. See you tomorrow at practice," Razah said as he stood up. As the coach was saying goodbye, Razah waved and walked out of the locker room and headed straight for Mizz's crib.

Twenty minutes later, Razah knocked on the door and waited for Mizz. A few moments later, Mizz opened the door.

"Let's go to the pizza spot and talk," Razah suggested as Mizz walked out the door.

"Cool, I'm hungry," Mizz agreed. They headed across the street and up the block to their favorite pizza joint. They walked in and ran into their friend Marty, the

"Pleasure without conscience
Knowledge without character
Life can change with a single drop."

pizza shop owner. "Hey guys, if it ain't the world's two best athletes," Marty said smiling.

"Marty, what's good bro? How's everything?" Mizz asked.

"You guys got the good life. I'm just tryin' to live," Marty said with a smile.

"Yeah right, you straight," Mizz said.

"You do mad business." Razah added, "You always packed."

With a big smile Marty said, "You two are alright. Not like most of these clowns," he motioned outside referring to the wanna-be thugs that roamed the 'hood, some of whom had probably robbed Marty at one time or another. "What can I get you guys? It's on the house. It's always on the house for you two."

"We got you when we get on," Razah promised.

"I know brothers, I know." Marty said shaking his head. "Don't you worry. Now, what you guys want?"

"The usual," they said.

"All right guys, be good," Marty said as he headed back into the kitchen.

"That Italian dude be lookin' out," Razah said as they sat down in an empty booth.

"No doubt." Mizz wanted to get down to business.

"You know we got that National Honor Society convention coming up in California," Razah started, "And I'm unofficially visiting USC too."

"Ok and what?" Mizz inquired.

"Well, I've been talkin' to my cousin, Nico. Remember, he came out here in July?" Razah continued.

"Yeah, good dude," remembered Mizz.

Razah nodded, "Yeah, so, I was tellin' him about

"Pleasure without conscience
Knowledge without character
Life can change with a single drop."

38

my idea and he said he'd be down for whateva'. And my other cousin, Cuzzo, put me down wit' this dude wit' plans for the bank and everything..."

Mizz interrupted, "Bank?" Mizz whisper-shouted in disbelief. "You done bumped your head?"

Razah ignored Mizz and carried on, "I gotta meet him tomorrow. Here's the idea; the bank is in Cali and we'll have the perfect alibi. Why not take it down while we out there, Mizzzzzz?"

"Bank?" Mizz's lips moved but no sound came out.

"Bro, trust me for real," Razah said tapping his chest.

"Are you serious?" Mizz asked half laughing.

"Man listen," Razah said, just a little too loud, "Trust me."

"Ok, Ok," Mizz backed down as he could sense Razah getting upset with him, "I feel you. Hey, your cousins, are they wolves?"

"Most definitely, this is our chance. I will find out the score when I meet the dude tomorrow. You know how to handle a Mac 10?" Razah asked seriously.

"Dude, neither of us have handled hardware before," Mizz said as a matter of fact.

"True and hopefully we ain't gotta use it," Razah agreed.

Mizz now saw that Razah was serious about this, "You real wit' this?"

"No doubt. My plan is to a T. One shot. It's like a buzzer beater and a Hail Mary touchdown pass rolled into one. We will own this city!" Razah calmly exclaimed staring straight into Mizz's eyes. Just then, Marty brought out their order, so they quickly changed the subject.

"Pleasure without conscience
Knowledge without character
Life can change with a single drop."

That night, even though exhausted, Razah still could not sleep. His mind buzzed with anticipation of what was about to happen. He felt it in his blood. The next day he would meet up with Cuzzo and the man that would help put his plan into action. After that, there was no stopping them. He closed his eyes and let himself think about what life would be like with real bread in their pockets. With visions of a Money Team lifestyle, Razah finally succumbed to exhaustion and drifted off to sleep.

The next day Razah met up with his cousin, Cuzzo, outside an old office complex. The abandoned building had been boarded up for years. Stripped and burned-out cars dotted the landscape, making this a perfect place to meet in private since no one in their right mind would make the mistake of walking back there. Razah and Cuzzo gave each other a quick hug and then got right down to business.

"Razah, this is my man, a real old G. They call him Wiz," Cuzzo gestured toward the man standing at the building's entrance. The man stood about six feet tall and looked to be in his fifties. Dressed in a black suit with a black shirt and black shoes with a diamond stud in both ears, his mere presence commanded respect. "We used to think he worked at the parliament, all this money he used to get."

"Hey, young blood," Wiz spoke shaking Razah's hand. Razah noticed that Wiz spoke with a very distinctive style. Educated, yet wise to the street. "Your cousin has told me much about you. So tell me, why do you want to deal with the inner thieves?" He gazed at Razah to gauge his response.

Without hesitation, Razah responded, "Well, its simple arithmetic," he began. "I can continue to prosper

"Pleasure without conscience
Knowledge without character
Life can change with a single drop."

and struggle or I can continue to prosper and get money, too. I prefer havin' the best of both worlds, feel me?"

The old man looked at Razah intently, considering what he had said, "Ok young blood. I feel your 'gangsta.' Step into my office." The wizard opened the door and motioned for Razah and Cuzzo to step inside. Wiz relaxed in a nice leather office chair behind a solid oak desk as he continued to speak.

"Please, have a seat," he offered. "Ok, youngin, I have everything planned to a T. If you were to not succeed, than I am sorry, but you're not as intelligent as Cuzzo says you are. Oh, and if you were to snitch on anyone, well the consequences would be grim," Wiz said with a cold stare. "I'm sure you are aware so there wouldn't be a need to emphasize that point, you dig?" Wiz's face changed to reveal the hardened interior that existed under the soft fabric of his designer suit.

"I dig," Razah quickly replied.

"Ok, now down to business, young blood. Here is the deal. The operation will commence toward the end of the week," the Wizard said as he began to layout the plan.

"Thursday?" Razah asked

"Of course. You are a shark. Certain locations are currency clearinghouses, which stock the other area financial institutions with paper so they're prepared for Friday's payroll. You understand?" Wiz asked.

"Yes. How many dudes?" Razah asked.

"Remarkably, there are only two to a maximum of four. That's it. Bypass them and you're free, clear as day," Wiz smiled.

Razah paused a moment, thinking perhaps he was missing something. Although helpful, this information

"Pleasure without conscience
Knowledge without character
Life can change with a single drop."

didn't seem to be worth the price. "So Wiz, you want a hundred and fifty stacks just for that?" His tone changed, "That ain't right G. And ten percent of the earnings? Dang, Wiz! Man listen, you bumped your head. Word, 'cuz the tellers are gonna hit up the bank alarm. I gotta bounce before the 5-0 show up. What the !!! is that Wiz?"

Wiz sighed. Obviously, the young man did not grasp the finer details of this business operation. "Son, they hit up three hold up joints. In case you don't know Spanish, two telecoms plus a cellular."

"Word," Razah was beginning to understand.

"Yes, check it out though. The signals won't be going anywhere because the night before, you and your crew cut into the system and trigger program the system to turn the video cameras and records off 30 mins before you do your thing. You'll also hijack the security and surveillance system. Those bankers can hit the silent alarm all they want. They'll get nothing. You understand?" Wiz asked.

"Yeah, I feel you old G," Razah replied as he was seeing the big picture.

"Furthermore, these are the architectural, electrical and engineering plans. Also 'lil' G, I have all the schematics. I had some associates build the boards. You'll need to acquire a PC for the boards. It's not logical to take a whole computer with you across country.

"Dang, dude! You got all that?" Razah was beyond impressed. The suspense was killing him so he had to ask, "What's the take, Wiz?"

"It varies from week to week but the consistent range is 10.1 to 10.2 million dollars," came the calm and confident reply.

"Pleasure without conscience
Knowledge without character
Life can change with a single drop."

Razah looked at Cuzzo in disbelief. Cuzzo simply smiled, knowing that the Wiz had his stuff together.

"No doubt old school, you on!" Razah's eyes almost popped out of his head in excitement.

"That is the estimate, son. I have a print out if you want to check it out, though," the older man offered.

"Word?" Razah asked still amazed.

"Why do you think they call me Wiz? Anyway, congratulations on your endeavor young blood and best of luck. Remember, I either have everything or access to it. Of course, you'll have all my contact information," confirmed Wiz.

"I see. Thank you. We'll be in touch," Razah turned and started towards the door.

"Ohh, I know you will, young G ... I know you will," Wiz spoke almost under his breath as he watched Razah and Cuzzo leave. With the plans for the bank job all set, Mizz and Razah had to sit tight for the next few days until they left for California. So they went over the plan excessively.

"Yo Mizz!! We good. Look at all this madness!" Mizz looked at Razah in disbelief, "Bro, is this the plans for fort knox!! Mannnnn!!!" he said laughing.

The day before they were to leave, they got together one last time to go over the plans. Razah was confident that they were ready. He told Mizz to go home and get a good night's sleep. Tomorrow was the travel day and once in California, then they'd really get down to business.

The following morning they met before heading out. They looked confident on the outside, but they had a certain level of uneasiness on the inside. They had memorized the plan to a T.

"Pleasure without conscience
Knowledge without character
Life can change with a single drop."

The trip went smoothly. Shockingly, their flight was actually almost on time. Razah's cousin, Nico, picked them up using his Dad's truck.

Time is Money

Later, Razah sat down in his hotel room with the paperwork that Wiz had given him and went over the plan step by step. He felt like something was missing. He knew there had to be something else to make sure that this would look like an inside job. He needed a way to speak with his crew without it being traced. 'A burner phone would work,' he thought to himself and he headed out to find one.

After picking up the burners at a local store, he went in search of a pay phone; he found one outside a gas station. Looking around to make sure no one could hear him; he picked up the receiver and called the crew. He gave them the password that Wiz had given them, and he laid out the plans for them using Pig Latin to throw off any would-be listeners.

Three hours later Razah spoke with his crew and he went over the plan with them once again. This time he called from a different pay phone. Then, using the pre-paid, he shot Wiz a text asking for a list of the security guards on-duty in the bank, with their addresses and phone numbers. Wiz texted him back that it wouldn't be a problem to get the info, but he'd need about an hour.

An hour later, Wiz texted the information Razah had requested. Razah then dumped the prepaid phone in a nearby alley, dumped the battery in the sewer, then pocketed the SIM card. After getting back to the payphone, Razah then called the security guards that would be on duty the day of the heist and informed them there was a last-

"Pleasure without conscience
Knowledge without character
Life can change with a single drop."

minute schedule change. They were needed to cover a city conference an hour or so away from the bank. Because of the short notice, as a bonus, they would get paid time-and-a-half and mileage. They all agreed.

Razah also went online and checked out the security company's website. Razah's cuzin's homie happened to work at the spot where the companies get their uniforms made, so they were straight with the look of authority that they needed to place them in the bank.

Once they settled in, Razah and Mizz made plans to do a couple of recons of the bank. They made sure they weren't in the vicinity too long so they wouldn't be able to be identified by the host of regulars that frequented the area.

For the final recon, Mizz and Razah planned to scope out the bank from the underground garage located directly beneath the bank. It was simply a matter of determining which concrete wall concealed the wires, and tie their equipment in so when the time was right, they could bypass the bank's systems. Once they figured it out, one of the team hacked the security camera in the corner and made a couple playback loops from week-old footage. It was basic stuff, but the team wouldn't be seen by anyone monitoring the garage.

Under the cover of the video loop, they parked Razah's uncle's truck where the plans indicated there was an access point. Wearing work hats and coveralls, the two of them looked like utility workers doing routine maintenance. While Mizz drilled through the concrete, Razah stayed in the truck working on the computer. The plan was to open up a hole large enough to stash the computer, then tap into the power and data lines to override the bank's security system.

"Pleasure without conscience
Knowledge without character
Life can change with a single drop."

Mizz drilled an access point that was big enough for the computer. He quickly tied in to the supply wires running past, and the computer linked up without any problems. They then covered the hole in the wall with a façade that matched the concrete so it would be difficult to notice.

Next, they located the access point to a service tunnel which ran under the bank's floors to the corner of the main lobby. While reviewing the bank's blueprints, Razah had remarked that this was a bank begging to be robbed, noting the relatively easy access.

Mizz texted Cuzzo, who was parked on the street in a van he had stolen the night before at a trap house. Mizz directed him to their location, the idea being to use the van to block the area Mizz needed to work, and then leave the van overnight to keep the access point hidden. Cuzzo had swapped the plates of the stolen van to plates to those of an identical vehicle so if the squad car happened to do a search; the van wouldn't come back stolen.

Once Cuzzo parked the van, he quickly exited the garage and headed back to the crib. Meanwhile, Mizz started drilling and cutting through the concrete low on the ground to make it less obvious to the casual observer. Once he had removed enough material, he was able to look into the tunnel. Rebar rungs were spaced evenly all the way up and down the tunnel, acting as a ladder. Since they still weren't sure what they would encounter in the tunnel, the plan was for Mizz to scout the tunnels above using the measurements they had paced off from inside the bank.

Razah stayed back as a lookout while Mizz entered the tunnel. He was quickly able to ascend the ladder to the cross-tunnel under the bank, and determine it was big

"Pleasure without conscience
Knowledge without character
Life can change with a single drop."

enough to crawl through. The electric conduit ran in the top right corner of the tunnel, carrying electricity to outlets in the bank's floor. Two of these outlets had access points up through the floor. The bank's floor was tiled in 18" ceramic tiles, so they would have to cut away the subfloor and most of the grout from the tiles on either side to make a gap big enough to fit through. As Mizz quietly moved along the tunnel, he kept track of the distance he travelled so he would know where he needed to tie in from above later. He came upon the first location and was surprised to find that the tiles above him were not supported by subfloor, only an access hatch anchored by a twist-latch that drove rods into the case on either side. Using a sidecutter, Mizz cut the bolts holding the electrical box, revealing the outlet and electric wires. He carefully unscrewed and capped the connections, then turned the rusty latch and removed the access panel, hoping the tile would not drop in. He then cut into the grout surrounding the tile, leaving just enough material to hold the tile in place. When the time was right, a solid hit would break the tile loose, and they would have full access to the bank's main lobby. After he finished the first access point, he replaced the panel and moved to the second location, and repeated the process.

Once both access points were modified to his liking, Mizz moved stealthily back through the tunnel and made his way down to the garage. He stuck his head out to see Razah standing there patiently.

"What's good?" Mizz whispered.

"It's all good," Razah quietly replied. Mizz crawled out and they put the façade back into place. Hardhats, coveralls and tools went into the stolen van. A final sweep assured them that everything looked like a normal parking

"Pleasure without conscience
Knowledge without character
Life can change with a single drop."

garage. They walked over to their truck, got in and headed off to Razah's uncle's crib.

That night Razah, Mizz, Cuzzo and Nico went out for some grinders at the local bodega. This spot had a lounge inside where you and your homies could chill and talk, roll dice, play cards, gamble, anything goes at this spot. Mizz and Razah reviewed what they had done that day in the garage.

Razah spoke up, "Ok fellas, here it is," he began. "You all know the plan and you know everything is in place. What y'all said before doesn't matter. I need to know now, who's in? If you in, you in. If you out, walk away now and no hard feelings. Either way. This is still popping off you feel me!! Razah said violently. He looked at each of the other three, settling on Mizz. Knowing the answer, he had to ask anyway, "Mizz?"

"Pfft. You know I'm in. Ride or die, G," he replied as he bumped his chest twice.

Razah looked at Cuzzo next and before he could ask, Cuzzo looked at him in the eye and said, "Cuz, you don't even need to ask, I'm in."

That left Nico, the quiet one of the group. Razah looked at him and Nico spoke up, "Yeah, ma' G, y'know I'm in." The conviction in his voice was proof enough to Razah.

"Let's get this money!!!!

The Heist

Cuzzo stood in his room admiring how he looked in the security officer uniform. He wondered if he would have a better chance of scoring with the ladies if he showed up dressed like that. He laughed, realizing he was wearing

"Pleasure without conscience
Knowledge without character
Life can change with a single drop."

what was essentially a toy soldier's uniform. He straightened his clip-on-tie, put on his plastic badge and left.

Only a few blocks away, Nico was just about to leave when the lady he picked up at the club the night before pulled him back inside. She ran her hands up and down his sky blue shirt and tugged at his tie. "I don't know what it is boy, but this uniform is getting me all excited. I wish you didn't have to go to work," she purred sweetly while playfully pouting. He looked at her thinking, if she only knew what he was actually about to do, she'd be pushing him out the door.

He wasn't going to keep her around long enough to share anything with her anyway. Wearing nothing but one of his shirts, she stood there tempting him to stay just a little bit longer. He thought about it a second, but then green and nothing but green filled his mind. Chilling was one thing, but paper was quite another and he was not going to blow his chance at the kind of haul he stood to gain with the heist. He kissed her on the forehead and bounced, and told her to lock the door on her way out.

Once at the bank, Nico and Cuzzo alternated taking turns at the front door while the other performed rounds. They had decided to hold off until the morning rush of customers cleared out, but to initiate the operation prior to 11:00 a.m. to avoid the lunch rush. They wanted to minimize the number of customers in the bank. The purpose of one of them performing rounds was so they could determine who was in charge. This information would be passed to Razah and Mizz so they wouldn't waste precious time once the robbery began.

By 10:15 a.m. the bank only had three customers in it and most of the tellers had also gone on break. Cuzzo

"Pleasure without conscience
Knowledge without character
Life can change with a single drop."

contacted Mizz, who was waiting patiently with Razah below the floor. They had managed to score some walkies with earpieces so no one would overhear their transmissions. "There are three Chevy's, two Toyotas, and one Mercury in the garage," Cuzzo informed Mizz, code for three customers, two tellers, and one manager.

"Tell the mechanic that we'll be there in five minutes," Mizz replied. Everyone marked the time on their watches. Razah set the power failure countdown clock on his computer to five minutes, and clicked on run.

Razah and Mizz pulled the stocking caps down, double checked their ear pieces and switched the safeties off the fake Mac 10's they were hoping not to fire. They waited as time seemed to move more slowly than waiting for the last class bell before summer vacation. With about thirty seconds to go, Mizz looked back at Razah.

"This is it Razah," Mizz said, "Ride or die."

"I'm here, G!" Razah replied. They dapped each other up, ready to get busy. Right on schedule, the lights in the bank went out, and immediately the people inside started screaming. Razah set the timer on his watch to go off in five minutes.

Mizz and Razah popped the tiles and rolled two smoke grenades toward the center of the lobby. As they popped up from the floor, the emergency generator kicked in and the bank lighting was partially restored. In the dim lighting, Razah and Mizz emerged from the smoke like The Dark Knight (Batman).

"Everyone down on the ground. We want the bank's money, not yours. Your money is insured by the federal government," Mizz said trying to calm the situation down.

"Pleasure without conscience
Knowledge without character
Life can change with a single drop."

You can thank your illustrious President Barack Obama for that. So don't forget to vote for him!! The couple of customers immediately complied with Mizz's request as did Nico and Cuzzo. The bank employees stood still, unsure of what to do. As expected, one of the tellers stepped on the floor button to trigger the silent alarm.

Razah spoke up next, "We don't wanna hurt anyone. Please do NOT be a hero. You will be dealt wit' harsh, to quote the great Busta Rhymes, please believe. Now everyone put your hands behind your heads and interlock your fingers so I can see them. Good, good," he said as people complied with his demands.

Keeping their covers, Cuzzo and Nico complied with Razah's demands. Razah walked over to them and removed their guns. He then pretended to kick Nico in the side in plain view of the others in the bank. Take that you clown! I said don't move!" A collective gasp was heard throughout. Nico pretended to writhe in pain.

Razah looked at the bank employees and called out, "Jerry?"

Instinctively, Jerry shuddered at the sound of his name being called out by a bank robber. Razah saw this and immediately knew which one was the supervisor. Razah vaulted over the counter. The nearest teller cowered in fear as Razah walked by.

As Razah made his way to the supervisor, Mizz went to the front door and locked it. From his backpack he pulled out a sign and adhered it to the door. The sign read, 'Bank closed due to power outage.' He hung it between the handles with an emergency lockout tag they had swiped from a construction site.

Razah approached the older gentleman and looked

"Pleasure without conscience
Knowledge without character
Life can change with a single drop."

at his nametag to verify that in fact this was Jerry, the bank supervisor, the holder of the key.

"Jerry?" Razah asked, as the man gazed at Razah with a blank stare, neither showing bravado nor fear. "Jerry, I'm going to ask once and I expect you to cooperate," Razah said with an unwavering tone. "Jerry, where's the vault key?"

Jerry's expression changed as if he did not understand Razah's question. This was Jerry's thirty-fifth year with the bank, and only had a few months left until retirement. He wasn't going to let some punks get away with the first robbery in the bank's history. Finally, in a shaky voice, Jerry asked, "Wh-wh-what key?"

Razah's shoulders drooped as if disappointed. He raised the gun and sternly said, "Jerry, stop pranking. Now where's the key?" Without waiting for an answer, he cracked Jerry square in the face between the eyes. As Jerry reached up putting his hands to his face, Razah saw the chain around Jerry's neck. In one swift motion, he grabbed the chain and ripped it from Jerry's neck. As blood spurted from Jerry's nose, Razah yelled, "How you like that Jerry, you dumb old goat, see what you made me do?" shaking his head with remorse. He tossed the key to Mizz who was making his way toward the vault. Jerry fell to the floor in obvious pain.

Mizz entered the vault and pulled four large duffle bags from his backpack. He quickly and neatly filled them to maximize the amount he could put in each bag. As he filled each one, he'd slide them to Razah, who in turn tossed them over the counter. As each bag was filled, Mizz checked his watch to check their progress.

Razah was keeping an eye on the employees and the

"Pleasure without conscience
Knowledge without character
Life can change with a single drop."

customers. Aside from Jerry's stubbornness, the group as a whole was well-behaved. There were no screamers and no heroes, much to the relief of the four robbers. Mizz finished filling the final duffle bag and carried it with him as he exited the vault.

Razah's watch timer went off and he announced into his microphone, "We gotta bounce."

As Razah and Mizz jumped over the counter, Razah told everyone to wait at least five minutes before exiting the bank. He explained that they had a sniper across the street and if anyone tried to follow them... He didn't finish the thought.

Mizz unlocked the front door and removed the sign. He pulled out two more smoke grenades from his backpack, pulled the pins, and rolled them on the floor just as Razah triggered the backup generator to go off-line, killing the lights again. Razah and Mizz put a twist on the escape route. The two rejoined their partners as each grabbed a duffle bag full of cash and in turn, dropped through the holes in the floor. The last two through realigned the tiles and access panels. Upon close inspection, it would be obvious to the investigators how the robbers gained access to the bank, but by then all four would be long gone.

Earlier when Mizz was checking out the tunnel there was a last minute game change. He found another escape route. This tunnel route led to the alley where Razah dropped the prepaid phone earlier that morning. Mizz figured everyone didn't need to go to the same route. They climbed out of the sewer, then pushed open a pothole to see if anyone else was around. It was clear, so they just climbed out and walked to the corner and waited for the other crew members. By then it was a tight fit. Each full

"Pleasure without conscience
Knowledge without character
Life can change with a single drop."

duffle bag slid through the tunnel as it was pulled by one of the crew. As they reached the vertical tunnel, they'd unwrap the strap from their ankle, get on the ladder and then dropped the duffle bag as they made their way down to where the van was located. Once they reached the garage level, they tossed the bags into the van. After Nico deposited the last bag into the van, Cuzo covered the access hole with the cement façade. They climbed in the van and Nico began driving as he and Cuzo changed their clothes.

On their way to pick up Razah and Mizz, they wondered why the two took a different route, which would be discussed on the way to the crib of course. Once they reached Nico's dad's truck, they simply tossed the duffle bags in the back, they picked up Razah and Mizz, who already had their clothes changed and had them in their book bag. Just across the street was the getaway truck. As Razah and Mizz threw their book bags in the van, Nico poured gasoline all over the interior and under the hood, and then Cuzo ignited it. A couple seconds later, as they began to drive off in the truck, the van blew up in flames. Razah sped off because he had the escape routes from the plan Wiz gave him.

Sitting in the back seat, Nico said, "That was hard, but what was good wit you two going the other route."
Razah said, "It didn't make sense for all of us to go the same way. It would have just took longer."

Nico and Cuzo looked at each other again and at the same time said," True story!"

Razah said, "But when we get out of this ride, let's not mention it again."

"My G, my adrenaline was crazy," Mizz said.

"That plan was to a T," Razah proudly declared and

"Pleasure without conscience
Knowledge without character
Life can change with a single drop."

righteously so.

"Razah!!! Razah!!! Cousin!!!" Cuzo said shaking his head.

"Word Razah, word," Nico added, still disbelieving they actually pulled it off without a hitch." They soon reached Razah's uncle's crib, a small house located at the end of a dead end street in an even more dead end neighborhood. If you weren't from this area or weren't with someone from this area, your chances of survival were pretty slim. Mizz and Razah lived in a pretty rough area back in Waterbury, Pearl Street next door to the ABC Park. But this was Compton and they knew its reputation well. Everyone knew, you don't mess around in Compton. They got out of the truck and hustled the bags into the Crib.

"Yo, gonna head over to USC. The unofficial visit, that is... LOL. Uncle is gonna take me over there. In the meantime, get the money machine and count that dough," Razah motioned towards the basement.

"No doubt. I got you," Mizz said. "But Razah, how we gonna take this paper with us?"

"When you guys go in the basement, there are two big plastic bins filled with Styrofoam packing foam and books. My other cousin Casey, Nico's sister, is a manager at FedEx. In the morning, we bring it to her location and she'll overnight it to this old folks' home, y'know, where Leak's girl works at. When it arrives, Leak knows he's to pick it up," Razah explained.

"Dang B, you do got this plan to a T. A'ight, we good. We gonna handle the countin' and packin' that. Remember, don't sign," Mizz said as he punched Razah in the arm.

"Nope, 'cuz we goin' to the same school," Razah

"Pleasure without conscience
Knowledge without character
Life can change with a single drop."

reassured Mizz.

"No doubt, 100," Mizz agreed.

"100," Razah confirmed and with that, he headed out to meet his uncle.

USC

Razah's uncle came over and let Razah know he was ready to go. Razah grabbed his coat and headed out. When he arrived at the school there was a welcoming committee waiting for him. He felt like royalty as he climbed out of his uncle's ride and saw students with signs and shirts, even printed jerseys with his name on it. The coach walked up and put his arm around him.

"You are the best running back I've ever seen at the high school level. You're almost ready for the NFL right now but a few seasons as a Trojan would get you on the right track. I can see why they call you Razah, Mr. Sharp Dresser." Razah had made sure to look sharp to make a good impression even though he knew he wasn't going to sign that day. The coach seemed to be more of a fan than a guy set on recruiting him.

Razah chuckled to himself. "Thanks for the compliments, Coach. Ready for the NFL? You really feel that way?" Razah asked.

"Well, almost ready, son. Uncle, you gotta be proud of your nephew, Myshawn," addressing Razah's uncle. Turning back to Razah he asked, "By the way, where's your sidekick Mizzier?"

"He's chilling at the hotel. While we're here in California, we're also attending a National Honor Society Conference," explained Razah.

"That's good. I'm sure neither of you will have

"Pleasure without conscience
Knowledge without character
Life can change with a single drop."

issues with the academic eligibility requirements for student athletes," the coach laughed at his little joke. "I never heard of a tandem like you two before. Hopefully both of you will consider USC and become Trojans," Coach said as he patted Razah's back.

"Coach I really appreciate the kind words coming from a person of your caliber and success," Razah said, humbly.

"Well, what we have in store for you today is a football game so you can see how we work. Let me bring you both to the locker room to meet the guys," the coach said.

"Wow, I would love that," Razah said as they headed toward the locker room.

The coach introduced Razah and his uncle to all of the players who were suiting up for the game. They were clearly impressed with this young man, and acted more like his fans then potential teammates. The coach then led Razah to his own locker, where a jersey with his name on it was hanging inside.

"This is unbelievable. You've really gone the extra mile for me!" Razah said picking up the jersey.

"So what do you think?" the coach said, grinning.

"Well, if this is a dream, then I don't wanna wake up," Razah was getting a little excited seeing his name on the jersey.

"Ok, good," said the coach as he smiled to himself, "I'm going to give the pre-game talk and get them ready." The coach moved to the center of the locker room, waving to an open spot on the bench. "Please listen in."

Coach spoke to his team with conviction and motivation. He got them all hyped up. They were ready to

"Pleasure without conscience
Knowledge without character
Life can change with a single drop."

do work. Coach brought Razah aside and told him to walk out with them onto the field. Playing on the big screen were highlights of Razah making fools out of his opponents as the crowd chanted, 'We want Razah! We want Razah!' Razah stood speechless, mesmerized by the crowd.

'So this is what the fuss is all about,' he said to himself.

"You deserve this Myshawn, you deserve this." His uncle walked over to him and put his arm around him.

The coach called them over and asked if they wanted to join the team on the sidelines for the game. He couldn't believe the stops they were pulling out for him. He and his uncle watched from the best spot in the arena as USC trounced their rivals, UCLA. It was a great experience for the both of them. After the game, the coach called them back into the locker room.

"So what you think? This something here you wanna come to?" the coach asked, as he made no attempt at hiding his excitement.

"Of course, you're in my top 5," Razah replied.

Pulling a pen from his pocket, the coach offered, "Well, you can sign right now, if you want to, son."

Razah paused for a moment before responding. "Thanks Coach, but to be honest, I'm not ready to sign anything yet. I will be in touch though, regardless of my decision."

"I can respect that Myshawn," the coach responded as he tried to hide his obvious disappointment.

"Thanks again," said Razah as he tried to soak it all in.

"Do you need anything? Anything at all?" the coach asked with a hint of promise in his voice.

"Pleasure without conscience
Knowledge without character
Life can change with a single drop."

Understanding what the coach was hinting, Razah smiled and said, "Thanks Coach, but I'm good. You've given me something to think about."

"Thanks for considering USC. Good luck and remember, anything you need, anything at all, just pick up the phone. In that packet I gave you are all my numbers, including my home and cell," the coach told him.

"Coach, thanks again for having me," Razah said as he and his uncle were leaving.

Razah and his uncle left USC and on the way back to the crib, they discussed the school and their visit. Razah was only half listening, because while the visit had been good, it had also been an eye opener as to what schools might be willing to do to get him to attend. Now, all he could think about was the paper waiting for him back at the crib.

When they got back to his uncle's house, Mizz was waiting for Razah.

"So how was it? Coach didn't trick you into signing anything?" Mizz joked.

"Yo, Bro, that joint was hard. Check it, we watched the game from the sidelines. Dude even had a jersey with my name on it. Fo' real though, I don't know if I wanna go there," Razah confided.

"I don't think it would be a good idea," Mizz said in a somewhat serious tone.

"Me neither," Razah said laughing, knowing exactly what he meant. "So how's it going with the count and packing?" Razah asked referring to all the paper.

"It's going," Mizz said as he let out a whistle, "zero to a million."

"Enough to buy 90 Maybachs and a Bugatti," Razah

"Pleasure without conscience
Knowledge without character
Life can change with a single drop."

said as they both laughed.

The rest of the night they spent in the basement, counting and packaging all the paper. They checked the news, which mentioned the robbery, but the reporter said that the police didn't have many leads to go on. Mizz and Razah looked at each other and smiled, "Ewwwwwwwh!!"

Michaela L. Rivera

The next morning the boys woke up and prepared to attend the National Honor Society conference. Even though they were just juniors, both of them had been actively involved in Honor Society functions since their freshman year. Combined with their athletic prowess, academic achievements and nationally known name recognition, the Society board was more than eager to invite and subsidize the trip to bring the two scholar athletes to this year's convention.

As both were sharing a mirror to tie their ties, Razah smiled and remarked, "USC coach said I'm a sharp dresser an' that's why they call me Razah."

"It's true. If it weren't for my natural good looks, I'd be embarrassed to be seen next to you," Mizz replied as they both laughed.

"Real talk, I hope there's some talent at the conference today," Razah said wishfully.

"Dude you always got the ladies on the brain. Talent, I like that, Bro. That's a new one. That's hard. Good thing no ladies were around yesterday's joint. We'd be in jail right now," Mizz joked.

Laughing, Razah responded, "Oh you tellin' me you didn't see that one teller? Ooohh, she was fine. Still kept my focus."

"Pleasure without conscience
Knowledge without character
Life can change with a single drop."

"For real, I hope there are some talent, but I ain't holdin' my breath." Mizz said as he headed outside to Razah's uncle's truck. As Razah's uncle drove them to the conference, the boys sat quietly staring at the various sites along the way.

Razah's uncle parked on the side of the building as he remarked that there were too many people out front. The boys got out and saw the banners displaying the National Honor Society LEAD Conference and knew they were in the right place. They thanked Razah's uncle for the ride and told him they'd call when they were done. As the uncle drove away the boys walked to the front of the building. Razah's uncle was right as there were a lot of people milling about the entrance to the conference center.

Razah checked his watch and remarked, "We're not early but it looks like the doors aren't open yet."

"Strange," Mizz replied as they continued toward the entrance.

Suddenly a buzz started rising from the crowd and the boys started hearing their names. They looked at each other as they realized most of the people near the entrance were reporters and photographers. Everyone was calling out their names to try and secure an interview. It was all a bit overwhelming but they did offer a few comments as they eased their way inside.

"That was strange," Mizz said.

"You called it," Razah replied as they made their way to the registration table. Once they registered, they pinned their nametags on as they made their way to the stage. They both had been asked to say a few words to start the conference and they cordially agreed. Neither of them shied from the spotlight, regardless of the audience. They

"Pleasure without conscience
Knowledge without character
Life can change with a single drop."

felt it was important to illustrate that not all intelligent students were 'nerds' and not all athletic students were 'dumb jocks.'

As they made their way to the dais to take their seats, they both stopped dead in their tracks as the most beautiful girl they had ever seen made her way to the podium after being introduced. With each long stride, her jet-black hair flowed, barely brushing her shoulders. Her big brown eyes glistened in the bright stage lights. Her form fitting black dress accentuated her well-toned body and natural curves.

As they sat down, Mizz whispered, "You see that gift? Oh my God, she is tough," and Razah nodded in agreement. From their seats directly behind her, neither of them missed the fact that the view from the back was just as nice.

After adjusting the mic to her height, she introduced herself as Michaela L. Rivera. She welcomed the attendees and explained that these conferences were designed to encourage interstate communication among student leaders and advisers, to strengthen leadership skills, and to prepare those attending for leadership roles on the local, state and regional levels.

"We have a special honor at this year's conference. Perhaps when you all arrived you noticed the reporters and news station cameras at the front entrance. I think the two gentlemen that I'll be introducing to you may have something to do with that," she began.

Continuing, she added, "These two student athletes are from the same school, both carry 4.0 GPA's while taking advanced placement courses, and are also the president and vice-president of their student council. One

*"Pleasure without conscience
Knowledge without character
Life can change with a single drop."*

will undoubtedly be the number one college recruit in basketball while the other will be the number one recruit in football. It's my pleasure to introduce Mizzier "Mizz" Sanders and Myshawn "Razah" Greene."

With that, the two stood up, smiled and waved to the audience. "We'll hear from both of them," she paused as she turned toward them. "Mizzier Sanders, would you come up and say a few words?" she asked while joining the audience in applause. Razah sat down to await his turn as Mizz approached the podium.

As she shook his hand, he leaned in and whispered, "I'd like to speak with you after."

"I'm here for the whole conference," she whispered back while smiling. She turned and took her seat as Mizz adjusted the microphone.

"Thank you," he began as the audience's applause subsided. "First, I would like to thank God, my family, and my homie, Myshawn. I would also like to thank the beautiful Miss Michaela Sanders, excuse me Rivera, for that warm introduction." There were several laughs from the crowd, and he then continued his short but poignant speech emphasizing the importance of being true to yourself and doing what you can to improve your life and the lives of those around you. The audience listened intently to every word and at the conclusion gave Mizz a standing ovation.

Miss Rivera returned to the podium to introduce Razah. She smiled warmly at Mizz as he returned to his seat. She then introduced Razah in the same manner as Mizz. Razah's speech focused on planning for the future but not forgetting to live in the present. He expressed the point of never being afraid of failure, quoting Michael

"Pleasure without conscience
Knowledge without character
Life can change with a single drop."

Jordan, "I've failed over and over and over again in my life. And that's why I succeed," and added that fear will always interfere with achieving greatness. As he concluded his speech, the audience also gave him a standing ovation.

After the opening session of the conference, Mizz and Razah mingled with the other attendees while keeping an eye out for Miss Rivera. Razah caught sight of her standing by the door and he called Mizz over. "Yo Mizz, there she is. Watch this," Razah said, as he left to approach her. He cleared his throat and put on his best game face.

"Hey, what's good?" he asked with a smile.

"Hey, what's good?" She mocked, while shaking her head. "Nothin to you, you clown," she said as she rolled her eyes and neck.

"Clown? Ow! Word! I guess you're one of those I'm into myself chicks, a feminist, huh?" Razah shot back.

"What?!? That's no way to talk to a lady," Michaela scowled.

"I'm sorry, Madame," he said backing off.

"Razah, chill, chill," Mizz said as he quickly approached to bail out his friend, who seriously just played himself.

Michaela stood there shaking her head in disbelief. "Wow," was all she could muster.

"He didn't mean anything by that. He's been going through some things of late, so...," Mizz said in an apologetic tone.

"Well, you need to check him before...," she replied standoffishly.

"Beautiful, don't let anyone take away from your smile and charisma. Now, can I talk to you for a minute? Let's start all over," Mizz suggested, trying to smooth

"Pleasure without conscience
Knowledge without character
Life can change with a single drop."

things over.

She rolled her eyes as she sighed, "Okay, go ahead." It was obvious that much of her time was spent rejecting the advances of wanna-be players.

Undeterred, Mizz continued with sincerity, "Excuse me. I'm sorry to bother you, but you're simply the most staggering woman I have ever seen in my life. My name is Mizzier or Mizz for short, if you want to be part of my world." He said with a big smile.

She laughed as she shook her head. A laugh filled with disbelief and a hint of embarrassment.

"Why are you laughing?" he said defensively.

"That was so corny. Stop pranking," she said while giggling.

"No it wasn't. You were just trippin' when my man said 'hey.' What is it?" he asked.

"So what if I was like, 'Dude, you hot, oh my God I had to say something', would you believe me?" she asked.

Mizz paused for a moment then confidently responded, "Um...well...yeah."

Again, she laughed but this time it was a warm laugh, "You're too funny, Mizz." She smiled. "Oh, I'm sorry," she said as she glanced at her watch, "but I have to go. Maybe I'll see you tonight at the award ceremony?"

"Yeah, I'll be looking for you," came the quick reply as she smiled and turned away to leave. Mizz stood there for a moment watching. As she turned the corner and disappeared from his sight, he couldn't help but hope that they would see each other later. Coincidently, she had the same hope.

Mizz saw Razah standing by the refreshment table. He made his way over and picked up a cookie. Razah,

"Pleasure without conscience
Knowledge without character
Life can change with a single drop."

already knowing the answer, asked dejectedly, "What happened?"

"Probably get at her later or whatever," Mizz answered flatly not wanting Razah to feel any worse.

Razah figured that he'd changed the subject, "Everything is straight wit' the situation."

"Word? Everything?" Mizz questioned.   Razah smiled.

"Let's get it poppin'," Mizz suggested.

Just then, Razah's uncle pulled up and they headed back to the crib. When they got back to the house, they thanked his uncle for the ride and went into the house and straight down to the basement. Cuzzo and Nico had finished counting and they were just sealing up the second bin. They were waiting for the truck to get back so they could load the bins into the truck and take them over to Carey's FedEx location. The final tally was a cool 10.3 million. Even after Wiz's $150,000 plus 10% of 10.3 million, they were still walking away with 9.12 million or 2.28 million each.

Mizz knew what he and Razah would be doing with theirs, but he was curious what the cousins would be doing with their shares. That conversation could wait for another time, but right now everything was straight, as Razah said.

Mizz and Razah needed to change clothes and get ready for the award ceremony. Once they were ready, they packed their bags because they were staying at the conference center hotel, near the airport. They planned to attend some conference activities the next day, and since their flight home was early the following morning, they didn't want to impose on Razah's uncle any longer. Once they were packed, they thanked the uncle for his hospitality.

"Pleasure without conscience
Knowledge without character
Life can change with a single drop."

Nico brought the two back to the convention center, Cuzzo planned to stay another week before heading back east. Nico and Cuzzo's next stop was FedEx, once they dropped the two back to the conference.

After arriving at the conference, they immediately started looking for Michaela. Soon they saw her having a conversation with another knockout. She spotted them and motioned for them to come over. She introduced her friend, Tess, to them just as the lights flickered letting them know that the ceremony was about to start. They all agreed to meet later. While Michaela made her way to the stage, Mizz and Razah went looking for their seats.

After the ceremony, Tess bumped into Mizz. "Hey, you look lost. Can I be of any assistance?" Tess offered with a smile.

"I'm looking for Michaela," Mizz replied as he continued to scan the crowd.

"Oh, you like her, huh?" Tess said dejectedly.

"Why you think that?" he asked trying to sound surprised at the question.

"'Cuz most dudes sweat her. I mean, just look at her, she's hot," she said, not sounding jealous.

"I would expect you to say that 'cuz she's your friend," he said, quickly adding, "and you hot too." Then he saw Michaela walking up the stairs. He grabbed Razah to speak with Tess, "Razah, you remember Tess?"

"How you doin' Madame?" Razah said looking Tess up and down.

"Madame?" she said, shaking her head a little.

Mizz hurried up the stairs and caught up with Michaela at the top.

"Good evening, Ms. Lady," Mizz said trying to

"Pleasure without conscience
Knowledge without character
Life can change with a single drop."

catch his breath. It wasn't the stairs that had gotten to him, it was her stunning good looks and the chance to speak with her again that had him a little choked up.

With defiance came her response, "Please don't call me that. I want you to look upon me as your equal." After a brief pause, she continued. "Oh, even though your boy called me a feminist earlier. So, tell me something, how does it feel being the most popular kid in the world right now?"

"I didn't come up here to talk about that. I came up here to get to know you and express my 'G'," Mizz quietly stated.

"Oh really? Well, let me hear it, but first, I gotta tell you something. I'm not looking for a relationship and I don't date National Honor Society guys," Michaela intoned flatly.

"Then I'm your friend and I quit." Mizz said, without hesitation.

"You can't quit, I need you," she said, her eyes and voice softening as she took a step closer. "Wait, let me see. You got something on your lip," she said.

"What is it?" he asked, thinking the worst, like it might be a booger.

She leaned in and kissed him.

"You seducing me? Hmmm, girl, you got game," he said as she stepped back again.

"Let me tell you something. When I seduce you, if I decide to even seduce you, believe me Mr. World renowned Mizzier, you will know," and with that, she smiled and then she kissed him again. "I'm in your world now."

"Pleasure without conscience
Knowledge without character
Life can change with a single drop."

The Director

A few minutes later, he went to go find Razah. Razah had stopped talking to Tess and was engaged in what seemed to be a deep conversation with some random dude. Mizz walked up to them and Razah introduced him. The dude, it turned out, was a movie director and had been following Mizz and Razah in the news for quite some time. He wanted to do a movie about their lives and their journeys over the next year. The boys said they would think about it and get back to him. The director gave them his card and invited them to check out his studio the next day. They were down with the idea and he agreed to pick them up at their hotel in the morning.

The next morning, Mizz and Razah waited in the lobby for the director. He arrived a few minutes late in a black Escalade with full tinted windows and the freshest rims that they had ever seen. They climbed in and the interior was decked out with TV screens, a mini bar and plush leather seating. They were riding in style.

When they arrived at the studio, they received the royal treatment. 'We could get used to this,' Mizz and Razah thought to themselves. The director, who asked the boys to call him Chase, brought them onto the set of his latest movie, a slasher film being done in the classic style. Mizz said he had always wondered how the makeup and special effects worked, so Chase took them into a back room where several masks were lined up each next to a computer. Over the next hour, he explained to them in detail the process of taking a person and turning them into someone or something else. Mizz, who had always been fascinated with this, took mental notes.

After the tour, Chase dropped them back at the hotel

"Pleasure without conscience
Knowledge without character
Life can change with a single drop."

and told them to call him when they were interested in discussing his idea further. They let Chase know that they were interested in discussing his idea further about them and it was something they would get back to him. They agreed and got ready to be out for their flight.

Keepin' it "G"

Early the next morning they sat on the plane and chatted about everything, well almost everything. Airplanes are not ideal locations to discuss ten million dollar bank heists.

"So you bag shorty or what?" Razah asked, really wanting some detail.

"She straight. She was frontin'," Mizz replied, "You know how the chicks do."

"I feel you. You think you going to beat?" Razah pressed.

"Maybe. I ain't stressin' that girl. Far as I'm concerned," He got serious again, "Cali was Cali and we should leave it at that, feel me?"

"I feel you. That's why you my dude," Razah sat back in his seat and put on his headphones. Mizz sat looking out the window, thinking about the events of the past few days. Real paper was waiting for them back home, no more bull. When they touched down, Razah immediately hit up Leak to see if everything was cool.

"Holla at me," Razah said into the phone.

"You young clowns are geniuses," Leak replied, almost in disbelief that the two of them were actually able to pull it off.

"So, we good?" Razah questioned, already knowing the answer.

"Pleasure without conscience
Knowledge without character
Life can change with a single drop."

"Yes sir. Meet me at my spot," instructed Leak.

"Ok," Razah hung up and looked at Mizz who was eager to know what was up.

"What's good?" Mizz asked.

"Everything is a'ight," Razah said with a big grin.

"Cool?" Mizz was confirming.

"No doubt," Razah assured Mizz. "We gotta go to Leak's crib and handle that."

"We there," Mizz replied as an equally big smile came over his face.

As they approached Leak's house, the two of them remained cool, calm and confident as if nothing had happened. They climbed out of the cab and walked up to the old run-down duplex that Leak called home. Now it wasn't that Leak was poor. No, he had plenty of green, but he had learned a long time ago that one could use their money for many things and he just didn't see the point in spending it on his crib. Besides, he had to keep close to his clientele.

"What up, kids?" Leak said as he invited them inside.

"Chillin'," they said in unison.

"Did you do what I ask?" Razah continued.

"Of course cuz', of course," replied Leak.

"Where the bins? I know you didn't bring them over here as hot as the spot is," Mizz said.

"Mannn" no, you two ain't the only ones that are smart," laughed Leak.

Razah informed Mizz, "I told Leak to go to a storage spot. He had some couches, chairs, tables and stuff. So when he left his shorty's job, he went to the storage spot."

"Pleasure without conscience
Knowledge without character
Life can change with a single drop."

"Ok. You surprise me more and more. But I got something for you. Razah, remember when I went to York (United Kingdom) to play on that tour team and to visit my homie Ross, the foreign exchange student that worked with me that summer in the pharmacy? Well, Ross and I have stayed in contact over the past year. It just so happens his pops runs a bank in Gibraltar.

Razah responded, "Where's that?"

Mizz said, "Let me finish. The border of Spain. I had set up an account at his dad's bank for us. So the money we make here goes into that account. So this money that we just obtained is going in that account. Bro, the ill stuff is that Gibraltar has not signed any double tax treaty with other countries. The tax haven on Gibraltar has not signed any information exchange with any other countries, which means any information regarding offshore clients is safe and will not get back to their country's authorities. This is all a part of Gibraltar's way of maintaining privacy for their offshore clients."

Razah said, "So we should just take some paper for our living expenses and needs and just let the rest of the interest build up."

Mizz replied, "Exactly. For a rainy day they also offer a flat rate of low tax of 10% to all non-resident individuals. And bro, no worries, they have all your info so you have equal access like me." Mizz wanted to explain to Razah so he had no doubts. "

Razah said, "Dude, why? You my dude. I would never doubt you. I trust you."

"Ross' pops is looking into some other investments for us. So 10% of the money will be used for that. Maybe we could find a way to open a chain of businesses in the

"Pleasure without conscience
Knowledge without character
Life can change with a single drop."

UK and then in the states to help the unemployed in our neighborhood. Or maybe in the city to do something good with this paper. Feel me." Mizz replied.

Razah says, "I agree Bro. Mizz, you a genius my dude. That's what's up. I'm cool with all of that."

Time for Change

Time is money and football season was ending. Basketball pre-season was just around the corner and it would soon be time for Mizz to showcase his stuff. Mizz looked at the calendar and smiled, tomorrow was the first day of the practice. It seemed like a decade since Mizz balled out. He couldn't wait to be back out on the court.

"Mizz, your season is pretty much here," Razah said coming up behind Mizz and putting a hand on his shoulder.

"I know dude. I hope to have a season like yours bro. You just have the states left. You set mad records," Mizz praised.

"No doubt, but we got the paper, so what we gonna do about your idea?" Razah asked, changing the subject.

"I know. Get Leak and his people together and let's meet later on tonight in the abandoned building on Bishop," instructed Mizz.

Later that night, Leak and a few of his goons met up with Mizz and Razah at the abandoned spot on Bishop. The rundown building was tucked away in a remote section of the neighborhood with broken-out windows and 'decorated' with graffiti both inside and out. The old Scovill warehouse had been abandoned for years and served as a perfect spot for the kind of business transactions that were best done in secret.

Mizz pulled open a makeshift door that was nothing

"Pleasure without conscience
Knowledge without character
Life can change with a single drop."

more than an oversized piece of plywood and led them inside.

"Pfft, you don't trust nobody, word," Leak commented as he look around, "No bugs, nothing. You're a smart young dude, bro. Good move choosing this spot too, abandoned building and everything."

Mizz gathered everyone around, "Well, let's get started."

Mizz stopped and looked at one person, "Oh dang, Meneto. What brings you down here cuz'? I haven't seen you in years. You must like broke dudes! What would make a high price insurance agent like yourself come and hang wit' low income people like us?"

"I'm no fool. It's basic common sense and arithmetic. It's a difference from them paying me $1,250 a week and you paying me $12,500 a week," Meneto replied bluntly. He had long since left the street game and had gone legit. He had a job as a salesman for a well-respected insurance firm. When he heard about this opportunity to make some real paper, he decided to rethink his current situation.

"Good, 'cuz you gotta rob and steal to get ahead wit' the way Bush killed this economy. For real," Mizz saw this was the time to lay it down for everyone. "Anyways," he began, "there is enormous growth of African Americans wit' no paper, disenfranchised, disinterested and disgusted. Then these Republican jokers act like we don't exist," Mizz continued with genuine sadness.

"Meanwhile, the corporate fat cats get richer," Razah joined in.

"And the rest don't get a penny," Meneto chimed in.

"When the world like this go down, people wanna

"Pleasure without conscience
Knowledge without character
Life can change with a single drop."

get high, dumb high, and wild fast and please believe me," Mizz said holding up what looked like a piece of candy, "this is going to do it and make us rich and it's completely legal."

"What? That look like a peppermint your moms gives you in church to keep you quiet," Leak's girlfriend, Chantress, said doubtfully.

Not yet wanting to get into the specifics and ignoring Chantress' comment, Mizz continued, "The white folks, white collar crime, Bernie Madoff, that's not how we do. The 'great get money' hustlers like Freddie Myers, "Freeway" Ricky Ross, Guy Fisher, Rich Porter, Rafer Edmonds, and especially the last crew to do it, like no other than *BMF*..." Mizz paused in a moment of reflection.

More animated, Mizz continued, "Black Mafia Family! Shout out to Big Meech, hold your head. They all showed us the way. My dude's way is hardcore and how they freaked it. But fam, we doing this different, all of us working on the beeper and cell phone. You change the product, then you must change the marketing strategy. We ain't gonna worry about territory or what corner or projects we got. The game ain't about territory no more. It's about product. We got the best product and we going to sell no matter where we are. Check this out, half the real estate, twice the product, the territory don't mean nothing if the product is whack. PRODUCT PEOPLE! PRODUCT!" Mizz's voice had almost reached a fevered pitch. He took a moment to catch his breath.

"These fake thugs having the projects and corners. For example, dudes play b-ball here in the states, but go overseas to get that cake. Territory ain't nothing. It's about product and family and we have the product. We taking

"Pleasure without conscience
Knowledge without character
Life can change with a single drop."

this game to another level and thinking like some white collar corporate cats, not some ghetto hoodbooger on the corner," Mizz declared sounding more and more like a leader with every word. "So the concept is basically this, the whole family has to be put together as a black army. We going to take over the east and west coasts! But we going to do it our way and change the game. You feel me? Not like some of the other crews that did come up 'cuz wit' time brothers got smarter and wiser. Times have changed. For instance, the illegal acts of Y.B.I., Young Boys Inc., B.G.F, Black Gorilla Family, Bloods, Crips, Vice Lords, Gansta Disciples, Junior Black Mafia. They may have worked together, but that won't be the path we follow. Check this. Every day, I walk by the Soul to Soul Art Gallery owned by the good brother Najee Rasheed. He's always spitting that real knowledge I appreciate when I see him. One day I went into his place of business and family, I was taken aback by how dope the meanings of the paintings in the gallery were. Frank Morrison, Edwin Lester, Henry Lee Battle, and Kevin Williams, to name a few iconic painters, have shown me a different, positive way of thinking through their epic depictions. So we can do the same thing with this new product when we flood the streets." Mizz was rolling now.

Mizz looked out to those listening to him, they were starting to hang on his every word, "The list goes on and on but again the crew that did it like no other was Black Mafia Family...BMF. We need to take a little bit from all of these crews and build our empire to the fullest. Failure is not an option. Everyone in our family will move like brothers and sisters and will move as one. Everyone will prosper in his or her own way, but it all starts with the head of the body,

"Pleasure without conscience
Knowledge without character
Life can change with a single drop."

the leader. So a good leader," Mizz, speaking in third person just in case, "has good people behind him. If you a whack leader, you going to have whack crews behind you, not loyal dudes, just straight bum grimy ones."

"A real leader takes the good wit' the bad and shows you how to come up out of it. That is the meaning of a real leader and it formulates into *The Black Enterprise.* Trust me, there will never be another crew like this one and if there is, they won't be black, not in this lifetime. Like I said, BMF was the last and they didn't know it but they passed the torch to us and we gladly taking it. On the other hand, what is important is that we all came into this together, we all making money but money ain't nothing if we don't got each other and we not going to fall out over no chicks! I don't mean no disrespect to the ladies in here, but again, we ain't falling out over no broads.

"We all done some dumb things over one girl or another, turned on each other over rumors, so let me repeat again, we not falling out over no broads. Look at all the kinds of different people in this room. Dark, light, short, tall, nasty, fat, big heads, braids, dreads, beards, bald and you all got money, yet we can't get along cuz of some trick? Be for real! Not happening. Plus it's too much talent out there, you got money so you can have your pick of them. Fat, ghetto, hood rats, white, models, chicks wit' weaves, whatever you want. Please, I'm emphasizing, I don't want no beefing, no drama, just business and no unnecessary attention to us."

"One thing for sure, you wanna trick, watch your purchases 'cuz it will turn against you. That's what them people want you to do. If you wanna get anywhere and get any real money then don't mess wit' the street dealers.

"Pleasure without conscience
Knowledge without character
Life can change with a single drop."

Like I said, you change the product, you change the marketing strategy. You take out one of them fake thugs out; it's a thousand of them jokers right there to take their place. We going to deal wit' those that have clout, something to lose. We not dealing with Willie and Nut Nutt getting shot up in the hallway over a dime bag. Nah, we ain't going out like that. We going to deal wit' people that can make us rich and then turn around and we supply them. Feel me! Here's the deal."

Mizz reached behind him and took a board with a bunch of names and pictures on it, "Here we go. Check this out. Rashod Anderson, he's the middleman. He supplies the dudes who supply the streets. This joker gets his stuff from the importer Jerome Massifield. He is the number one importer on the east coast. Fifty percent of all the drugs in New England goes thru this guy. He is able to do this 'cuz his step-father, Carlos Rodriquez Gomez' is the first cousin of the Latin, self-promoting, and influential politician Felix Sanchez."

Mizz said, pointing to one of the pictures on the board, "Sanchez is the one that helps Massifield get the drugs into the country. Our goal is to get at these cats and have them buy from us, like how the old 'G' Frank Lucas did to the mob in that movie, _American Gangster_, smell me?" Mizz stopped speaking for a minute to get the reaction from his friend and potential business associates.

"So we going after the Felix dude first?" asked Razah as he was trying to understand all that Mizz was saying.

"Not right now, he too big. That's like saying CJ Miles versus Jordan," replied Mizz.

"Who?" Razah asked

"Pleasure without conscience
Knowledge without character
Life can change with a single drop."

Mizz continued, "Exactly, but we will if we can get to that step. Then we holla at the cousin and hurt him financially. Now my G's, that would be good for us and make a name in high places, feel me? But everyone listen, we get to Johnson and then Massifield, in that order. Why? 'Cuz it protects us and word of mouth and money is the plan. What it is, is trust. Fam, we goin' to change the whole game. Just imagine tons of this in worldwide distribution. Plus, we doing us here in this spot. It's crazy. We will have loyal customers. We going to set up the lab here on Bronson to make the product."

Pointing to one of the guys, Mizz instructed, "Jesse, you could find the two spots on Bronson wit' the real estate, ya know, one place to make the product and another place to collect our money. Oh and hook up PC systems 'cuz that's what you do." Mizz was thinking as he spoke, the wheels of the plan coming together. He wasn't about to overlook anything and was happy to see that everyone was paying attention and taking mental notes of their responsibilities.

"Watch out for the workers, money and product. Leak, we need muscle to watch out for the haters and screen the customers. Soon, we going to need look outs to holla on every block," Mizz was hitting on all cylinders.

"Fam, the world is gonna be ours. It's not like ecstasy, crystal meth, or pills. What's crazy is that this drug is completely legal and absolutely safe. It's made from all natural and legal ingredients. It's not a drug that's going to get you wasted. People will go to work and do their job better than they did the joint when they were sober or straight."

As Mizz holds up the candy, he looks directly at

*"Pleasure without conscience
Knowledge without character
Life can change with a single drop."*

Chantress and continued, "For real though, I have been taking classes and worked in a pharmacy the last two summers. This peppermint candy is a chemical barrier. It increases your attention, energy, contemplative powers and yet with a smooth transformation. Inside the red strips is where it takes place and you feel like you about to blast off. For example, one night in the pharmacy I had the opportunity to test the candy. A friend had been working all night and needed a fix. He didn't want an energy drink or pills or anything with any kind of extra caffeine because he wouldn't sleep." So I asked him, "I have some candy, you want a piece?' The moment to test the candy was finally here with great timing. I then said, "Here you go Bro. I don't know how much it will do for you but make your breath smell good." LOL. "You need candy anyway with your whitelips. Looks like you been eating powdered donuts all day."

This dude then said, "Shut up, Mizz. Just give me the candy. You always got jokes."

Mizz hadn't tried the substance at all, but as far as he was concerned it should be FDA approved.

Within seconds, the dude said, "Dang Bro. What kind of candy is this? Wow! Either I'm hungry or this is the best peppermint candy I have ever had. I am wide-awake. Man, you got more?"

Mizz then continued, "So, after this experience, to reiterate, it's completely legal and I'm the only one that knows how to make it. Yo, this whole east coast is ours. I did a lot of research on this substance. The candy identifies the receptors in the brain that activates specific circuits, but as humans we only supposed to be able to access 20% of the brain. This candy lets you access all of it, and if you're

"Pleasure without conscience
Knowledge without character
Life can change with a single drop."

smart it works even better. That's one of the benefits. Also if you're broke and depressed, it gives you motivation and drive, a new way of thinking, a new way of living life. It's not a hallucinogen so no one will be having bad trips or jumping out of windows. People will have record memory of things that happened 10 years ago like it happened yesterday. It doesn't make you drunk, drugged up, high, or bent. It makes you have an open mind, a sense of worth on Earth. You can work at a high level and not crash. That's the difference between this and other drugs. That's why it's called *Immortality*. So there isn't a down side. I tweaked and engineered the substance to get the bugs out and complete the process."

"Yo keeping it 100, all of you or most of you have sold crack!" he said stating a fact, "What is crack? Some of our family is on crack, true story. We all grew up in this life whether we like it or not, we street, real talk. Crack is an addiction most people can't kick and it's a lost cause. Ever since crack came on the scene in the late 80's early 90's, it's been going strong and getting stronger by the minute. Crack fries the brain and your will! Forget about it. In my opinion, a crack addiction is worse than nicotine. People can't cope and the after effect! We already know the result. It's dumb illegal and yet, you can get it on any block or street corner. That's why *Immortality* will change the game and take over!"

"Yo, and another thing," Mizz continued, "Yo fam!! You ever see a newborn crack baby, a new crack baby, seven hours old yelling and screaming 'cuz the withdrawal is so bad? That crack baby probably not gonna be able to do things on time like walking, talking, crawling or even laughing 'cuz all the drugs that mother did. He won't never

"Pleasure without conscience
Knowledge without character
Life can change with a single drop."

be right, can't never catch up, be having temper tantrums all the time 'cuz he so frustrated. Most likely by the time the kid is ten years old, it is already in the foster care system. Where we come from, there are mad babies like that 'cuz these fake gangstas are bringing that mess in this country."

"Like I said before, the majority of you here have hustled crack and maybe still doing it now. Regardless, that ends now. There's no need for you to be messing with that. We don't need the heat if you're caught and wit' what we doing you won't need that chump change either." The expression on Mizz's face conveyed how dead serious he was about this.

"The majority of our people are being murdered before they get the chance to live their own lives. That's gotta stop and that's why we going to change the game. *Immortality*!!" He said as he stands up holding the candy which reveals this new name clearly written on its wrapper.

"Yo Mizz... You serious wit this Homie!! Unbelievable plan," Razah exclaimed shaking his head and almost clapping.

The Black Enterprise

Mizz held up the piece of candy again and laid out his business plan.

"I know you're wondering how we gonna get this on and popp'n. Hear me out and you won't be disappointed. From this point on, loyalty and trust will define our family and not the love of money, though there be plenty of that," Mizz said as he began laying out the groundwork of the plan.

Continuing, he said, "Those that succeed remember

"Pleasure without conscience
Knowledge without character
Life can change with a single drop."

that it's always business, never personal. The whole operation will be called, 'The Black Enterprise'. 'The Black Enterprise' will be a Fortune 500 Company made up of black geniuses. The model is 'I failed ova and ova again, therefore, I succeed.' This means, there is no more room for failures, so no bad decisions exist in 'The Black Enterprise.' The company will be broken down like this."

Without pause, Mizz began outlining the particulars of the plan, "You will have to punch a clock with shifts like, day shift 7am-3pm, evening shift 3pm-11pm, and overnight 11pm-7am. This will be at all our locations and I will appoint lieutenants for each shift." At this point, Mizz saw among them those who would be his first picks, but opted to save that news for after the meeting.

"Let me give you some numbers so you know what I'm talking about. Each of these little 'candies' goes for five bucks. Trust, once word gets around we could charge more but we ain't gonna. We charge five, got it? It cost two bucks to make. That's three bucks profit each. Each case holds 2,500 so each case sells for $12,500. That's $7,500 profit each case. There's twenty cases on a pallet. So each pallet sold is a profit of $150,000. Once we totally popp'n, there's no reason wit' our product we won't be able to sell one pallet a day to start. Doesn't sound like much does it? Guess what fam, that's $4,500,000 a month. $4,500,000 a month profit! In one year that comes out to fifty-four million dollars." This brought a few surprised looks and quiet comments murmured amongst a few.

Undaunted, Mizz pressed on, "Never, and I mean never, write stuff down. And at the end of the week you'll pay all who worked at each location, $2,500 for the week. Trust, we're gonna monopolize the game because we can."

"Pleasure without conscience
Knowledge without character
Life can change with a single drop."

He paused to take a break and to observe the reaction. He was looking for the doubters because they would be the first ones to go. He was pleased because he saw none. He knew he had them and proceeded.

"Once we start hittin' numbers, then those makin' $2,500 a week will be making more, much more. You, my fam, getting in on the ground floor, what they call 'charter members' will be rolling. Razah and I aren't gonna be like those corporate fat cats takin' millions in bonuses 'cuz they can, trust, you will all profit too as long as you're cool and can follow the rules," Mizz paused again to see the big smiles light up the room.

"We will be the only ones who know how to make this candy and we're gonna supply the whole Tri-State with it. So what we're gonna do is give our Columbian connection fifty thousand pieces as a test. And they're going to give it all away. Give everyone a taste. And then we'll have our customer base," pointing to one of his family crew members for emphasis. "If everything goes according to plan, and he proves to be worthy, then we will supply him whatever he wants. For example, another fifty thousand, hundred thousand, fo' real, I know we'll need to supply them with a million pieces," Mizz said with his ever present confidence.

"Supply and demand will bring in *millions of dollars*," Mizz slowly letting those last three words roll off his tongue. Again, this brought on more whispered comments and a couple of whistles of shock from the listeners. "That's enough to fill my crib and Razah's crib combined! Oh, and of course, your cribs as well," Mizz added with a smile and a nod. "My family, this is gonna happen fast, like no one's ever seen before. It's not a

''Pleasure without conscience
Knowledge without character
Life can change with a single drop.''

stretch to say that we will be the largest manufacturer in New York City and on the East Coast. Oh, that's right, 'cuz we'll be the only manufacturer. Word, if everything is to a T, this plan could easily be pulling in 200 million dollars a year...if not more. Even I don't know where the ceiling is on this." Certain he had clearly stated their motivation and earning power, Mizz again raised the candy in front of them and signaled the meeting had come to an end.

When Mizz wasn't playing ball, he was giving samples of his *"Immortality"* candy out on his block. When people started coming back and had to have more, he stayed true to his plan and continued to charge only $5 apiece. With business popping, he designated locations to the family members and close friends he had brought in with his impassioned speech and solid business plan. With this candy being more popular than cocaine, crack, heroin, crystal meth, etc., and a lot of local dope dealers getting bagged, Mizz and his crew took over blocks during the early stages. Mizz and Razah used wearhouses and abandoned buildings to package the candy for distribution. This was looking like a regular drug operation. The selling of ounces, half ounces, 50s, 20s, 10s, round the clock. It wasn't unusual to have 50-60 transactions an hour. On each block, when the runner got low on his supply, he'd go to his car and beep the horn 6 times signaling the supplier to drop more *Immortality* for him out the window of the project building. Lookouts were posted on the rooftops. Leak, who was the most trusted out of the group, had his girl rent several apartments in the projects in her name where they held large amounts of money for the crew. She and Leak were their main carriers for their distribution activities and for quality control, using their Colombian

"Pleasure without conscience
Knowledge without character
Life can change with a single drop."

connections. For instance, since Mizz was the only one that knew how to make the product, they did a test run with Mizz giving Leak's girl 17 keys of candy which she hid in her luggage. She came back with a small lump sum of money compared to what they were about to receive.

The Columbians had to almost test the feedback from the loyal buyers and other distributors. The next run was for 300 keys worth 3 million dollars. Leak transported the keys along with his wifey who rented the U-Haul to travel around the country to meet the Colombian connection in Washington State. Though the candy took over cocaine in popularity, it was creating a drug epidemic in its own right. No one knew it was, by nature of the formula, completely legal. It was widely available in every ghetto and suburb. With business growing, Mizz's organization grew with it, and large amounts of the candy was being made and supplied in the tri state. Mizz was able to specify and allocate a large amount of the candy because he made it for retail and wholesale. Mizz only entrusted his fam and closest friends with the cutting and wrapping of the candy for all sales. Even Mizz hadn't expected this much success this quickly. He and Razah would simply look at each other in amazement, overwhelmed by the amount of paper rolling in. They were happy, the members of The Black Enterprise were happy and the Columbian's were happy. The best part of all was the fact that they weren't doing anything illegal. Well, not entirely illegal, that is.

What's Really Good

Mizz and Razah met up the next morning and headed to school. Mizz couldn't wait for the day to end and his first practice to begin. He missed his team, his coach,

*"Pleasure without conscience
Knowledge without character
Life can change with a single drop."*

his court and this season's promise of greatness. Regardless of all the success of The Black Enterprise, Mizz's true passion was that of being on the court. The Black Enterprise began as a vehicle to get paper until he made it as a pro. It was as pure and simple as that. Now his goals were loftier but the bottom line was he missed being on the hardwood. Razah tapped him on the shoulder shaking him from his thought.

"It's finally here," Razah said encouragingly.

"I know. It seems like I was just at your first game and now we 'bout to start my season," Mizz said thinking about the upcoming season.

"You deadly," Razah replied.

Mizz's tone became serious. "I needed to tell you something from the other day. Word, well Bro we have been thru thick and thin, I love you. That's why the money we make with this other stuff; you and I will be straight even if neither of us end up going pro."

Razah looked puzzled. "What you sayin' B?" he asked.

Mizz explained, "Remember when I went to Botswana in Africa a couple of summers ago to study and play ball? I told you about my friend Kitso down there. We've stayed in contact over the last year. It just so happens his pops runs a bank in Gaborone. Anyway, I had him set up an account at his dad's bank for us. So, the money we make here goes into that account, I mean aside from the paper that we need for living. And if we really need, we can get loans from the bank secured with our account."

Razah nodded in full understanding.

"No worries B, they've got all the info on you so

"Pleasure without conscience
Knowledge without character
Life can change with a single drop."

you'll have equal access to the money just as I do. Word," Mizz added to allay any concerns that Razah may have had.

"I never doubted you. I know you've got my back," Razah quickly interjected, sensing Mizz might have thought that he was concerned about the money.

"Well you know it's cheaper there so I'm having Kitso and his pops looking into some things that we could invest in down there too. So like ten percent of the money will be used for that. Maybe the money can help some local businesses and if it works out, we'd be making even more money. So you cool with that, B?" Mizz asked.

"Straight up Mizz, you really are a genius. And yeah, I'm cool with all that." Razah said with a nod.
"But anyway," Mizz continued, "'cuz like I was saying, just wanted you to know."
"A'ight, Word! I love you too G." Razah nodded.
"Word!" Mizz thumped his chest.
Razah thought for a moment and looked at Mizz and said, "Man B, we're gonna be all entrepreneurial and all that, huh?" Then they both laughed.

After walking for a bit in silence, Mizz changed the topic back to basketball, "Of course, the team starts practice at four today. No balls!! Just conditioning. Then tomorrow we play pick up, so those bums get one more day before I give them work, feel me?" Mizz said mimicking a cross over ight!!!

"What's really good though, my G, is with the other piece. That plan you got is on and poppin'," Razah knew that their wait for the real paper would soon be over.

"Yeah, thanks. Oh, that reminds me, I've got to get to the library today. I'll have one of the other kids log on and get online and order that stuff we need. I'll tell coach

"Pleasure without conscience
Knowledge without character
Life can change with a single drop."

that I ordered the gun and it'll be in next week. I'll have everything shipped to the school. But the gun already came in. I've got it hiding in plain sight," Mizz said.

Razah changed the subject hoping to get some juice, "By the way Mizz, you been talking' wit' shorty from the convention?"

"Ooooooh, you mean that fly shorty, Michaela?" Mizz smiled thinking about their kiss.

"Yeah, that fly joint," Razah confirmed.

"I speak to her every now and again, but nothing serious tho' she asked for a game schedule," Mizz smiled.

"Where she from? She from Brooklyn Park Slope?" Razah asked and then answered his own question.

"Word! How you know? It said it in the program or something?" Mizz asked in surprise.

"Yeah," Razz answered.

"One. The Brooklyn girls are crazy tho'," Mizz said thinking about a girl from Brooklyn that he chilled with the year before.

"A chick that bad, B," Razah paused as he pictured Michaela in his mind, "can do whatever she want."

Mizz agreed.

"Word!!" They laughed, dapped each other up and agreed to get at each other after school.

Later that day, Mizz met up with his coach to discuss the upcoming season. Even with what could be the season of his life just around the corner, his mind kept going back to The Black Enterprise and the paper they were gonna be making.

"Mizz, what's good player? I heard you the best thing since sliced bread," somewhat teasingly said the coach while thinking about a potential championship.

"Pleasure without conscience
Knowledge without character
Life can change with a single drop."

"Coach, you crazy. Just workin' hard. You know how I do," Mizz said.

"I know buddy, I just want you to stay focused. There are going to be a lot of haters and leeches trying to get on and get next to you," the coach always admired Mizz's work ethic. He wished all his players worked that hard. True, none of them had Mizz's talent but most of them could be better players just by following Mizz's lead.

"Thanks, Coach. Not only are you my coach, you're my friend," Mizz said with true sincerity.

The coach smiled. No matter how great Mizz was now and how great he'd be in the future as a player, the coach always sensed that he'd be a truly great person off the court as well. "Thanks, Mizz. That means a lot to me. Just remember, no matter what; always be true to yourself and the truly important people in your life."

"Good advice, Coach, thanks again," Mizz nodded in agreement.

Thinking about Mizz's work ethic gave the coach an idea. "Listen Mizz, I want you to lead this year, run preseason training and keep the team focused and ready. There will be a scrimmage next week, then the first game the following week. It's moving fast. The first game is on local TV too." Coach always got excited about the games being on TV. He was able to convey his excitement to the team and they seemed to perform better. He knew it was being televised to showcase his star player but that was okay with him too.

"How's your sidekick?" Coach said thinking about Razah and his upcoming game.

"He's chillin'." Mizz shrugged.

"They got state championship game this weekend,

"Pleasure without conscience
Knowledge without character
Life can change with a single drop."

huh?" the coach asked.

"Yeah, they should win. Razah's got mad schools after him tho'. More than me," joked Mizz.

Coach all knowingly chuckled, "You and he got the same schools chasing you. I watch ESPN too Mizz."

Mizz laughed out loud, "You right. Just makin' sure you be paying attention. Oh Coach, just so you know, I ordered the gun. It'll be in next week."

"Alright, thanks, stupid budget delays. We should have had that equipment already," the coach sounded annoyed for a moment but then his tone changed back realizing it wasn't worth getting upset about. Not as if his star player needed the equipment anyway. "Well, just wanted to holler at you. See you later in practice." Coach patted him on the shoulder and left.

"Ok, Coach. Thanks man, see you later." Mizz called after him.

How About Some Hardcore

The weekend finally arrived, bringing with it all of the hype that talent like Razah's commands. He was expected to bring home the championship and everyone was on hand to witness this phenomenon make history. The stadium was filled with mad scouts and TV cameras. Razah's mom couldn't believe that all of this attention was for her son.

She felt a deep sense of pride flood over her as she heard the announcer's booming voice fill the stadium as he introduced her son, "Myshawn Greene is leading the nation in rushing yards, kick-off return yards and touchdowns. He is by far the number one rated prospect in the nation. Many of the experts have compared him as a combination of

"Pleasure without conscience
Knowledge without character
Life can change with a single drop."

Barry Sanders and Reggie Bush. This kid is serious and he's only a sophomore."

The game started and the crowd went wild as Razah returned the opening kickoff 98 yards for a touchdown. His mom joined the crowd as they started the familiar chant of "Razah! Razah! Razah!" Mizz and Mikey went nuts waving their signs yelling right along with the crowd. Razah didn't stop there as he led his team to a 28-7 victory rushing for 325 yards and running for 3 touchdowns, breaking all high school records for a single game. His teammates carried him off the field on their shoulders as scores of reporters tried to be the first to speak with him.

The next day was Sunday and it was Razah's time to chill. He sat eating breakfast, thinking about the game when Mizz showed up at his door. As he got up to answer, he realized he hadn't gotten a chance to speak with him after the game.

Mizz was smiling, "Yo!! Razah, you nasty."

"Thanks Bro," Razah smiled. 'Yeah, I was nasty at the game,' Razah thought to himself. It felt good.

"B, you were surrounded last night. Couldn't get to you. Dang, you're *that* dude fam," Mizz said proudly. "Your mom dukes was in the building too."

"No doubt. It felt good too," Razah thought about how great it felt to see her in the stands rooting for him. He then changed the subject, "How's practice been going?"

"I've been dragging cats. It's real light, you know how I do. Same ol', same ol'," answered Mizz. "Word! I saw Leak at the game. He was chillin'. He was wit' the Goon Squad."

"Yeah, I peeped it," Razah confirmed.

"We 'bout to get it on and poppin' B, as soon as the

"Pleasure without conscience
Knowledge without character
Life can change with a single drop."

season starts," Mizz started going over the plan. "Chantress and Leak getting the muscle together so we should be straight in the next few weeks. Word, oh I forgot to tell you, the initial supplies got delivered so we straight. We just waitin' on the machinery which will be ordered once Jesse's got the spots. I spoke wit' him and he's almost set."

"Word," Razah acknowledged.

"Just trying to be like you, B, word! Have you been back to the storage?" asked Mizz.

"Nah," Razah answered sounding shocked, "We going together right?"

"Right," Mizz replied.

"I spoke to the fellas and we straight," Razah recalled the conversation with his cousin. "That mess had been on the news but now, no leads nothing. It's like the whole thing never happened."

"Say word," Mizz shook his head and smiled.

"Word!" Razah nodded in return.

"Razahhhhhhhhhhh! Cuz', that dope," Mizz said excitedly.

"Bust it. They are trying to trace the calls to the security guys," Razah cocked his head.

"One, word?" Mizz sounded concerned.

"Word. There's no way they can trace the number or if they do wit' all the technology stuff, the phone is in the sewer and the SIM card is wit' me," Razah said assuring Mizz that they were straight.

"Guard the SIM card wit' your life cuz', for real, word," Mizz's tone got serious.

"That was gangsta tho', how it went down though cuz'!" Mizz replayed the heist over again in his mind.

"Word," Razah agreed as he looked at the clock.

*"Pleasure without conscience
Knowledge without character
Life can change with a single drop."*

His mom was due home soon, "But I will holla later. My mom's doing something nice 'cuz of the game, Word!"

"Ok," Mizz got up to leave.

The next day on the way to school, they saw Murdock on the block chillin'. He told them to get in the whip as he wanted to talk. Murdock was a little guy but had worked out most of his life, so no one bothered with him. Mizz and Razah got into the car to see what he wanted.

"Yo, that was hard. The plan and everything and I was thinking on how we can..." Murdock started but before he could finish his sentence, Razah screamed.

"Yo!" and reached to blast the music in the car.

"Cuz', stop the car and let's take a walk," Mizz demanded, "Yo, come on. You're new muscle," Mizz said after they got out of the car.

"What's the rules?" Razah looked at Murdock almost angrily staring him down.

"I know the rules," Murdock said defensively.

"Say it," Mizz demanded. He wasn't playing around.

"Don't talk in the car or on the phone or to anyone that ain't down wit' us. But it's just you guys," Murdock answered as Razah just stood there glaring at him. "Ok, ok, I got it, I got it," Murdock put his hands motioning surrender. They got back in the car and Murdock dropped them off at school. "Good luck today, dudes, do work," He said as they got out of the car.

"Yeah, good look Murdock. You do the same," Mizz replied. As they walked up to the school, he turned and watched Murdock drive away. "That's one dumb dude," he said to Razah shaking his head as they walked into the building. Razah nodded in agreement and they headed off to class.

"Pleasure without conscience
Knowledge without character
Life can change with a single drop."

The season opener came and as expected, was jam packed with fans and reporters. ESPN was covering it for their high school game of the week and for the first time in his life, Mizz would be playing live on television. Every coach in the area eagerly waited to see what Mizz would bring in the first game. Mizz was hyped to be playing at the coliseum and couldn't wait for the game to start. During his warm-ups, he scanned the crowd and spotted Razah. He then noticed Leak, Chantress and their 'muscle.' He then saw someone else he hadn't expected, 'Oh dipp, it's Michaela,' he said to himself, his mind forgetting about the rest of the crowd and focusing on her. He looked over to make eye contact with Razah who was sitting behind the team's bench. After layups, as Mizz walked over to the bench to sit, he tapped Razah, "Look," he said while gesturing in Michaela's direction.

"Ohhh, worrrrdddd!!" Razah was surprised.

"Word, she looks dumb good cuz'," Mizz's mind had now completely forgotten about the game.

"Word, she's definitely a 12," Razah agreed.

"I'm droppin' fifty," Mizz said confidently.

"Say word," Razah answered nodding.

"Word," Mizz confirmed without hesitation.

He walked out onto the court and before the opening tipoff made eye contact with Michaela. She winked, smiled and waved while mouthing, "Good luck." Mizz did not disappoint the record crowd that had come out to see him. Toward the end of the third quarter, he had forty-three points, ten assists and ten rebounds. He was a fierce competitor and a driving force. He felt that he could easily have been playing pro ball. As he sat on the bench waiting for the fourth quarter to begin, Mizz looked to the

"Pleasure without conscience
Knowledge without character
Life can change with a single drop."

stands and saw Jesse point to him and then whisper to Leak and Chantress. They all hugged. He knew that Jesse had found the spots. Razah tapped Mizz on the shoulder, "I believe we good. I'm going to walk over there and see what's up."

"No dooke, stay here. You'll draw too much attention to yourself. I don't know why those fools over there doing that nutty stuff, feel me?" Mizz's tone was serious.

"Yeah, you right," Razah nodded. "They trippin.' I'll handle those clowns after the game, word! Forget about them. You still need to drop seven for your fifty. Take care of biz here and I'll see you later at the crib."

The fourth quarter started and by the end of it, Mizz had another thirteen points giving him fifty-six for the game. He hit thirteen three pointers and broke the school record for the most threes in a single outing. He ended up with a triple double adding twelve assists and thirteen rebounds. After the game, as if he were already playing pro ball, he gave a press conference and sat down for interviews with ESPN and local TV stations that had covered the game. After the interviews, he showered and dressed. Upon leaving the locker room, he was pleasantly surprised to see Michaela who had been waiting to see him.

"Wow, you a bad boy on that court. Excuse me, can I have your autograph?" she said playfully.

"Of course you can. That's all you want?" Mizz replied looking into her eyes.

"For now, fresh boy," she smiled as he laughed out loud. They walked and talked about the game while Razah was elsewhere talking to the crew about the rules.

"Fellas, what's good? My dude was killin' them

"Pleasure without conscience
Knowledge without character
Life can change with a single drop."

word," Razah said.

"A'ight, a'ight, word," they answered in unison.

Razah looked around to make sure the coast was clear and then got down to business, "Ok, let's keep it real. What was really good wit' y'all huggin' and pointin'. You remember the rules, no kind of anything. We all gotta be cool at all times. Come on, we workin' too hard to get here, all of us." Now how about some hardcore." He paused a moment to make sure they all understood to what he was referring. Their expressions on their faces assured Razah that they understood, so he continued, "So again. How about some hardcore!! Referring to the great M.O.P. This cannot happen again. We family, we won't self-destruct, trust! Nothin' will bring us down. We will own this city," and with that they all nodded and mumbled words of assurances that all was cool.

Meanwhile, Mizz and Michaela continued to walk and talk to get to know each other better. "So what made you come to my game?" Mizz asked.

"I got an aunt that lives out here, so on the weekends I take the train from the city to come visit her. Her daughter is my best friend. Besides, how could I not come? Your face is on every magazine and TV station," she said touching his arm.

"Word!! And I thought you forgot about me," Mizz said feigning sadness.

"Nah, you was cool. I like your style," she said.

"So you was feelin' my G? Ight!" Mizz said nodding confidently.

"You're a funny dude," Michaela said almost laughing.

"So how many dudes you deal wit?" he asked

"Pleasure without conscience
Knowledge without character
Life can change with a single drop."

"A few, nothin' serious," she replied.

"A'ight, that's cool," Mizz commented.

"And you?" she said raising her eyebrows.

"I'm chillin'. I got friends, same deal," he answered calmly.

After an awkward silent moment, Michaela blurted, "Well it was good seeing you again. My aunt is waiting for me. I'll see you around," Michaela turned to leave.

"Can I get a number, an address or something?" Mizz said almost begging.

"No, I'll see you again," She answered as she walked away. She turned and gave Mizz a smile and a quick wave.

'Ewhh!! Wow, you played me,' Mizz said to himself watching her as she got into her aunt's car. As she drove off, he memorized the license plate number.

The next day, Michaela was enjoying a relaxing day when she heard a knock at the door. 'Who can that be?' she wondered as she went to the door. She peered through the peephole to see Mizz standing on her porch. Michaela opened the door. "Mizz, what the !! you doin' here and how you know where my aunt lives?"

"Hey beautiful," He said as he smiled at her.

Perplexed, she repeated, "How do you know where my aunt lives?"

"I know that it's crazy that I just popped up here," he replied, seemingly avoiding the question.

"What did you do, follow me here?" she asked suspiciously.

"Nah!" he answered, "Well nothin' like that girl. I did memorize your aunt's license plate and called a friend who was able to tell me your aunt's address," Mizz offered

"Pleasure without conscience
Knowledge without character
Life can change with a single drop."

while looking down sheepishly realizing how crazy it sounded.

"Dude, are you loony?" she asked incredulously.

"No, but I just wanted to give you tickets to the next game," he said while offering a couple of tickets.

"Oh that was nice of you, thanks," she said as she took the tickets. She looked at him as he stood there looking at her and into the house. "You lookin' all around like you tryin' to come in or somethin'," she said, still unsure what to make of the situation.

"Nah," he replied while shrugging but then changed his mind, "I mean yeah, but if you don't want me to it's cool. If you're not busy, I really wouldn't mind," he rambled. He seemed more nervous than he thought he'd be. Things were never this difficult with any other girl before.

"I'm not busy. You can come in." She relented, figuring he was harmless enough.

"You ight. I mean, you cool for real," he smiled.

"Yeah, it's fine," she said coolly, not totally warmed up to his charms.

"I hope I'm not barging in," he said as he walked in.

"Too late for that, don't ya think?" she said cocking her head.

"Your aunt's crib is hard. Where is she?" he decided changing the subject would be a good idea.

"She took my cousin to a college tour for a couple of days. I'm here house-sitting and feeding the pets," She glared at him and finally pressed, "Ok, Mizz, question. Why is your black butt here?"

"You came to my game, I had career numbers and I want your support. I was hoping that if I asked you to come to the next game, you might say yes. If not the next game,

"Pleasure without conscience
Knowledge without character
Life can change with a single drop."

maybe the next game after that and I'd keep asking 'til the next game became the right game," he explained.

"Aw, I see, a man who is not willing to take no for an answer. Persistent," She coyly said as she slowly nodded.

"You never know how far it can get you. I see you're into fashion, huh?" He said as looked at her hoping another subject change would mellow the situation. She was dressed in tight blue Armani jeans with a white Dolce t-shirt that accentuated her upper body perfectly.

"You know about fashion?" She asked, sounding surprised.

"A lil' something, feel me. Gucci, Prada, Armani, Coach, Louis Vuitton, True Religion, Dolce and Gabana, Vogue," as he rattled off some top designers confidently.

"Really, you go boy. So you're like a Renaissance black man, basketball, honor society, stylist, presidential and all that," she responded, trying not to sound too impressed.

"You can say that! There was a quote by a famous actor, '*The world is yours*,' Wesley Snipes in *New Jack City*. I guess I live like that," Mizz said now sounding a little too confident.

"Ooohh, ok Mizz. You clown; you think you *know* your actors and movies? Well, it was Al Pacino in *Scarface* who said that. Now I think you're tryin' too hard," Michaela said as the expression on her face changed slightly. She seemed to be warming up.

Mizz laughed, "I'm startin' to feel you, Ms. Lady."

"Well, don't feel me too much," she said with a slight smirk.

"A'ight, for real though. Tomorrow night, my fam is having a little surprise party for Razah for winning the

"Pleasure without conscience
Knowledge without character
Life can change with a single drop."

state championship and I want you to come and chill with me. Maybe we can start to get to know each other better."

"Are you trying to ask me out Mizz?" she asked playfully feigning surprise.

"You can say that Ms. Lady, I definitely am," was his quick reply.

"I'm not too sure," she hesitantly replied while curiously thinking what a date with Mizz would be like.

"I can't take 'no' for an answer. It will be a great ending to a beautiful day. So, what do you say?" Mizz persisted, holding out his hands.

"Since you put it that way, ok, ight," surprising herself as she agreed to the date.

"I'll pick you up 9-ish, if that's cool?" he asked.

"How 'bout I meet you there. I'd be better with that," she replied still not ready to fully commit herself.

He started to object but she stopped him short, "You want me there, don't you?"

"Yes, I do," he conceded. He told her the time and location. "So, I'll see you then," he asked just to confirm.

"Yes, you will. Oh and Mizz, next time you intrude, call first, 'cuz I know your ghetto butt got the house number."

Mizz laughed. "You right, I got your number," he said as he winked at her, grinning from ear to ear. "I'll see you tomorrow night, Ms. Lady," he said as he headed for the door.

Upon closing the door behind him, Michaela took a deep breath, held it for a moment and slowly let it out. Then a smile came across her lips as she already began thinking about what she would be wearing tomorrow night.

At the party the next night, Mizz waited for

"Pleasure without conscience
Knowledge without character
Life can change with a single drop."

Michaela to arrive. He was determined to be on his game with her that night. As she entered the doorway and stopped, it seemed as if every guy in the place paused and stared. Dressed in a very low-cut red Louis blouse and a pair of black Prada jeans that looked like second skin, she stood at the door looking for Mizz.

Mizz saw her and immediately made his way to her, not too quickly as to seem over anxious in front of his fam, but quickly enough so she'd know he was waiting for her.

As he approached her, it suddenly struck him how hot she looked. The best he could muster was a simple, "Hi," that sounded to him as if he had stuttered.

Smiling, knowing that her ensemble had achieved her intention, she replied with an equally simple, "Hi yourself."

"Come with me, I want you to meet everyone," he said as he took her by the arm and led her over to introduce her to the fam. She saw Razah standing there and it was love, as if nothing happened the first time they met.

"Congrats to you on the championship," she said sincerely to Razah making him smile.

"Thanks. I see you chillin' wit' my man," Razah leaned in close, "You better treat him right."

"We chillin', he's cool," she said. Then with a wink, she added, "and I think it's him that should be treatin' me right."

Seeing that all was copacetic, Mizz interrupted, "ight, I see you two made up, no doubt."

"Yeah, we straight," Razah caught Mizz's cue. He excused himself and left them alone. Mizz introduced Michaela to the rest of the group in the immediate area. They all hung out for a little while longer until Mizz

"Pleasure without conscience
Knowledge without character
Life can change with a single drop."

decided to break out to spend a little time alone with Michaela.

"You hungry? I know a pizza place we can go," Mizz asked. There wasn't much food at the party and Mizz was feeling pretty hungry.

"Cool, I'm starving," Michaela calmly replied. She really was starving too. She hadn't eaten all day. Even though she wouldn't admit it, she was actually quite nervous about tonight.

They made their way to the restaurant. They chose a booth away from the other patrons. Mizz was happy to learn that she liked the same kind of pizza that he did. After the waitress took their order they began talking. Once the pizza arrived they continued talking. They ate and talked and even when the pizza was history their conversation continued. They talked about the basketball season, the honor society and even a little bit about fashion. Mizz listened intently to every word that flowed from her beautiful lips. Surprising to himself, he discovered that he was actually listening. He had never met anyone like her before. He learned about what she liked and what her hopes were going forward. Mizz felt the chemistry between them starting to grow. A couple of hours later, realizing the time, they left the restaurant.

As they walked to her aunt's house, they continued talking. Mizz had lost count of the number of different subjects they had discussed. He had known many intelligent girls before but most were not able to keep his attention this long and none looked as good as Michaela. At one point Mizz had considered holding her hand but for some reason, thought he maybe shouldn't. So, he didn't.

The whole walk back to her aunt's house, Michaela

"Pleasure without conscience
Knowledge without character
Life can change with a single drop."

had wondered if he would hold her hand. She had thought about taking his hand but thought that might be too forward. So, she didn't.

Mizz walked her up to her aunt's door, disappointed that they had arrived. He really was enjoying the evening and didn't want it to end. They stood there for a few seconds in silence, while Mizz contemplated his next move. Michaela spoke first, breaking the stillness of the moment.

"Thanks, I had a wonderful time tonight," she said trying to hide exactly how great the evening was.

"Me too," Mizz sincerely replied, looking into her eyes. "I haven't felt like this in a long time. Actually, I've never felt like this," as he leaned forward and kissed her, actually catching her by surprise.

She pulled back and looked at him, "Umm, Mizz."

"My bad, I should break," Mizz said hoping that she wasn't really upset.

"Mizz, I had a good time, I just can't go out like that on the first date," she said, trying to sound sincere, although she was longing for another kiss.

"I got you, I feel your G," Mizz replied. After a moment, they embraced and started kissing again. Mizz stopped suddenly and as he pulled back he blurted, "Oh Ms. Lady, my bad an' plus it's mad late," Mizz said, as he pointed at his wrist like he was wearing a watch, which he wasn't. "I'll call you."

"Yeah, you right, call me," She agreed while making a poor attempt to catch her breath. They both stood there for a moment.

Mizz decided to take the chance to see what would happen. "For real, I just wanna come in and talk."

She laughed, knowing that was the last thing he or

"Pleasure without conscience
Knowledge without character
Life can change with a single drop."

she wanted to do. "Ok, just talk," she said, pretending to sound serious.

Mizz took her hand, "Is that cool?"

She opened the door and pulled him inside. Mizz had gotten his answer. After another quick embrace and kiss, they went upstairs to her room. She turned the stereo to some slow jams (*RAIN by RAZAH*) to set the mood. They kissed again and fell onto the bed. Mizz took his time and it was exactly what Michaela had hoped it would be. She was in love for real.

The Morning After

The next morning Michaela woke up to some delicious smells coming from the kitchen. She put on his shirt and headed downstairs. As she entered the kitchen she remarked, "Yo, you really a Renaissance man making omelets and french toast." Realizing she was looking even better than she had the night before, Mizz smiled, "I didn't know what you'd prefer so I made both. You ok with that?"

Smiling, Michaela was impressed. "I love both and look forward to tasting your fine cuisine, Chef Mizz."

Turning serious for a moment, Mizz changed the subject, "For real though, I'm feeling you. I hope you don't look at me differently or feel we moved too quickly."

"Please, I wanted it to happen," She kissed him. "It takes two to tango," was her quick and reassuring reply.

"So that means I can see you again?" Mizz asked hopefully.

"Of course," she was surprised at the question.

Mizz pressed a bit more, "So you ain't going to front on me, then don't call me back. I hate that bull, for

"Pleasure without conscience
Knowledge without character
Life can change with a single drop."

real. Anyway, you want something else?"

"Don't ask me that," She said as she walked up to him and pulled him in close and whispered in his ear, "Mizzwerk."

"Ight," Mizz smiled and feeling her body close to his, bad memories of past relationships just disappeared. After a couple of warm kisses, they decided to sit and enjoy the fine breakfast Mizz had prepared. After breakfast, they both decided it be best if Mizz left as Michaela wasn't exactly sure when her aunt would be returning.

Mizz decided to head over to Razah's crib, unable to stop thinking about the previous night. He couldn't wait to share the details. He knocked on Razah's door and waited impatiently on the porch.

He called through the door as he heard Razah approaching.

"Yo, be right out," Razah called back.

"Cool." A few seconds later Razah opened the door and they headed down the street.

Not wasting any time, Razah got right to the question at hand, "What happen last night? You two just disappeared."

"Yo! We had pizza," Mizz smiled.

"Say word," Razah said wanting details.

"Word. Then I spent the night," Mizz smiled. My G she put it on me dooke!!!!! "I even made breakfast," Mizz contently said.

"Breakfast? You can't cook dude," Razah was almost in shock. Lol!!! U are nutttttty!!!

"I was so hit, yo!! I woulda fried some cereal," Mizz joked.

Razah laughed hard and loud. After a minute, he

"Pleasure without conscience
Knowledge without character
Life can change with a single drop."

then switched to a more serious tone.

Mizz looked at him, "Yo, don't get it twisted. I just said we had a good time. I'm on my G. Please believe dude, this ain't no love thing, we just chillin'," Mizz said, trying to reassure his partner in crime that all was cool.

"One thing for sure my G, when that kitty start calling it's a mutha!" Razah pushed Mizz in the chest, "Word! But remember, you're a criminal mastermind not a lover!"

"I got you, I got you," Mizz replied but in his thoughts, he couldn't get last night's events out of his mind.

While Mizz was recounting last night, Michaela was having a leisurely morning in bed reliving last night's events. She couldn't get Mizz out of her mind. It had been better than she had expected and now she couldn't wait for it to happen again. She reached for the phone and called her best friend Tess to share her excitement.

"Hello, what's good? How was your weekend?" Tess answered, sounding like she had been up for a while.

"Girl, guess what?" Michaela said excitedly.

"What girl?!" Tess knew her best friend had something juicy to tell her. "Oh, Sugar, what happened?"

"I saw him....Who? You know who!" Michaela knew Tess was playing.

"Mizz? Ooooooh that Mizz!" Tess said, as if she had actually forgotten whom Michaela may have been speaking.

Michaela laughed out loud, "That brotha' was chocolate. I was wit' him! I was wit' Big Mizz himself, but I was front'n' being all shy and stuff, like I wasn't feeling him."

"Did he....did he?" Tess's question hung in the air.

"Pleasure without conscience
Knowledge without character
Life can change with a single drop."

Rather than answer, Michaela just laughed again.

"You bad girl! Wow! How was it?" Tess wanted details.

"It was like all I saw was Fourth of July fireworks. Get this, that man even made me breakfast this morning," Michaela's voice jumped excitedly.

"No, he didn't!" Tess couldn't believe what she was hearing. Tess didn't realize at first that breakfast this morning meant that Mizz had spent the night. "Wait a minute... did he?"

"Spend the night? He surely did," was Michaela's satisfied reply.

"What the...? I wish I could find me a dude like that! Hey, what's up wit' you and Marcus?" Tess asked, referring to Michaela's last on-again off-again so-called boyfriend.

Michaela paused for a moment, "Girl, you know the story. He drank too much, priorities was out the window, couldn't help him. I know, I didn't want it to happen but it did. I had no control. Marcus and I are done." Michaela thought for a moment about what she had thought was a good thing before things got bad and before she met Mizz.

"Yeah, he was a loser. I loved him, but he still wanted to drink, get passed out and do dumb stuff. He put his alcohol before me, and all I did was try to help him. He was too old to be doing that dumbness. He finished college and still lived at home with his parents at twenty-six years old, come on! He'll never change! That's why I had to move on, but he will realize, I hope, someday and get his life together. He don't know a good thing till it's gone. And now I'm gone," again, Michaela paused, reflecting her time spent with Marcus and truly realizing it was over. She also

"Pleasure without conscience
Knowledge without character
Life can change with a single drop."

realized that it seemed as if a huge burden had been lifted off her shoulders.

"Hey girl, I know it hurts. Just focus on Mizz now. I'll call you later after school girl. And I'm glad you let Marcus go," Tess said offering her thoughts on the matter.

"That's the thing Tess, there is no pain, just relief," Michaela giddily replied. "Give me a call later, byeee," she said before hanging up.

'Byeee?" Tess said to herself staring at the phone in disbelief. 'Oh girl, you got it bad,' she thought to herself, shaking her head and smiling. That certainly was not what she expected to hear when she had picked up the phone.

Heat Around the Corner

The dimly lit interior of the aging police station buzzed with activity. Regular patrolmen, neatly clad in blue and detectives in their suits, seemingly all holding a cup of coffee in one hand and a cell phone in the other, snaked their way around each other as if walking assigned routes throughout the station. Newly arrested perps slovenly sat awaiting their turn to be processed. Once processed, then they would move downstairs to the holding cells.

In an overcrowded office in the back of the drab squad room, the captain's face contorted into an even angrier shape than usual. The shade of red was darker than normal as well. He glared at his lieutenant and not wanting any misunderstanding as to what he wanted and when he wanted it, roared, "Three days! I want information on my desk in three days! Don't let me down, Lou! Or heads will roll and sure as heck one of those heads won't be mine." He walked out of the lieutenant's office and slammed the door so hard that it sprung back open.

"Pleasure without conscience
Knowledge without character
Life can change with a single drop."

"Wow!" The lieutenant's mouth hung open. 'Good morning to me,' the lieutenant quietly said to himself.

"Captain is mad, huh?" The young baby-faced detective was known for his mastery of stating the obvious.

"He should be. Man, someone leaked some stuff to the chief and the captain had no answers. The chief lost it."

"About what stuff, Lieutenant?" asked the detective.

"Some substantial amount of wrappers with the name *Immortality* on them. Drugs and a high profile hustle named Leak Martin. Look everyone. You and I know that the system wasn't ready for this epidemic, this *Immortality*. It came on the scene like wildfire. But now I got the chief, mayor and the governor on my back. I need results and I need them fast."

"You see this piece of candy Lieutenant?" asked the young detective. "This stuff ain't your everyday stuff. This *Immortality* is twice the potency. I hear people in my building talking about it. It's the purest thing in the streets. And as you can see these wrappers are everywhere but no one knows what it's made of. I also hear people love it because you're not snorting it, smoking it, or using needles. You sucking on it cuz' it's a piece of candy and it's 5 bucks. Like I said, it's everywhere, on every corner out there.

The lieutenant replied, "Wow. How's that possible? Who could afford to sell a product twice as good for half as much?"

"Look at the wrapper, how it's packaged," Petey stated. It's like a Mentos, a Now & Later, or even a SweeTart wrapper," Petey said.

The lieutenant said, "Wait. I see these wrappers in my neighborhood. I never would have thought they were a drug of some sort. That is real clever."

"Pleasure without conscience
Knowledge without character
Life can change with a single drop."

Petey agreed, "Real clever. Sorry, I got off topic. Who is Leak?"

"He's the cousin of that high school basketball star, Mizz Sanders," replied the lieutenant.

"Really? That kid is nice," the detective expressed. He was a big basketball fan and had even been to the season opener after seeing that piece on ESPN.

"But let me tell you something that ain't so nice," the lieutenant, continued as he got up and closed the office door. "Word on the street is Mizz and his friend, Razah Greene, those high school star athletes, got something to do with Leak and they're saying Mizz is the mastermind of the whole organization."

"You gotta be kidding! Wait! Mastermind? Mastermind of what?" the detective asked incredulously.

"According to the Captain, they have the High Rises and the Terrace mostly. But apparently they're expanding."

"Sounds like bull," the detective interjected, afraid to repeat his previous mastermind question. He still wasn't clear to what 'organization' the lieutenant was referring. Actually he wasn't clear about most of what had been discussed even when the captain was screaming. He wasn't even sure why he had been called into the office to begin with.

"Maybe, but Captain was real mad and wants a file with answers in three days," the lieutenant answered.

"But what I'm wondering is why he would think those kids have something to do with it and with Mizz as the mastermind? He just plays basketball," the detective commented.

"No clue. Here's the file," said the lieutenant as he

"Pleasure without conscience
Knowledge without character
Life can change with a single drop."

handed the file to the detective.

Opening the file the detective remarked, "Not much of a file. One sheet. What's all this chicken scratch?"

"Those are the notes the captain took. It's hard to focus on penmanship when you're getting your butt chewed by the chief. Believe me, I've been there. You better get things answered quickly because I don't want to be there again," said the exasperated lieutenant. "And trust me, you screw this up and you'll find out for yourself how mad the chief gets. You think the captain was mad…that was a walk in the park. Now hurry up and review those notes," instructed the lieutenant, "You have algebra class in an hour."

"What?" asked the young detective with a puzzled look on his face.

"You're going back to high school, Petey," informed the lieutenant. "Undercover, now get going. And I suggest losing the 'look at me, I'm a detective' attire. Report back as soon as you get anything."

The young detective's stomach churned. He hated high school the first time around. He couldn't imagine it would be any better the second time.

He's Sheisty

Monday rolled around and Michaela was back at her school. The day was going by slowly. Finally, it was lunchtime. While at lunch, she started flipping through a newspaper that someone had left on the table. To her surprise, there was an article on Mizz. She was totally immersed in the article when a boy she did not recognize interrupted her and introduced himself.

"Excuse me. Hi, I'm Petey. Can I see that paper?"

"Pleasure without conscience
Knowledge without character
Life can change with a single drop."

he asked with a smile.

Apologetically Michaela replied, "Oh I'm sorry, is this your paper? It was…"

Petey cut in, "Oh no, no, I just wanted something to read. When you're finished, take your time." Then he spied the picture of Mizz and realized she was reading about him. "That dude is great and in a few years, an NBA superstar," Petey said, believing it to be true.

She smiled.

"Do you know him?" He asked her, knowing she may, according to one of the notes that he was able to decipher from the captain's chicken scratch.

"Yeah, you can see the paper, no problem. And yes, I know him. I'm Michaela, by the way," she said.

Petey's heartbeat quickened thinking perhaps this could be a break. He was there undercover to see if he could get any information or find someone with a connection to either Leak or Mizz. If she really knew Mizz as more than an acquaintance then she could be the lead he was looking for.

"Do you think I can get an autograph from him?" He asked trying to find out exactly how well she knew him. "It's kind of a hobby for me and I know he's going to be a superstar someday. Never too early to start," he added.

"Sure, I don't see why not," Michaela responded, not thinking the request was strange as she had seen Mizz stopped and asked for autographs. Realizing she had seen Petey before, she asked, "Hey, aren't you the new kid in my algebra class?"

"Yeah, I'm new here. Today's my first day," he replied.

"Oh? Welcome. Where you from?" she asked.

"Pleasure without conscience
Knowledge without character
Life can change with a single drop."

"Staten Island." Petey blurted out. Not sure why he said Staten Island as he had only been there a couple of times. He was hoping she wasn't familiar with it and begins asking him questions.

Michaela's face brightened as she had an idea. "I'll tell you what Petey. Mizz gave me tickets for their Christmas tournament game. The tournament is being held here. I got an extra ticket you can have. Consider it a welcome to the school present," she said with a smile.

Petey was caught off guard with her generosity and finally stated, "Those tickets been sold out."

"It's ok. I have three tickets. You can come with me and my girl, Tess."

"Really??? Wow! You're the best!" he said trying to contain his excitement but failing miserably.

As the bell began to ring, she told him, "I'll talk to you more about it after last period. Meet me here." With that she got up from the table to head to next period.

"Ok. Cool. Thanks so much," he said while thinking that this was going so much better than his first time through high school.

After the last period ended, Michaela saw Petey hanging out by the cafeteria. She headed over to him. "Hey Petey! Good first day?"

"Thanks to you, much better than I thought it would be," he replied while smiling.

"It's cool. This way the ticket won't go to waste. The game's in a couple of weeks. Meet us right over there," she said pointing to a spot near the entrance to the courts. "Cool?"

Again not trying to sound too excited, and failing, he blurted, "Yeah, yeah!! Anything!"

"Pleasure without conscience
Knowledge without character
Life can change with a single drop."

She smiled, being polite but was thinking, Petey certainly was an excitable dude.

After he left the school, Petey took a roundabout way back to the precinct station to update the lieutenant. He wanted to make sure he wasn't being followed. He was a young detective but he knew you could never be too cautious when you're undercover. As sincerely excited as he was about seeing Mizz play, that was not his purpose at being in high school...again.

"Hey Lou," Petey said upon entering the lieutenant's office.

"Petey? I didn't expect to see you for a day or two. You got something?" Asked the lieutenant curious as to why Petey was here already.

"Well Lou, here's the thing. I met this girl who seems pretty tight with Mizz. She's giving me a ticket to Mizz's tournament game being held at her...ummm... my school. She says that he gave her tickets to the game, which was sold out right after that ESPN piece aired. It's in a couple of weeks. I'll keep working it 'til then but I don't know how much I'll find out. I think going to the game might give me a better idea of who the players are in this so-called organization. And also who's calling the shots," concluded Petey

The lieutenant thought for a minute. "When's the game?" he asked Petey.

"In a couple of weeks," Petey replied.

"Dang. The captain's not gonna like waiting for a couple of weeks. But you're probably right. Big game like that would probably bring all the crew together, especially if Mizz is the 'leader,'" concluded the lieutenant. "Alright Petey, I'll talk to the captain. Still work it from other angles

"Pleasure without conscience
Knowledge without character
Life can change with a single drop."

and send me some reports over the next couple of weeks. Something. Anything, so I can keep the captain off my back."

"Ok, Lou," answered Petey.

"Better get going Petey. I'm sure you have homework to do," Lou said while chucking.

Petey scowled, "Ugh, don't remind me, Lou." He turned to exit the office stopping at the doorway peering into the squad room to make sure no one was there from the school that might be able to ID him. The coast was clear and Petey left the precinct house to go home and do his homework.

The next couple of weeks were uneventful for Petey. He wasn't really able to get any more information from anyone regarding Mizz. He'd see Michaela in Algebra or in the halls and they'd exchange a friendly hello. Once he did ask if everything was still cool for the game and she said that it was all set.

His reports to the lieutenant were sparse at best and Petey knew that he better turn up something from the game or else the captain was going to blow a gasket. He was sure the captain's fuse was smoldering from the two-week delay, recalling the captain's demand for information within three days.

Finally, game day arrived. Petey eagerly waited for Michaela and her friend at the agreed upon spot. He watched as the crowds made their way into the school and milled about awaiting the tip-off. He thought to himself how the atmosphere reminded him of being at a Knicks game at Madison Square Garden. He couldn't believe the excited buzz just for a high school game. As he looked at his watch thinking that he was being stood up, Michaela

"Pleasure without conscience
Knowledge without character
Life can change with a single drop."

and Tess arrived. Petey noticed that Leak and his crew were not far behind.

Michaela approached Petey. "Hey Petey, sorry we're a little late. This is my friend Tess. Takes her forever to get ready," she said with a smile. "Tess, this is Petey, the new kid I told you about."

Unimpressed, Tess nodded a hello.

"Hi Tess, nice to meet you," Petey said politely, noting that Tess was equally hot. Fortunately, before his mind wandered too much, Leak and his crew approached them.

"What's good girl, how you been? I haven't seen you in a minute." Leak said looking at Michaela.

"I'm good, just school and studying. How you doin'?"

"Hi, I'm Tess. Michaela is so rude! Psych! Just kidding, girl," interrupted Tess before Leak could answer.

"I'm Leak. What up? Who's your boy?" he said, staring hard at Petey.

"What up Bro? How are you? I'm Petey." Petey's voice cracked like he was shook to death.

"So Tess and Petey, you friends with Mizz?" he asked with a hint of suspicion in his voice.

"I know Michaela from school," Petey answered.

"Michaela is my best friend," Tess chimed in.

"She is good people." Leak said smiling referring to Michaela.

"What brings you here?" Tess asked, noting that Leak seemed a bit old to be attending a high school game.

"Mizz is family. I do anything for him. I mean anything," he said emphasizing the word anything.

"Wow, you guys must be tight?" asked Petey.

"Pleasure without conscience
Knowledge without character
Life can change with a single drop."

"I said I'd do anything. I been around him his whole life, Mizz is like a son. Anyways, enjoy the game," Leak and his crew turned and made their way into the gym with the rest of the crowd as tip-off time was just a few minutes away.

Petey sat down next to Michaela and tried to piece together the connections that Michaela had with Mizz and Leak. He liked that he was getting some information but still had to get a lot more.

Razah found Leak and his crew and sat down to chat for a while. He wanted to make sure that there wouldn't be a repeat performance of what had happened at the opening game. Feeling like he had made himself clear, he went over to see Michaela and Tess.

"Dang, you girls are definitely the finest in the building!" He said being his typical charming self.

"Who's your boy?" Razah asked Michaela.

"What up my dude? You chillin?" Petey raised his hand in a half-wave.

"Yeah, I'm chillin'. The question is who you here wit', dude?" Razah said cool-like as he intently looked at Petey.

"It's not like that. It's cool. We all friends. I just came to see the game, Homie," reassured Petey.

"Ok, cool. No disrespect. Just wasn't trying to step on your toes 'cuz I'm about to bag Tess. Feel me my dude?" Razah said laughing trying to lighten the mood.

"I got you," Petey nervously laughed also.

"You crazy!" Tess said, hitting Razah's arm.

"Razah, you going to sit wit' us?" Michaela asked.

"Nah, I'm going to sit with the fam tonight and talk business," came his reply.

"Pleasure without conscience
Knowledge without character
Life can change with a single drop."

"Business? What business your ignorant behind got?" Michaela jokingly asked.

Razah just rolled his eyes. Looking at Tess, "Holla at me, girl!" he said.

"Ok, whatever you say boy! I'll call you if you lucky!" she laughed.

Razah walked off and headed back across the stands to discuss business with Leak and the crew. He dapped the crew and leaned in whispering something in Leak's ear. Leak nodded, whispered back and called Michaela over.

Michaela told Tess and Petey she'd be right back as she headed over to Razah, Leak and the crew. Petey was intently observing all the activities as discretely as he could.

When Michaela approached the group, Razah spoke up, "Hey, after the game we going to chill at the crib. If you wanna come chill, you and your friends," Razah said nodding in the direction of Tess and Petey.

"Ok, Cool. I'll hit you up," she said smiling as she was hoping she'd be able to see Mizz later.

"Cool," Razah said as Michaela turned to get back to her seat. The teams were lining up for the tip-off.

The game started and Mizz continued with his usual routine leaving players in his dust as he hit shot after shot. As he was driving for a layup, he was fouled and went to the line for a couple of free throws. Just before he took his first shot, he scanned the crowd looking for Michaela. He found her and to his surprise, sitting next to her was Tess and some dude he'd never seen before. 'Who the!!! is that,' he thought to himself as he drained the second foul shot. He then called a timeout. Mizz spotted Razah and gave him a nod. Razah caught Mizz's drift and made his way to the seats behind the bench.

"Pleasure without conscience
Knowledge without character
Life can change with a single drop."

The coach showing some concern for his star came over and asked, "Mizz, you ok?"

"Yeah Coach, no problem. I just needed some G2," he replied, referring to some Gatorade. "It's all good," he assured.

When Razah got behind him, Mizz asked suspiciously, "Who that clown wit' Michaela and Tess?"

"Some nutty dude from Michaela's class," Razah replied.

"Word, B. He look mad sheisty. Something about his look I don't like. I don't trust him," Mizz hoped he was making his point.

"Ok. Word," Razah replied, understanding perfectly. "I'll handle it," Razah added.

Michaela looked at them wondering what they could be talking about in the middle of the game. "Did you see that?" She asked Tess.

"That was weird. They both looked over here and started talking. Those two boys are something else. They seem up to no good," Tess answered letting the word 'something' hang in the air for a minute.

"Yeah, that was weird." Petey remarked, "Like they saw something that they didn't like."

The game ended and Mizz had yet another stellar finish with forty-three points, nine assists and eight rebounds. Mizz and Razah met courtside after the game discussing Petey. As the crowd was making their way out, Mizz would hear the frequent, "Good game" or "Nice playing" and Mizz would nod or wink to acknowledge those that made the comments.

Razah gestured to Leak and his crew to come over. Mizz looked up at Michaela as she, Tess and Petey made

"Pleasure without conscience
Knowledge without character
Life can change with a single drop."

their way down. He signaled that he would call her later. Mizz and Razah bumped fists and Mizz headed into the locker room. When everyone reached Razah, he spoke up, "Ladies and gents, sorry tonight won't be good. Maybe next time," he said.

"Ohhh! I wanted to chill." Michaela was genuinely disappointed.

"Me too. Dang, oh well. Guess we can get up another time." Tess said.

"For sure, Homies for sure. I'll tell Mizz to holla at you M-Easy," he said smiling at Michaela.

"Ok, sweetie," Michaela replied to Razah, still disappointed. Michaela, Tess and Petey said their goodbyes and headed out. Petey followed right behind the girls wondering when he would get another chance to hang with Mizz and his friends. He too was disappointed but for very different reasons. Once outside, the girls decided to grab some pizza and asked Petey if he wanted to join them. He wanted to but had to decline. He had a more important concern, as he wasn't sure what he'd be able to report to the lieutenant, if anything. He had delayed the captain two weeks and now he wasn't sure if he had anything more than he did two weeks ago.

They said their goodnights and went their separate ways, the girls getting pizza and Petey alone with his thoughts. He had considered trying to follow Leak and his crew but figured there were so many of them, no doubt he'd be spotted.

The next day Petey waited outside the lieutenant's office thinking about his next move. The lieutenant was on the phone but he acknowledged Petey's presence. He was hoping Petey had something because the captain was not at

"Pleasure without conscience
Knowledge without character
Life can change with a single drop."

all happy about waiting two weeks for anything solid. Over the last two weeks, Petey's reports were nothing but fluff and everyone knew it. One thing was for sure in the lieutenant's mind, if Petey had nothing but smoke, then they both were in hot water.

With his call ended, he called Petey in. "How was the game?" He asked as Petey entered the office closing the door behind him.

"On the court, that kid's all that they say he is," Petey replied almost sounding in awe of Mizz's talents.

"Tell me you got something," Lou was never much for chitchat when he was anxious to hear about a case.

"Well my suspicions were right about Michaela being Mizz's girl…" Petey began.

"Petey, I'm not interested in the love life of two teenagers," interrupted Lou.

Unfazed, Petey pressed on, "…so I'm waiting for her to show up with my ticket and as she walked in with her friend, right behind them came Leak and his crew."

That got the lieutenant's attention. "That's the son of a gun I want to hear about," he commented. "Go on."

"Well I got introduced to them all and everything was cool. Razah invited us to chill out wit' Mizz and Leak and all them but, here's the odd thing," Petey paused for dramatic effect, "During a timeout I saw Mizz whispering to Razah. They both then looked at us. After the game, Razah came back and said it wasn't going to happen."

The lieutenant nodded, "During a timeout? Yeah, that is odd." The lieutenant thought for a minute hesitant to say what he was thinking because it would mean the whole case was in jeopardy. "Petey, any chance you were made?"

"No, no way. They'd have no reason to be

"Pleasure without conscience
Knowledge without character
Life can change with a single drop."

suspicious of me," Petey replied without hesitation.

"Ok then, what else you got?" Pressed the lieutenant, hoping there was more.

"As we know, Leak is Mizz's cousin. When I talked to Leak he said he practically raised Mizz and he'd do anything... and he stressed 'anything' for him," Petey continued.

"That's the thug I want to get off the streets, that'll keep the captain quiet," Lou interrupted again.

"Yeah but Lou wait. The word on the street is that Leak has five of the seven towers in The Terrace. That's ten stairwells in five high rises, plus you got the low rises and I'm sure the corners are theirs as well. But here's the thing, what I'm hearing is that Leak is just the muscle. Mizz is the mastermind behind the whole thing. I mean we can easily go after Leak and get him but that's small time," Petey paused to allow the lieutenant time to process this.

The lieutenant let out a whistle and leaned in to concentrate on what Petey was saying because if what his gut was telling him was right, they had stumbled onto something huge. "You can't be serious," he finally said. "Petey, any idea what they're actually into?"

"Lou, it's gotta be drugs but no, I don't have anything hard yet. Still working on that. They're tight and from what I've seen and heard, very organized. Lou, Leak's a thug and is scaring anyone that looks at Mizz wrong. Petey said expressing his opinion. "Last night Leak was there with his crew, Jack, Murdock, Rondo, Jesse and some hottie named Chantress. Aside from her they're all muscle, nothin' more than two-bit thugs. No Lou, Leak is small time. Don't we want the big fish?" Petey posed the question.

"Pleasure without conscience
Knowledge without character
Life can change with a single drop."

"Dang, if that is true, there would be an all-out drug war," the lieutenant said, stunned. "What I don't get is why are we not hearing anything rumbling from the Columbians? I spoke to Resnick over at narcotics recently and if anything, he said the Columbians are almost acting like model citizens."

"Maybe Mizz and Razah are the new power, not only in their sports but on the streets, too. Regardless of what it is, you couldn't even call this a war." Petey said as he stood up and walked around the office.

"Why not?" asked Lou.

"Because wars end!" Petey said, pounding his fist on the lieutenant's desk.

The lieutenant jumped, surprised by Petey's outburst. "Maybe this one ended before it started?" asked the lieutenant almost thinking out loud. There was an awkward pause.

"Petey, here is a true fact, if you follow the drugs you got a drug case but truth is, if you follow the money you don't know where you'll end up," stated the lieutenant.

Petey got the message, don't focus on the drugs but focus on the money trail.

"Good work Petey. I'll take this to the captain," he said as he walked to the door to open it. "Now stop wasting time and get back to work." With that, the meeting was over.

Loyalty is Key

Later on that evening, Mizz wanted a meeting and asked Razah to gather the peeps at the abandoned spot. An hour later Mizz stood and addressed his crew.

"How's everyone doing? I don't have to ask, I see I

"Pleasure without conscience
Knowledge without character
Life can change with a single drop."

see, yo," He looked around at each of the members. Some were dressed just a little too nice and wore just a little too much bling for his comfort. He continued, lowering his voice so that they had to focus on what he was saying, "Remember, be careful wit' your purchases. Oh yea, the machinery came in so we really poppin and ready to supply everyone now!! But real talk, anything too flashy is gonna bring attention and with attention comes heat. We don't need heat," he paused to make sure everyone understood what he was saying.

Once he felt that they all got it, he continued, "Now, let's get down to business. I just want to reinforce something so we not slipping. I just want us to remember, we family and loyalty is the key."

Mizz continued, "Loyalty, this part of the game you got your peoples. If you don't have family in this world what do you have? We gotta run a tight ship out there. You feel me? You don't hand money to no one that matter and don't take no product from no one that matters. If you do any of this nonsense, you done bumped your head and we all are done. So until we meet again, may all your jumpers hit nothing but the bottom of the net," he signed to the crew and he and Razah left.

Mizz sat in his room after the meeting thinking about everything but mostly about Michaela. He decided to call her to find out who he had seen her with at the game.

"Hello, Ms. Lady," he greeted her in a soft voice.

"Hey boy, what's up? I see you been killing," she said, still impressed with his performance in last night's game.

"Yeah girl, you know how I do," he got right down to business. "Hey, quick question for you? I peeped ya at

"Pleasure without conscience
Knowledge without character
Life can change with a single drop."

the game last night, looking dumb good as always by the way, but who was the dude you was wit'?"

"Who Petey? He's a new kid in school," she said, wondering why he was so interested.

"Really? I never heard you speak about him before. What's good wit' him?" Mizz casually pressed so as not to concern Michaela.

"He's harmless. He came up to me one day. I was reading an article about you in the newspaper. He noticed your picture and he said he was your biggest fan," Michaela said, recalling her first encounter with Petey.

"Word, a'ight, just like that huh?" commented Mizz.

"Yeah, just like that. Dude was sweating you real hard too, like you important or something. Don't let that go to your already big head. Anyway, those tickets you gave me, I had one left cuz my aunt couldn't come. She was busy so I said he could come. Why? You all jealous?" she asked teasingly.

He laughed, "Nah, not jealous. So that is how it went down huh? No under the stands kissing?"

She laughed. "You are the funniest dude I know, you have nothing to worry about."

"You straight, we straight, I was just trying to holla at you and see what was good. I'll holla in the a.m. girl," Mizz said in his usual manner.

"Ok, Mike Air Jordan. Sleep tight," she said kissing him through the phone.

"You too," he said and kissed back. He hung up.

Immediately, he picked up a second phone he used only for business and called Razah.

"We might have a problem for real," Mizz said without saying hello. He continued, "Remember the dude

"Pleasure without conscience
Knowledge without character
Life can change with a single drop."

that was at the game wit' Michaela and Tess?"

"Yeah, what up?" Razah asked wondering what he was saying.

"Watch out, he might be a pig. He look like one," Mizz said matter of factly.

"Huh??? Ewhhhh word, how you figure?" Razah asked, surprised by Mizz's comment.

Mizz was in no mood to argue. "Just watch him, he look corny, word. You see his face? It's corny. Just watch him. Somethin' ain't right, especially the way Michaela said she met him and the way he's sweating me like some groupie. Plus I wanna see how he play and see if he interacts wit' anyone in the crew, feel me?"

"No doubt, I'm on it," Razah replied, now equally as concerned as Mizz was.

Things were pretty status quo as the Christmas break finally arrived. Business was booming and Leak decided to throw Mizz a little birthday party at his new club. He decided to call his new club, "*Just Us*," in respect to the family.

Mizz walked into the club not expecting to see everyone there, especially Michaela and Tess. They all wished him happy birthday. He mingled his way around saying "hi" and "thank you" to everyone in his usual gracious manner. He then called the family together for a little meeting upstairs in Leak's office, which was actually Mizz's office.

"A new American dream, anything can be accomplished as long as you are loyal to those who are loyal to you. Don't forget where you come from and where you are going! This is hard work and this is what you get. I wanna get a toast to my family," raising a glass, he added,

"Pleasure without conscience
Knowledge without character
Life can change with a single drop."

"To death do us part." He tipped the glass to each of them. He signed to the crew and went downstairs to rejoin the party.

Later on that night, he pulled Razah aside. "One of the reasons for our success is you. We're probably the smartest sixteen year olds in the world. You and I, let's keep it that way. We workin' too hard to go out like Alpo and Rich Porter over some B.S., you feel me? We gotta hold each other down. When it's time to get, we will walk away on top. Believe me, on top," Mizz emphasized by raising his hand as high as he could like it was a jump shot, "None of this 'cuz of me, it's we," he said gesturing to Razah and back to himself, "We gonna do things the right way. Failing is not an option. Razah, brotha', it's not all about success. It's also about survival and loyalty. You remember the Jordan commercial, 'I fail over and over again that's why I succeed'? Nothing and no one will come between you and me. I love you man," He hugged Razah tightly.

"I love you too," Razah said hugging him back.

Petey had heard about the party from Michaela and Tess and had decided to try his luck at crashing it. He stood outside the club and knocked hoping someone would hear. Leak looked out the door and saw that it was Petey. He told Mizz then waited for instructions. Mizz gave the okay to let him in. Petey stepped inside the club not knowing what to expect. Mizz just looked at him. Michaela saw Petey too and was surprised to see him. She had mentioned the party but hadn't extended an invite.

Petey figured he would seize the opportunity and approached Mizz directly, "Although we have never met I just wanted to say happy b-day. I'm a good friend of

"Pleasure without conscience
Knowledge without character
Life can change with a single drop."

Michaela's."

"Yo name is what Bro?" Mizz asked, being cool.

Petey ignored the question and continued, "And I'm a fan of yours too, Bro."

"Ok, well enjoy yourself." Mizz said pointing to the food and other refreshments.

Petey mingled while scoping out everything and everyone. He was searching for anyone that might not be family and that might fold under pressure, if enough pressure was applied. He made mental notes of several potential targets, chatted with a few and observed the rest.

Mizz and Razah hung back in a corner and observed his every move. Curious was the fact that he left only 20 minutes after he arrived. They both looked at each other, knowing what the other was thinking. Deciding to keep things under wraps until later, they rejoined the party. Even though they enjoyed themselves, Petey was never far from their thoughts.

Petey the Thinking Man's Rocket

The next day at the station, Petey stood at the dry erase board in front of the lieutenant and the other detectives. He had written a bunch of names and circled several.

"You guys won't believe what I came up with, it's amazing but this is how I see it," Petey started.

"Ok. Go ahead. Show us what you have," the lieutenant directed.

Petey looked at the other detectives and took a deep breath before starting to lay everything out. Pointing at the first name on the board Petey began, "Does the name Mizzier Sanders ring a bell? Or should I say Mizz?" A few

"Pleasure without conscience
Knowledge without character
Life can change with a single drop."

of the detectives expressed familiarity with the name. Petey continued, "He was born up in Waterbury, Connecticut. He is the number one ranked high school basketball player in the country as well as the number one ranked student-athlete with a 4.0 grade point average (GPA)."

"His main crew consists of five others, which are all family and the rest are workers. His right hand man is Myshawn Greene, aka Razah," he said letting the detectives make the connection in their minds. "He is the number one high school football player in the country and the number two student-athlete in the world, also with a 4.0 GPA right behind Mizz. And yes, both are only sixteen years old." He then pointed to the four other names on the board behind him and pointed to them in succession before continuing. "Leak is the cousin of Mizz and has been in the game hustling for years." Again, a couple of the detectives acknowledged knowing of Leak. "Murdock is the hit man and muscle. Chantress is the runner and also a model for *EDIB TV* and Jesse is their tech and acquisitions guy."

Mizz chills wit this girl and her name is Michaela Rivera. Anytime she's not hanging with Mizz then you can find her with her best friend, Tess. Michaela's the one I made initial contact with. That's why I chose to go undercover at her school figuring if I could get in with her then she'd lead me to Mizz. If I went right at Mizz at his school he would've made me right away and the case would be dead. In speaking with Michaela, I get the impression she has no involvement in the operation. Her friend Tess won't give me the time of day and Tess's interaction with any of the people I mentioned earlier is basically non-existent. I don't believe either of these two girls is worth investigating but I will use them to get me

"Pleasure without conscience
Knowledge without character
Life can change with a single drop."

into Mizz's inner circle.

At this point one of the other detectives spoke up, "Petey, where you going with this? So far you're telling us about a couple of high school athletes and a couple of two-bit small time thugs."

Undeterred, Petey simply said, "Guys, hear me out and you'll soon understand where I'm going with this. Cool out!! Patience, okay?"

"Go on Petey," the lieutenant said.

"Thanks Lou. Anyway, Mizz seems to be an ordinary kid but you will only ever see him at his basketball games. He is like Mr. Untouchable. I have been following this kid for a minute now and make no mistake he is still a kid. He gets up every day, he and his neighbor Razah walk to school and after school, he goes to b-ball practice. Then after practice, he walks home with no contact with anyone. He is a very low-key kid and doesn't draw any attention to himself. Oh and by the way, he's the leader of the fastest growing drug organization and it's based right here in our backyard."

After a moment of stunned silence, the room was filled with grumblings and murmurs. The detectives looked at him and then each other shaking their heads. The lieutenant spoke, knowing that he was not alone in his thinking.

"Dang, are you sure Petey? I know we spoke a couple of weeks ago and you had some suspicion of drug activity but now you're telling us that this organization is that big and growing? I mean these ain't your local dumb lame household kids hustling dime bags. We're talking future superstars of their perspective sports, very public and well known especially in this area."

"Pleasure without conscience
Knowledge without character
Life can change with a single drop."

"Yeah Lou, that's what I'm saying," Petey replied with conviction.

"Petey, using your words, he's an athlete, he's a genius and you say he's low-key and yet he's running a major drug operation?" asked the lieutenant just trying to be absolutely clear with what Petey was saying.

"Lou, don't trip on the 'low-key' aspect of this. Don't forget Marcus Robinson was low-key and ran this city for years," commented Petey defending his theory.

The lieutenant thought for a moment. "So what you're saying is this kid Mizz replaced Marc Rob and he is the new drug kingpin of these parts? Petey are you smoking dust? That sounds crazy, better yet nutty."

Petey ignored the comment and continued, "Everything he does is like Marcus and who is a better teacher than the one you looked up too. Like I said, the details are sketchy but I'm getting closer. Street talks I know they moved 500 at least to a thousand keys of whateva' they selling as a family. Dope, coke, heroin, who knows but I will find out!! Trust!! Check it, that equals 70 to 90 people on both sides of the street. It's like the 1st and 15th of every month but every day! I do know this young cat has it set up like a Fortune 500 corporation. He's got round the clock shifts with dudes punching time clocks, even overtime. You have the option of morning shifts 7am-3pm, second shift 3pm-11pm, then graveyard shift 11pm-7am. These jokers were selling like 9-10 keys a day. I haven't been able to pinpoint where they're stashing their stuff yet but I will. This Mizz dude is a mad scientist, his intellect is crazy, has the brains and leadership skills to build an empire bigger than Nino Brown. I mean, he's like Scarface. He's doing what a lot of the old timers are scared

"Pleasure without conscience
Knowledge without character
Life can change with a single drop."

to do. I'm telling you guys, we've never seen anything like this before," Petey paused to gauge the reaction. What he saw were blank stares.

"With what they're selling, word is they're moving up two thousand keys a week with gross profit up to seventy million dollars. It's estimated that these young masterminds are bringing in thirty million a month. The scary thing is the fact that they just started less than three months ago," added Petey.

"What do you mean, 'With what they're selling'?" asked one of the detectives, "What are they selling?"

Petey hesitated, "Well, I...ummm... haven't exactly... narrowed down what drug or drugs they're actually selling," Petey replied sheepishly.

A collective gasp of disbelief emanated from the group of seasoned detectives. They turned to look at the lieutenant to check his reaction.

The lieutenant paused before he spoke. Unlike the captain, the lieutenant was one to formulate his thoughts and words before speaking. "Petey," he began, "You've been on this case for a while now. And it seems as if you've made progress but at this point can you prove to me that there are any laws being broken?"

"Lou, trust me, these guys, this organization... yeah, there are laws being broken. What we have to do is take them down sure, but with these kinds of dollars we also have to take down the supplier. We do that and the drug activity in this whole region will be crippled," Petey was getting excited.

Again, the lieutenant thought before he spoke, "Ok, so what do you have besides instincts that will hold any weight in court? 'Cuz let me tell you, this is nothing. This

> *"Pleasure without conscience*
> *Knowledge without character*
> *Life can change with a single drop."*

sure ain't going to do the job. Without the drugs, informants or confessions, none of these scumbags are going to jail, Petey. We will just be wasting our time and a lot of police work. As of right now we couldn't even issue a jaywalking ticket with the garbage you're presenting," the lieutenant said angrily. "I mean c'mon Petey, step back and look at what you got. Names on a board won't lead to any convictions. Might as well put Santa Claus and the Easter Bunny up on that board 'cuz with what you got, those two are just as guilty. This meeting is over. These other detectives have actual prosecutable cases they're working on."

"Lou, you'll see," Petey said confidently. "This whole organization is going down. Going down hard."

Cautious is Survival!!

Wanting to be more cautious and to avoid any potential problems, Mizz went over some new ideas in his mind as he waited to hook up with Razah. Since this had truly become a real 'business' and not just a standard drug operation, he wanted things to be more efficient. Eager to share his ideas, he met up with Razah and they headed off to school.

"Yo, Razah, we need to build an exact replica of a drug lab," Mizz said as Razah was closing the door behind him.

"Really? Why?" asked Razah, a little puzzled at the remark, "Just trust me," Mizz said with a nod.

"Ok, fam," Razah shrugged. "Anyway Bro, you got a big game this week."

"Yeah! A couple more games then we have the state tourney. But I feel like I'm forgetting something dumb

"Pleasure without conscience
Knowledge without character
Life can change with a single drop."

important," Mizz said, looking as if he was trying to remember.

"Uh yeah, the East Coast NHS convention G. Dang, you forgot that?" Razah was surprised Mizz had forgotten.

"Oh right, thanks. With all this other stuff on my mind," Mizz sighed. "Especially the other night, that Petey mess. Bro, whatever. I gotta get back on track. I'm slipping. So, meet me at Tiny's at 4 pm. I need a cut bad."

"OK Homey. I gotta go to 7-Eleven anyway so on the way back we could stop there." Razah said.

Mizz stated, "Matter of fact, I wanna slurpee. I'll roll with you 'cuz I wanna talk to you anyways."

"No doubt. I'll meet you after school," Razah said. After school they met in the courtyard. Mizz was signing autographs when Razah approached. "Dang Bro. You get more love than I do.

Mizz replied, "That's only because I was outside first." LOL.

Razah stated, "True, True. What's good? What u wanna talk about?"

"No doubt B. Yo, bro, I been thinking about this for a while. What you think about this? The other day I was walking from the bodega, ya know, the one off Bishop," Mizz started.

Razah questioned, "What you talking about, A1?"

Mizz continued, "Nah bro, that's Willow St."

"Oh yeah, my bad. What's good though?" Razah said.

"Ms. Murray's." Mizz responded.

Razah asked, "No doubt. On Bronson St?"

Mizz answers, "Yup. Anyway. I was looking at the court. Yo, the court is all messed up. Bro, cracks

"Pleasure without conscience
Knowledge without character
Life can change with a single drop."

everywhere. White lines are completely gone. Both rims are bent and no nets, man. It's all a wrap for the court." They reached 7-Eleven. Mizz got his slurpee. Razah just got some scratch offs for his mom.

"Yo. You right about that court. It's tore up. What you thinking?" Razah asked.

Mizz answered, "I'm thinking, remember I told you the mayor came to my practice last week? He told me anything I needed, come see him. I'm getting brain freeze from this slurpee."

Razah said, "You ight?" Laughing at Mizz. "Ya, I remember. What's good?"

"Well, I'm gonna tell him to fix up the court. Put some lights up for the night balling, so kids like Mikey and other kids get the same chance we had. And you know kids wanna ball out during the day. The football field too. No goal posts. And that field ain't had no lines since you balled on it, real talk Raz."

Razah responded, "No doubt son. I'm feeling your G."

"Raz, you should come and speak your piece about the football field. It will be better coming from you."

Razah stated, "Absolutely. Let me know when you're going Mizz, I'm there, trust."

Mizz stated, "Word, sometime next week."

Mizz and Razah finally got to Tiny's Barber Shop. A couple of old heads were inside chopping it up. One was in Tiny's chair and a couple others were chilling out talking about what's good in the hood or what's what.

Tiny said, "What's good fellas," with a grin on his face. Tiny was an old skool G who'd been cutting hair mad long. He's like the godfather of every barbershop in the

"Pleasure without conscience
Knowledge without character
Life can change with a single drop."

hood.

Mizz stated, "Tiny, what's up, Bro."

Razah said, "Tiny….."

There were some old players in the shop talking about how they were able to get health care. But they were disturbed about paying taxes and they had to fall back on some of the spending. Cole was a regular at Tiny's, always passing knowledge and was good people. He was Tiny's friend since a youngin'.

Cole stated, "What's good Mizz? How you been, young brother?"

Mizz responded, "I ain't seen you in a while Bro, where you been?"

Cole asked, "Razah, I didn't even see you young blood. How's your mom?"

"She chillin', thanks for asking." Razah responded.

"How you been, Cole?" Mizz asked.

Cole shrugged his shoulders in disgust and let the boys know how he felt, "Well little homies, I hope when you two make it you can make a difference in this community. Ain't that right Tiny."

Tiny responded, "Hell yeah. It's tough out here. People working eight hours a day, forty hours a week, and some have a third job."

Cole added, "Women can't afford to take care of their children, can't feed them breakfast, lunch and dinner Razah, ask your mom. You know, you live in a single parent home."

Tiny shared, "Shoot. Your folks main job is to supply a roof over your head and food on your table and, if you're lucky, a few dollars in your pocket."

"Man, listen, unemployment is crazy." Cole said,

"Pleasure without conscience
Knowledge without character
Life can change with a single drop."

"People can't afford to pay their rent, can't afford breakfast, lunch and dinner. Kids are starving right here in our community. I'm grateful we all have healthcare, but those taxes, Bro."

Tiny said, "Man listen, I didn't even get my refund check, cuz I owe, Homey."

Cole said, "Dang, I know you hit Tiny."

As the boys continued to listen to Cole and Tiny speak about how times were going and making their lives be uneasy, Mizz and Razah were starting to feel a sense of conscience on how they believed it was all good and legal what they were doing. All their crimes being justified as victimless, but running a legitimized illegal enterprise. They felt it wasn't a major burden on honest tax paying citizens. Especially people like Tiny, Cole and other people in the neighborhood, people working hard to support their family. Everything was coming to the boys' minds.

Cole said, "Anyway Mizz, how you doing?"

Mizz responded, "I'm OK. Don't worry Cole. I'm gonna take care of the hood, trust."

Razah added, "You got my word."

Mizz stated, "Thanks for the cut Tiny, as always, you hooked me up. But Tiny and Cole, we got this, trust us."

Tiny stated, "We hear you talking, but you guys word always been good."

"That's how you both been raised," Cole added.

Mizz and Razah both said at the same time, "Good looking."

They both left with a new outlook on what they wanted to do to make things right. They walked up the block and Mizz started talking first. "Bro, my mind is racing. We doing everything wrong. We gotta make this

"Pleasure without conscience
Knowledge without character
Life can change with a single drop."

right."

Razah said, "Bro, tell me about it. Dang, I didn't even think about it, feel me."

Mizz stated, "Yo Bro, you know number 1 we ain't paying no taxes. We ain't got no business license, no certificate of occupancy, no insurance coverage. We gotta make this right. I gotta see the mayor tomorrow, forget next week. Cuz if he don't budge, I'm gonna get in touch with Wiz."

"Wiz? You ain't talked to him in udd." Razah said.

Mizz said, "I know, but I'll worry about that later. Let's see what's good with the mayor, Homey."

"No doubt," Razah said. "You always have a backup plan."

"No doubt," Mizz said. "That combo really got me."

Razah said, "I know you Mizz, you will make it right."

"That I will," Mizz exclaimed. "That is when Wiz comes in to play. Bro, the bottom line is I wasn't trying to work outside the system. I just have already outsmarted the system. Now I wanna give back to my community so they could eat too."

Razah responded, "I feel you."
Mizz stated, "My bad Bro. I was so overwhelmed wit' everything, now getting back to this Petey drama before I forget.

"I been thinking. I'm gonna get Tess on him, with her fine self, to see what's good wit' that crazy dude."

"Tess!" Razah blurted out. "Word? Dang, Mizz, I wanted to have a shot at that." Razah was looking disappointed.

Mizz laughed. "Take one for the team. Being

"Pleasure without conscience
Knowledge without character
Life can change with a single drop."

whipped is powerful. Stop being whack, a'ight. Besides, that chick is dumb bad and that's what we need to figure out this Petey dude's angle. Somethin' ain't right with that fool," Mizz added.

"Yeah, you right," agreed Razah. "I don't trust that joker face Uncle Tom anyway. Something ain't right with that dude." Razah knew Mizz was right in that they had to get to the bottom of Petey's intentions. Razah's chance for a shot at Tess would have to be delayed.

"I haven't pin-pointed it yet, but trust me, I will, feel me. I'll call Michaela and tell her what's good, smell me," Mizz relayed his intentions.

"No doubt, word," Razah said, nodding his head.

"I gotta talk to coach. I'll holla later!" They dapped each other up and Mizz headed off to see his coach. He hadn't talk to him since Christmas break, so he wanted to check with him to see what was good.

"Hey Mizz, how was your Christmas break?" the coach asked as Mizz entered the coach's office. "How's your family?" Coach was at the dry erase board drawing up some defensive plays.

"Well Coach, I'm Muslim, so we don't celebrate Christmas but if someone gives me a gift I will sure take it." Mizz laughed. "The good thing is it was a week off, so I enjoyed it."

"You're a funny dude, Mizz," the coach said with a quick smile. "On a serious note, we only have a few games before the state tourney starts. Mizz, it's our time this year," the coach put his hand on Mizz's shoulder. "If we are going to get a chip, it's this season. We're good at every position," the coach said with confidence.

"Coach, you right. Everyone on the team is working

"Pleasure without conscience
Knowledge without character
Life can change with a single drop."

hard and I'm staying focused, praise be to Allah," Mizz agreed.

"That's good, Mizz. I agree, as it's always good to have faith. Even if we are of different faiths, I believe you will always be blessed and successful, thinking and feeling that way. Nothing can be done without the faith of God," Coach said as he pointed to the ceiling.

Mizz looked up. "Why you pointing at the ceiling coach?" he asked.

The coach chuckled. "I'm Christian Mizz. We believe God lives in Heaven and Heaven is up there," he said again pointing at the ceiling.

"I know what you mean." The coach moved on to a different subject. "Just let me know the colleges that are in your main interest 'cuz they are overwhelmingly hitting me up. The funny thing, a few asked me about a package deal with you and your boy, Razah!"

"Word! 'ight," Mizz liked the sound of that.

"I thought you'd like that idea. Something for you guys to think about. But the whole reason for talking to you is to make sure that you're staying focused, Son," concluded the coach with sincerity.

"Thanks Coach," Mizz looked his coach directly in the eyes. "I will not let you, the team or myself down. Especially you, 'cuz I know all the trust that you have in me," Mizz thought for a moment about what his coach or the team would do if they knew about the operation.

"Good talk, Mizz. Thanks for stoppin' in. You better get to class. Can't have you missing practice 'cuz you got detention," the coach said with a smile.

Mizz said goodbye and left the locker room. The school day was uneventful, as was practice. After he

"Pleasure without conscience
Knowledge without character
Life can change with a single drop."

showered and dressed, he left the building. As he started walking down the street he called Michaela to talk to her about hooking Tess up with Petey. He figured this was the best way to find out what was up with him. He wasn't sure why but he knew something was all-wrong with the dude. His immediate concern was how to get Michaela to agree to get Tess to do it, without having to give her too much reasoning. He figured he'd try the direct route and then wing it from there.

After a couple of rings he heard, "Hello." Michaela answered in her usual sweet voice.

"Hey girl," Mizz responded in his usual suave manner.

"Hey stranger, where you been hiding?" She asked playfully.

"I'm sorry, just trying to stay focused and getting ready for the upcoming state tournament. The season's almost done, y'know," he said apologetically.

"Yeah, it's ok, I understand." She did understand but still felt a little neglected. "So what's on your mind, babe?" she asked.

He took a breath and got right down to business. "Babe, what's really good wit' that dude Petey? I'm not feeling this cat. For real, something ain't right wit' him. Just look at him. Look at his face. He's all corny!" said Mizz bluntly.

She laughed, "He's straight, he's cute, but Mizz you right, he is corny. Why don't you trust him though?" she asked.

Mizz sighed while rolling his eyes at the thought that Petey was trying to edge in on Michaela. "No, no, nothing like that, girl. It's just; he seems like a herb, sucker

"Pleasure without conscience
Knowledge without character
Life can change with a single drop."

for love dude, and a joke!! Something's up wit' that dude and I'm not trustin'," Mizz thought, so far so good. He continued, "Do me a favor, babe. Put Tess on him so she can feel him out, then we can see what's really good."

Michaela looked perplexed, "Excuse me, what?" She wasn't sure she heard him right. At least, she hoped she didn't, "Hook Tess up wit' him for real?" she confirmed.

"Look babe, Tess is fly. She got the goods, smell me, and a cute face. She's a perfect 10 plus. Everybody wants a relationship wit' her. The last dude she walked out on, I'm sure he ain't been the same. I can imagine that dude be crying and what not, wanting her back, '*Oh Tess, sniff-sniff come back to me sniff-sniff,*'" Mizz said, while pretending to be crying.

This caused Michaela to laugh. "You so crazy, Mizz," she said.

Mizz thought Michaela's laughter was a good sign. He continued, "Babe, I know Tess is the answer to lure this clown in, no doubt," he was hoping that he was getting through to her.

Michaela thought for a moment, "Ok crazy boy, what you want her to actually do? Lure him in for what?"

"Just make sure he wants to be closer to her and he trusts her completely. The more time they spend together, the better for us and the more information we can get," he replied.

Before responding, Michaela put the phone at arm's length and shook her head, "Mizz, that's kind of messed up. I just thought you wanted her to chill and hangout wit' him, not lead him on and then infiltrate. Then break his heart. She doesn't have the type of training for that."

"Pleasure without conscience
Knowledge without character
Life can change with a single drop."

"Dang! No disrespect intended Michaela, but what the freak? Let's be real, lie to the dude? Training for that? Are you serious? She's a broad, she's got all the training she needs," Mizz's outburst came from the experience of having his heart broken once or twice before.

"Oooh, all righty then," she liked Mizz and all but sometimes he surprised her with stuff that she didn't like. "Mizz, you messed up. Not all women are like that." she paused. She thought to herself that she should be mad at him for saying that but realized after hearing some of her friends talking about guys that he was partially right. She sighed, "You my baby Mizz and Tess will do anything I ask her to but I'm telling you he is straight."

"Thanks, babe. If he's straight then we cool but I'm telling you he's not," Mizz relaxed his tone with her. "I'm looking forward to seeing and chilling wit' you at the end of the month at the convention."

"Yeah, anytime to chill wit' you I look forward to as well, baby," wishing she'd be able to see him before but realizing he really needed to get ready for the state tournament.

"Cool, listen girl, I gotta jet. I'll hit you up later, beautiful," he said while thinking how much he was missing seeing her but almost as importantly, he had accomplished exactly what he had set out to do.

"Bye babe," she hung up the phone wondering what the heck just happened. What had that conversation really been about? She figured she'd get the scoop at some point, but for now she had to run this by Tess. She knew Tess would do anything for her. She picked up the phone and dialed her best friend.

"Hello," Tess answered.

"Pleasure without conscience
Knowledge without character
Life can change with a single drop."

"Hey girl, what's going on?" Not waiting for an answer as she saw no point in beating around the bush so she came right out with it, "Listen I just got off the phone wit' Mizz."

"Really, What that negro talking bout?" Tess asked.

"He's being all weird and he said he don't trust Petey. So he had an idea I wanted to run by you," Michaela began.

"Don't trust Petey, why?" Tess seemed surprised because Mizz was usually pretty easy going with everyone. "That's weird 'cuz Petey seems so innocent and sweet. So what was Mizz's idea?"

"Yeah, well y' know guys can be crazy like that. Mizz thinks Petey is a snake and he phony. The thing is that I haven't seen Mizz wrong about anything yet," admitted Michaela. "Anyway, he was thinking maybe you could get close to Petey, see what's what with the dude," Michaela said and winced waiting for an angry outburst.

Tess thought for a moment. "That's an odd request girl," Tess finally said. "But Mizz is your man and you're my girl so hey, ya never know, might be fun. Yeah, I'll see what's good wit' Petey. Not a problem,"

"Thanks, Tess, you're the best. Y'know you're my girl too," Michaela seemed relieved. Then she thought to herself how strange these last two phone conversations had been.

"Michaela, you know better than that, you my peeps." Tess laughed, "I'll let you know what up with our lil' Petey."

"Cool. Thanks girlfriend," Michaela said, smiling. "I'll holla at you later," and with that she hung up.

After she hung up with Tess, she texted, 'Tess dwn

"Pleasure without conscience
Knowledge without character
Life can change with a single drop."

W it' to Mizz letting him know that Tess was in. She then added, "she crz lk U lol," laughing as she sent it. Mizz read the text and laughed then he thought to himself, 'Word, no doubt.'

"One thing done and out of the way," Mizz said to Razah. "Remember we have to go see the Mayor." Mizz and Razah got the meeting set for the next day.

Mizz said, Mr. Mayor, thank you for seeing us on short notice. We know you are very busy."

The mayor responded, "The pleasure is all mine. How could I be of assistance to my future NBA and NFL pro athletes?"

"Well, it's like this. Myshawn and I have been doing a lot of thinking and we would love to see our neighborhood park renovated."

Razah added, "We want kids for the next generation, now and the future, to have the same opportunities we had growing up. And the way our park has turned out, it's not going to happen."

Mizz added, "It's disgusting to see how rundown and terrible the court and football field have become. We feel you are the only one who can help us."

The mayor replied, "Man, you guys, I feel terrible, but our budget is not able to let us renovate anything at this point. But if you want to use any city gymnasiums to raise money please feel free to do that, free of charge from the mayor's office. Please come see me again personally and we will handle it. "

Mizz stated, "Thanks Mr. Mayor, this is greatly appreciated."

Razah added, "That's fantastic. We will keep your idea in mind."

"Pleasure without conscience
Knowledge without character
Life can change with a single drop."

Mizz and Razah both said thanks again. Mizz and Razah felt good about the mayor even though they didn't get the answer they were looking for. But Mizz had the backup all in his head and was ready to execute.

The Backup

"Bro, plan B, my dude." Mizz said to Razah.

Razah responded, "What's that, Bro?"

Mizz said, "Wiz."

"Wizz? You ain't talked to him in udd long. He gonna think something up." Razah said.

"I know. I heard he's doing real estate. He cleaned up. All the way straight." Mizz said.

Razah stated, "Wooorrddd!!"

"Michaela works in the human resources department. I'll have her pull his file and see what's good." Mizz continued, "What I'm thinking is we give him the money and have him front a business for us since he all the way straight. That way we can have him employ folks in the community and renovate our park. He will only have to have his name on the paperwork and we will hit him off with the bread."

Razah responded, "I swear you a genius. Dang Bro, I'm with that."

Mizz said, "I'm gonna get at Michaela to get the info and pop up at Wizz's real estate office and explain everything to him."

"Sounds good, brother." Razah said.

"Gotta holla at Michaela. Holla at you later, Bro. 100." Mizz said.

"100. Hold up, wait Mizz. You just said Wizz all the way straight. What you mean by that?" Razah asked.

"Pleasure without conscience
Knowledge without character
Life can change with a single drop."

Mizz responded, "He the bank, Bro."

Razah questioned, "The bank?"

"Yeah, that means the bank plays it legit. He generates a good bit of honest income. But at the same time his money finances whatever it is he does but will never touch. Bro, he won't ever go near the street. He's isolated from the everyday money that comes in. The money that comes back in is then laundered through enough straight business investments that there's no way to trace it. Bro, to play a guess at that point there's no way working police can catch that dude." Mizz explained.

"Dang bro, he is straight." Razah said.

Mizz said, "He is straight Homey. I will holla later."

"No doubt." Razah said.

Mizz then met up with Michaela and he said he really needed to find out if Wizz was legit. He didn't want to go to Wizz if he wasn't all the way straight. Michaela did an internship at the courthouse in the human resources department so he wanted her to look up some information, a phone number on Willie Foote, aka Wizz.

Michaela said, "So why'd you want me to look this number up for this dude? It don't matter, I have the info for you."

"I have a reason. I just wanna make sure it's him." Mizz said.

Michaela said, "That's lame, why you just ain't call yourself? Anyway, was the number you were looking for (203) 555-6785?"

Mizz replied, "Yup. But was it like some real estate place or something?"

"I got a lot of info on this dude. I know you want everything detailed to a T so I got you." Michaela said.

"Pleasure without conscience
Knowledge without character
Life can change with a single drop."

Mizz laughed and said, "You think you know me? Let's see what you got."

"Well anyway, the number I pulled is the M&M Property Assessment and Lend Transfers from circuit court. He did say M&M when he answered." Michaela said.

Mizz replied, "Exactly."

Michaela said, "You know some of the paperwork you asked for a contact number so don't be surprised why your boy is using the cell phone so freely. Here is the list of the incoming and outgoing numbers on his phone. Mizz, the majority of them are downtown exchanges."

Mizz asked, "Downtown exchanges, like what?"

Michaela responded, "City licensing, agricultural firms, authorities, zoning officers."

So Mizz asked, "Really, that's his number?"

Michaela answered, "Yes. The number is correct. It's him. Whoever you are looking for. Accountant information confirms he has had this phone listed for quite a while."

Mizz said, "Thanks Michaela, that's all I needed."

Mizz, with that information, realized that Wizz is officially the bank and is straight and clean with washing his money. It was time for Mizz to go see the bank, aka Wizz. Mizz met up with Razah to break the news.

The Bank, aka Wiz

Razah said, "What's good, Bro. What you find out from Michaela?"

Mizz said, "He is all the way straight, brother. He's the bank, Bro. Check it, Wizz is out of reach as far as the game is concerned. Which is good for us, but Bro, remember a couple of years ago when they were renovating

"Pleasure without conscience
Knowledge without character
Life can change with a single drop."

downtown? Just building everything up."

Razah said excitedly, "Don't say it, hold up."

Mizz said, "Yep. When we used to see all of them thug dudes around those developments, it's like they were trying to get a flip for their cash when the houses were condemned to get the federal payout."

"Right. Go ahead Bro," Razah encouraged.

Mizz went on, "Yo, it was all Wizz. He is buying more and applying for building permits. Bro, Wizz is a Wizz, real talk. He is worse than a drug dealer."

Razah said, "Mizz, he is a developer. I think it is time for you to go see Wizz, Bro, since he is not in the open."

Mizz responds, "You are absolutely correct."

Mizz waited a few days to go see Wizz at the real estate business on Grand St. in downtown Waterbury. He had to make sure his game was tight. Mizz entered the door and the bell sensor went off and one of Wizz's employees came to the front. Wizz was looking through a side office window. After he saw that it was Mizz, he came out and said, "I got this." The employee walked away and Wizz said to Mizz, "Mizzier Sanders."

Mizz said, "Mr. Willy."

Wizz's eyebrow shot up in reference to his real name. "How can I be of service to you? Your folks looking for a new spot to rest your head? Apartment, condo, house...anything I can do to help."

Mizz responded, "I haven't seen you around the way."

"I am not around the way no more. You want to find me, I am right here." Wizz said.

"You right here, huh? I respect you and your G."

"Pleasure without conscience
Knowledge without character
Life can change with a single drop."

Mizz said.

Wizz said, "Appreciate you, young blood. This and some other endeavors I'm working on enough to occupy me really."

Wizz handed Mizz a card and on the back of it, it said, 'Meet me at the old spot in a half hour.' Wizz was smart. He knew Mizz wanted something and he had to put on a façade while he was in the work place. Mizz looked at the back of the card and smiled and said under his breath, 'My man."

Wizz continued speaking, "So Mizz, where are you and your folks living now?"

Mizz said, "Where we living?"

Wizz said, "Ya? If your folks want to move downtown, I have some condos about to come down the line in seven months. You say the word and I could hook you up with something nice, near the Courtyard Marriott. Loft apartments, real nice."

Mizz responded, "Thanks, I'll keep that in mind."

"Have a nice day superstar," Wizz said. Wizz walked to the back and Mizz walked to the door. Thirty minutes later they met at the spot and Wizz wanted to know what was good, why he came by the office.

Wizz asked, "So, What's up youngin', talk to me."

"All due respect, you're smart, I see that. I'm feeling your gangster I swear."

Wizz said, "Thank you. Get to the point. Time is money, young fella. But you're smart too and I appreciate that. What's good though."

Mizz continued, "Here is the thing Wizz. You know Waterbury has had its share of great hustlers. No need to name cuz you already know and you in my eyes are the

"Pleasure without conscience
Knowledge without character
Life can change with a single drop."

smartest. But as soon as their names rang out the feds was on them heavy, but you know the government don't want you to be organized or come out the ghetto. They want you to kill each other, fight, not to lead by example. At the end of the day, they want to be able to tame you. Not me, Wizz. I started out doing what I had to. Once you do what you had to they never let you do what you want to. That's why I'm coming to you about this change, brother. I wanna give back to the community. Open up new line of food chains where we can employ our own people and give back. No need for the money, I have it and I want to also renovate the park. The one where I grew up and it all started. So kids could have the same chance I did. I'm a front the whole thing; I just need you on the paperwork. Now that you all the way straight, big bro."

Wizz said, "Smart thinkin', Mizz. Anything you do, especially now with your career evolving and with you getting recruited, anything goes wrong with your name…they coming to get you. That's what they do. They turn your money, fame and image against you. Mizz, you a smart young brother. Of course I'll help you. Knowing you want to give back to those before you and those after you. I know you have everything on some paper for me so I could see what you want me to do."

Mizz opened up his book bag and pulled out his school notebook with all the information with the business plan and it had no name on it, so if it were lost it couldn't be linked to Mizz.

"The franchise will be called 'Courtside Deli' and employ the first African American culinary developer, Willie Foote. So you will get even more props. I have already started a chain in the UK, Homey. The United

"Pleasure without conscience
Knowledge without character
Life can change with a single drop."

Kingdom consists of four countries, England, Northern Ireland, Wales and Scotland. This is approximately 66 million people with a gross domestic product, GDP, of 2.4555 trillion. The UK is known for having avid coffee and tea drinkers. And last year alone, there were approximately 60.2 billion cups of tea drank which equates to nearly 100 cups per person in the country. Wizz, there are many advantages for doing a FDI project like this in our hood and around the city. But we both have experienced living here and we know what our people want. And on top of that, we can give back to the community that raised us and give them jobs." Mizz explained.

Wizz responded, "I'm feeling you, I'm really feeling you. Go on."

Mizz continued, "I can see a definite market for a Courtside Deli. We as a minority unit have a large conglomerate market that is well established. So we would just have to tweak the menu a little bit. Bust it, our city has a lot of corner stores, dollar stores, mom and pop stores, you know, the hood stuff. I can see that many business people, students, grandmas, church folk, families, or those with a little time to spare at lunch or in the morning would love more spots with people working that they know and trust and that's affordable."

Wizz said, "So, I get it. So it's like supply and demand, best food, best product at the lowest price."

"You're right, it's like supply and demand. And we will have the best dollar menu with the tax rolled into the cost. Draw the whole neighborhood in." Mizz said

Wizz shakes his head and said, "Tell me more."

Mizz said, "I have also chosen locations in these hoods, Hartford, New Britain, Manchester, Danbury, the

"Pleasure without conscience
Knowledge without character
Life can change with a single drop."

Valley, and New Haven. My reason for choosing these cities is cuz' they are the largest cities for unemployment among minorities. Soon we will build and expand also to the tourist sites. You got to take care of the hood first. Also at these locations, people will be able to try food and other products which could only expand the company's global recognition. Yo Wizz, check it out though, the UK and the US are similar with their products. But we just gonna add a few things, that's our main focus when the stores open here in America. Selling home cooked meals, homestyle cooking with ethnic flare from all backgrounds. You could get anything you want. We will cater to all ethnic backgrounds to touch everyone in the hood from Spanish to Italian, to Soul Food. Mexican and Chinese, and any other...we touching everything. And we will have the originals, coffee, tea, pastries, donuts, whatever you can grab on the go, all at the cheap rate. There will be a slight problem with some competitors, though. They will have the global brand loyalty customers. And there's no denying that they have combined revenues in the billions and thousands and thousands of stores in 62 countries. This is due to the fact that people like to go and eat locally and support their local business. Eventually we will be in that stream. Our benefit is that we will be offering similar products at a lesser price. This is with us establishing a new company within the US market. It is hard to gauge what price to place on our products outside of the dollar menu. As a guideline, I have researched what we should sell coffee and tea for. In the foreign country, how that equates with the current exchange rate from pounds to dollars is a regular cup of coffee in the UK is 3 pounds. In America it averages 2 dollars. Local coffee or specialty shops are

"Pleasure without conscience
Knowledge without character
Life can change with a single drop."

usually more expensive and location matters. In the UK I'm selling an extra-large tea or coffee for 1.50 pounds, which has many benefits and advantages. First, we are undercutting our main competitor by 50%, which seems radical but it's a similar case between the major competitors here in the US. Second, the current exchange rate is 1 pound = $1.60 American. We are actually selling the same product in another country at a higher price than its original home country as equates to $2.30. This will help enormously with making a profit. It would be a lot harder at the start of business especially with advertising and marketing aspects that need to be done when we launch in the 6 areas. Another benefit of this is due to VAT, value added tax, being 20%. The profits earned will help pay the difference of a higher tax rate as well as the shipment of products and import/export tax. Also I was going to transport and place in storage beans from the UK that will cost more because of the currency equivalence compared to the strength of the UK pound. But we are going to make everything a round number so the tax is included. Wizz, how you feel about this? Like I said, the name of the spot will be Courtside Deli. And it's similar to a Barnes & Noble setup. People will be able to read books, eat, chill, play chess, and have like a homey atmosphere. Most important will be the employee's introduction phase of the store. We will employ neighborhood folks mainly for the experience, because everyone knows everyone in the neighborhood. Also, that way, everyone respects and protects each other and the product. The best way of advertising in your hood is word of mouth. Once everything has taken off and the business is up and running, we will look at training and hiring outsiders to bring in a

"Pleasure without conscience
Knowledge without character
Life can change with a single drop."

different flavor that wants to support the local employment as much as possible. Our main goal with our staff and our customers is to build a great relationship that will lead to brand loyalty which is vital to creating this global enterprise. We will go with the old slogan, 'Rise above your surroundings' that's why the building is structured the way it is, feel me.

Wizz reflected on Mizz's plan and said, "I definitely do, 'Rise above your surroundings,' that's dope.

"We will pay our staff more than minimum wage," Mizz said, as well as a discount card for the stores, books, and accessories, and tipping system. Our main aim is to employ students, single parents, mainly local people. This will create jobs in the area which in turn will help the community as more people will be employed. Therefore more taxes can be gathered for the government and counsel these workers and the crime rate will go down. I feel that with this and everything going according to plan, we could rebuild the park and renovate where Razah and I started and call that Courtside Dreams. All I ask is that your name is on the paperwork and when I turn pro you can sign everything over to me. The good thing is that you don't have to go in pocket for anything. I will give you and supply you with everything. I just need your name on it and I trust you especially because of what we did before and that you turned straight, so we straight."

Wizz said, "That's a great idea young blood, I got you. I'll tell you how much for everything and my fee. We good money."

"That's dope Wizz," Mizz said, "I got you. Whatever you need. I am so grateful for this."

"I'm not going to front. I'd be a fool to tell you no

"Pleasure without conscience
Knowledge without character
Life can change with a single drop."

and about you turning pro and me signing the papers back over to you? Well…. we'll see. Sike! I got you. Thanks for giving me this opportunity." Wizz replied.

"No, thank you." Mizz replied, but in the back of his mind he felt that when he turned pro there was a chance that Wizz was gonna stick him. Mizz and Wizz dapped each other up; half hugged, and parted ways. An hour later Mizz met Razah.

Razah asked, "What's good family?"

Mizz said, "We good, I talked to Wizz. We all in. We straight and I'm feeling really good about this,"

Razah said, "You are a genius. I swear you are."

"Thanks Bro. This is what's up." Mizz replied.

A Dude Will Do Anything for Some …

A week later, Mizz met up with Razah before his game to discuss business and the Petey situation. "What's poppin' wit' the replica of the drug lab?' Mizz asked hoping to hear that it was about finished.

"It's all done!" Razah proudly said.

"A'ight!" Mizz was thrilled. "Yo, I was wondering if Tess and that Petey dude are coming to the game tonight?"

"You haven't spoken to Tess?" Razah was surprised.

"I spoke to Michaela but she wasn't sure. I thought you spoke to Tess. I been mad busy. What up wit' Leak and everyone?" asked Mizz.

"You know they will be in the building G, a'ight." Razah said.

"A'ight, word. Yo, Tess blessing dude yet? He's probably all lovey dovey wit her, word. Then the dumb dude will be telling her everything under the sun," Mizz informed Razah.

"Pleasure without conscience
Knowledge without character
Life can change with a single drop."

"Yeah. That clown probably dumb open, ole nutty negro. Razah agreed, both of them laughing hard thinking about Petey getting played!! But Razah still had mixed feelings about having Tess help like this, but deep down he knew it was best for the operation. He knew Tess was smart and wouldn't play herself.

"Yeah, you talk them up and there they go right there. Look," said Razah as he nodded in Tess and Petey's direction in the stands.

"I see that joker," Mizz said looking into the stands. "Let me hit these lay ups, B. I'll holla after the game."

Mizz stepped onto the court and started warming up. As usual, he gave buckets ending the game with forty points, seven assists, and nine rebounds. Throughout the game, Mizz would check the stands to notice that Tess and Petey were chatting on and off and not really paying attention to the game. He was cool with that. He also made sure he made plenty of eye contact with Michaela, who as usual, was looking dumb good.

After the game Mizz and Razah were talking courtside about the game but kept a watchful eye on Tess and Petey. As the crowd exited the gym, Tess turned around and gave Mizz a knowing smile and wink. She and Petey left the gym and headed out to the parking lot. Michaela came down to say hi to Mizz and let him know she'd be waiting for him after he showered and dressed. Mizz gave her a quick kiss and then Mizz and Razah dapped each other up. Mizz headed off to the locker room feeling that the Petey situation was in good hands.

Tess and Petey stood by his car and chatted. "Hey what's good? That game was a good one. Mizz really can shoot the rock," Petey said with true admiration of Mizz's

"Pleasure without conscience
Knowledge without character
Life can change with a single drop."

skill.

"Yeah, I never really watched much basketball but since Michaela and Mizz have been hanging out, I've seen more in the last month than in my whole life. I can tell he's good," Tess commented.

Petey opened the car door. "You want a ride to your crib?" he asked shyly.

"You don't have to bring me home." Tess said politely denying the offer. "I'll just walk home, okay. It's not far at all. Thanks for the offer, though."

"Well, I see you didn't want to wait for Michaela so I feel it's my duty as a gentleman. I don't mind," Petey countered, not wanting to take no for an answer.

"Michaela's aunt is coming to get her. Plus she is waiting for Mizz and I kinda do mind." She was getting a little annoyed.

"Dang, you been wigging all night." Petey started to get defensive. "What did I do to you?"

"Wigging, what's that?" She rolled her eyes at the comment, "Anyway you didn't do anything. I just wanna chill alone, a'ight."

"Well, I'm not feeling that, so I'm going to be a bugga boo and walk wit' you all the way to your crib," Petey wasn't ready to give up yet.

Tess smiled. "I think you should be going home. Anyways it's late and we got school tomorrow, plus I heard your pops be tripping."

"That's my uncle. That man crazy. I'm supposed to bring the whip back ASAP after the game, but bump it. I'll chill now and suffer later." They started walking towards Tess's home.

"But being in trouble can last forever, especially

"Pleasure without conscience
Knowledge without character
Life can change with a single drop."

what they sayin' about your peoples," Tess said thoughtfully.

"That's a true story. Punishments can last a lifetime. I remember one time I got grounded for sneaking a chick in the crib. Yo, he still talking 'bout that mess. For real, my uncle is cool but he just wants me to do the right thing," Petey responded.

"Michaela told me what happen wit' your mom and pops," Tess was showing genuine concern.

Part of Petey's cover was that his parents had been involved in a horrible auto accident recently. As a result, he had to move in with his uncle until they completed their rehabilitation. Petey had heard rumors that the kids in school had changed the story. Instead of physical rehab, the story became his parents were in drug rehab. Petey didn't care since neither were true anyway. As long as his cover wasn't blown, rehab was rehab.

"Yeah, that's why I live wit' my uncle. They were in a bad accident and they need special attention. Thanks, that was a while ago," Petey said shrugging. "That's enough about me, What about you? What your peoples do?" He asked, trying to change the subject. A good undercover operation is where the details are kept simple.

"Oh, my dad owns a couple of 7-11's," she replied.

"Ooh. Dang, I know you'll be getting it in crazy slurpees and chips," Petey said with a smile.

Tess laughed. "And my mom used to work in pharmaceuticals. Now she helps my dad run the business," she added.

"I'm surprised you don't work there and help out," he commented.

"I really don't have time wit' school and stuff. I

"Pleasure without conscience
Knowledge without character
Life can change with a single drop."

wanna get ready for college," came the non-defensive response.

Petey nodded in agreement, "So do I. I started going to official visits to colleges and filling out applications and stuff."

"Dang boy, you focused. Aren't those apps crazy? The Ivy League apps are a mess," Tess was reflecting upon the recent apps she had filled out.

"Dang, Ivy League? That's outta my league. You mad smart," complimented Petey.

They were nearing Tess's house. "Hold up, let me see if my light is on," Tess said as she touched his arm stopping them from moving on. She breathed a sigh of relief. "Whew, good, I'm home before them," commented Tess.

"So what's good wit' you and your girl? You two are the baddest tandem in school. I know you have dudes of all races in the palm of your hands." He noticed that she was smiling. "Anyway, on that note, I'm glad you let me walk you home tonight, Tess," he said with a smile awaiting a sign.

"You mad cool, too." She said remembering what Mizz had asked her to do.

There was a pause. Petey looked into her eyes and saw a signal so he leaned in to kiss her. She backed away, avoiding his approach. Oops, wrong signal.

"Hey, ain't you feeling Michaela?" she asked.

"I-I-I was," he stammered, quickly adding, "but I don't know her like I know you now and she got a man." He was back peddling, trying to recover from misreading the moment.

"Ok, cool," Tess said, hoping he got the point and

"Pleasure without conscience
Knowledge without character
Life can change with a single drop."

wouldn't try to kiss her again. "I'll see you later then."

"Ok, fine beautiful," he said trying to save a little of his dignity, "I will see you tomorrow." He was a little disappointed and his facial expression showed it.

Tess saw his expression and remembered about Mizz and her assignment. "Sorry, I'd let you in but my people are on their way home. And Petey," she added, "I'd let you upstairs, too." She was hoping that her earlier move didn't ruin things with Petey. She knew Mizz would be disappointed if she wasn't able to get any information.

Petey was totally confused by this sudden change of attitude but figured he'd play it cool and go slowly. He didn't want to risk misreading another sign.

"It's not a problem, Tess. For real, we straight," he said.

Before he knew it, Tess grabbed his hand and pulled him into her house. She led him up the stairs and they were in her bedroom hugging, kissing and slobbering on the bed. His hands were all over her body as were hers upon his. He moved his hand to her back and unsnapped her bra when she suddenly sat up and sighed, "Wait, wait, hold on Petey. Wait, this ain't right."

Petey shocked, stared at her. "What you mean? You getting' me all worked up ain't right. You being a tease," he said in an exasperated voice.

Tess stood up. "Word, Petey," she said raising her voice slightly. "Man, you was telling me fifteen minutes ago you was feelin' my girl, now you trying to get with me?"

Petey put up his hands looking like he was surrendering. "Look baby, real talk. I don't want you doing nothin' that you don't want to do. You want me to bounce?

"Pleasure without conscience
Knowledge without character
Life can change with a single drop."

Fine," he said frustrated but not angry. He was still trying to be cool.

"Yeah, you bounce, beat it, jerk," she yelled while awkwardly trying to resnap her bra.

Petey was all worked up and not ready to leave yet. He had to find a way to salvage this situation, if not for tonight but at least for the near future. "Hold on Tess, let's talk." he said trying to look deep into her eyes.

She scowled, "What is it that you want to talk about? Is it about what you want?"

Frustrated but not willing to give up, Petey responded, "You serious right now? You're buggin'. Look babe," Petey paused, choosing his words carefully, "both of you are extremely attractive and it seems like you want me to make a decision. There's no decision to be made. You are the one I want as a friend and I feel that if anything is going to work we should be companions first then maybe we should be lovers." She looked at him and he could tell by her body language that she liked what she heard.

Then Tess said, "First we try, then we trust." He smiled and said, "Now that that is out the way, where were we?" Seeing an opportunity, he pulled her back onto the bed and started kissing her again.

After a couple of minutes of passionate kissing, Tess whispered, "Do you have a condom?"

"Of course I got one," he said unable to hide his excitement.

Tess stopped him and looked, "Ok, dang! Is this regular for you? Are you always prepared like this?"

"My pops been making sure I've had one in my wallet since I was thirteen. No, it's not regular but it's better to be prepared," he answered. He pulled out the

"Pleasure without conscience
Knowledge without character
Life can change with a single drop."

condom from his wallet and tried to open it, but it got stuck to the wrapper.

Tess was shocked at what she was seeing. "Petey, please!" She blurted. "That condom is as old as the gold chain you wearin'. How long that been in your wallet?"

Petey had enough. "Man, this is whack! Told you this wasn't regular," he said frustrated, thinking he had blown his chance with Tess.

"It's ok Petey, there will be other times," She said as she kissed him on the forehead. She stood up and began straightening herself out and buttoning her shirt.

"It'll be a long time from now," he said disappointed that the moment had ended.

They were looking at each other when the neighbor's dog started barking. A beam of light shined into her room and Tess realized her parents were pulling into the driveway. They only had moments before her parents would be inside.

Petey, still excited, and now nervous also, looked at Tess. He whispered excitedly, "Wow, you're beautiful, but what am I supposed to do now?"

"Get your nutty butt out. My parents are home, silly!" she said laughing aloud.

They could hear her parents outside walking to the door and talking about the movie they had just seen. "That movie was excellent. You know, we need to get out more," her mom said as they were entering the house.

Dejectedly, her father replied, "Of course honey. I've just been so busy at work."

Panicking, Petey threw on his shirt and was going to try to jump out of the window. Tess, still laughing, told him how crazy he was and told him to take the side door. The

"Pleasure without conscience
Knowledge without character
Life can change with a single drop."

neighbor's dog continued barking loudly as Petey quickly went out the side door, through the yard and jumped the fence. Tess ran back up to her room and quickly got under the covers, pretending to be asleep as her parents checked on her. Fifteen minutes later when all was quiet, she picked up the phone and called Michaela to report on the evening's events.

"Hello?" Michaela answered sleepily.

"Wake up girl, I got something to tell you!" Tess too anxious to wait until tomorrow had to tell her what had happened.

"What time is it? What happened?" groggily asked Michaela.

"The time's not important. Girl, it's a Rapp, Petey!! He sweating me. Tell Mizz, we straight!" Tess was unable to contain the excitement in her voice but she had to be quiet so as not to wake her parents.

"Ok, cool Tess. Nice," She had no doubt her friend would come through. "I'll tell Mizz in the morning 'cuz it's gotta be mad late right now. Girl, tell me the rest in the morning. I want details but I'm too tired."

"Ok, girl goodnight." Tess hung up the phone thinking it wasn't that late. She knew Mizz would be pleased when Michaela gave him the news. She rolled over and went to sleep thinking about her next move with clown Petey.

You Can't Play a Playa

Michaela woke up early and called Mizz. She was really feeling him. Then she remembered Tess had called her after she had fallen asleep. No idea what time that was. She figured she'd call Tess first, get some details and then

"Pleasure without conscience
Knowledge without character
Life can change with a single drop."

call Mizz.

Tess answered on the first ring.

"You're up awfully early after such a late night," Michaela remarked.

"Girl, hate to tell you but it wasn't that late. Just after midnight when I called you. You be all snug in your bed. Were you alone?" asked Tess, knowing that Michaela was all alone.

"You know I was. So before I call Mizz, what's the story?" Michaela asked, wanting details and hopefully juicy ones at that.

"It was an interesting night, to say the least. Poor Petey, he's sweating me bad now. Pretty much gonna be able to do with him whatever I want. Things were cool, then warm then cool again then … hmmm … real warm," Tess said with a chuckle.

"Did you…" Michaela let her voice trail off.

"Girl! Nooo," came the quick reply. "For real, we was in my room and eventually things got pretty heavy. He's a wanna-be playa. He pulled out a condom that was so old it was stuck to the wrapper," now Tess was laughing recalling the moment.

"No!!! Ewwww," Dang Tess, he really whack like that!! Smh, that negro really playing himself!! LOL!! Michaela was laughing now too.
"So now I got Mr. Nutty right where I need him to be 'cuz he thinking he gonna get wit' me," Tess said, "but smh, that ain't happening."

"So it's cool to let Mizz know all that?" Michaela wanted to confirm nothing was a secret.

"Yeah it's all good," Tess answered. "I gotta get ready. I'll holla at you in school," Tess said as she was

"Pleasure without conscience
Knowledge without character
Life can change with a single drop."

hanging up.   "Ok girl, I'll talk to you later then. Peace," and with that Michaela also hung up. She then dialed the phone to talk to her boo. Even though she saw him last night she was already missing him.

"Yea!!" Mizz answered the phone ignorant as usual. "Great game again last night babe, very impressive. You already know that. No need to give you a bigger head." She said half-jokingly.

"Thanks princess, but you only telling the truth." Mizz laughed. "What's poppin' wit' the situation, girl?"

"Wow, no 'how are you?' or 'I miss you?' You just right to the point just like a typical insensitive negro," she was obviously annoyed. Sometimes he seemed to be always about business. She continued without waiting for Mizz to reply. "Gravy," Michaela said it wit her swag. "Well, she's got the dude right where she wants him. So I guess that means she has him right where you want him to be," she surmised.

"Cool, princess, you on your gangsta, but here is a true statement," Mizz said sounding even more serious than usual. "We don't know what we got, cuz we don't know what he got or his intentions for Tess or us. Why he wants to chill wit' us or her?" Mizz was thinking as he was speaking.

"Mizz, you so paranoid about everything, you would think you were a drug dealer or something," she said without thinking. "Why are you scary all the time? Loosen up babe. Maybe the dude just wants to hang with Tess 'cuz like you said, she's 9-10 and maybe he wants to hang with us 'cuz we cool to hang with," Michaela was making valid points for average people in normal situations. Mizz knew that Michaela and Tess were not average females and he

"Pleasure without conscience
Knowledge without character
Life can change with a single drop."

and Razah were far from being in normal situations. He had to be extra cautious.

"Present company excluded, but cupcake, I just don't trust people. Nothing is free and everyone wants something. You know it's just all about how they go about getting it." He backed off a little not wanting to give her any ideas. "I just don't trust people. My bad," he said apologetically.

"I guess you're right to some extent," her voice softened. "Well, she did what you asked. She is in the boy's realm now 'cuz he is feeling her now," said Michaela, speaking proudly of her girl.

"Good to hear, Michaela. Now, we just have to see how it plays out. I mean it's just like you go in a store and a dude is robbing the cashier, but then comes outside and tells the cops he ain't do it, but he got 10 stacks in his pocket. I guess somebody's gonna need to be calling *a Lawyer*. Patience is a virtue. People aren't always doing what they say they doing, not always who they say they are or what you think they are."

"Mizz, I don't understand you sometimes. I mean, where do you come up with these ignorant analogies? I'm getting off the phone. Talk to you later." She hung up without waiting to hear him say goodbye. She was starting to wonder about the true nature of Mizz and her relationship with him.

That morning instead of going to school, Petey headed to the station to update the lieutenant about the case and possible cultivation of an informant, meaning Tess. Tess, he thought, would lead him right to the inner circle or give him the information he needed without too much effort on his part and if he played his cards right, he would

"Pleasure without conscience
Knowledge without character
Life can change with a single drop."

get wit Ms. Beautiful in the process. Undercover work could have some benefits. He walked right into the lieutenant's office with a crazy heathcliff grin on his face.

"Hey, Petey," said a surprised lieutenant, "I didn't expect to see you. Aren't you supposed to be in school?"

"Hey, Lou, chill out brotha'," Petey said sounding as smooth as he felt.

The lieutenant's blood pressure rose immediately, "No clown, you should have your cocky self in school doing your job. You sure better have a good excuse as to why you're here." He wasn't in the mood for any of Petey's bull, especially after that meeting with the squad. "Petey, you have any idea what these thugs are into yet?"

"Lou listen, I chilled wit' Tess last night, y'know, best friend of Michaela, Mizz's girl. It was crazy and she is hot, Lou." He sounded like a boy who just saw his first Melissa Ford centerfold.

"Oh really? Detective, do I need to remind you that you're dealing with high schoolers? Just how old is this girl? Just 'cuz you chilled with her last night, suddenly she's going to tell you everything she knows about Mizz and get you invited into their scores and deals?" The lieutenant couldn't believe he had to deal with this amateur.

"Relax Lou," Petey sat down and stretched, "she's eighteen and no disrespect but it sounds like you hating on a playa."

The lieutenant had to do all he could to not burst out laughing. Composed, he said, "Playa? Petey, I'm paraphrasing your words but, she wasn't exactly sweating you a month ago when you met her, remember?" He decided he had to bring this lovesick puppy back to reality. "Did you forget we're dealing with a genius? How you

"Pleasure without conscience
Knowledge without character
Life can change with a single drop."

know Mizz ain't on to you? The question is do you trust her?"

Petey took a moment to reflect. "Well," Petey began, "it is kinda funny, of course, I mean with the timing and all. The whole situation is unique so I guess anything is possible." The lieutenant sighed thinking that maybe Petey wasn't such a dummy after all, "Well at least you're realizing the possibilities."

Petey leaned forward in his chair, starting to grasp the uncomfortable possibility that Tess was just playing him. "So what you're saying here, you don't think I should believe a dang word that she is saying, Lou? Well, she can be a spy of some sort, but I do think I can learn more from her than she can from me."

"I didn't say you can't believe anything she says," answered the lieutenant. "Just pay real close attention, she might slip up. I see your point too. I just hope you know what the freak you're doing," warned the lieutenant.

Petey got to his feet and his cockiness returned. "Lou, sorry if the well is dry at your house and my faucet won't turn off. I don't know why this chick is on me right now but rest assured, I will find out. Good day and see you later, Lou!" Petey walked out of the office slamming the door behind him. He heard the lieutenant yelling something about 'he had one chance.' He didn't care as he had to head home to get ready for his date with Tess. He'd show the lieutenant who the smart one was. In fact, maybe he'd make lieutenant after he busted this case wide open.

Oh, What a Nite

Tess arrived at the museum a few minutes before the agreed upon time. She felt good about the way she

"Pleasure without conscience
Knowledge without character
Life can change with a single drop."

looked and knew that he would be sweating her big time. She had chosen a *True Religion* black micro miniskirt and black and white *True Religion* bustier top. Both were equally tight and form fitting and she was confident that she had the form he'd be feeling. Her *Manolo Blahnik* shoes were ridiculously expensive, but Tess was a hardcore chick and swag was 100%. Her threads were perfect for this outfit and this evening. She felt good about her progress so far and figured that she would all but seal the deal that night. She actually felt sorry for him as she saw her reflection in a display window, poor Petey didn't stand a chance. She carefully took a seat upon a bench near the entrance to the exhibits. After a minute or two, just as she took out her phone to check the time, she felt a touch upon her shoulder.

"Hey, what's up Tess? What's good with you sweetheart?" he said as she turned and looked up at him.

"Hi, Peter. How are you?" she said with a warm smile.

"Please, call me Petey. No one calls me Peter." He said remembering how he hated the name Peter.

Tess laughed, "That is, no one except me. I'll call you Peter. Do you want to know why?"

"Why?" he asked.

"'Cuz I can," she said as she stood up, presenting herself fully for Petey's viewing pleasure. From the expression on his face, Tess knew her attire's mission was a complete success.

"Wow," was the best Petey could muster as his eyes bugged out of his head. He was thinking that she was right, she could call him Peter...Petey...Pete...Pedro. Honestly, he'd answer her regardless of what she called him.

"Pleasure without conscience
Knowledge without character
Life can change with a single drop."

"Whew Tess, I love a girl who can keep it funky," Petey was finally able to formulate a sentence.

"I do and always have," Tess said with a wry smile.

"Yeah, my girlfriend is the same way," Petey blurted without thinking. As the words were leaving his lips he was trying to get them to stop, but it was too late. The only thing he did right was not looking like he realized he had just screwed up in a major way.

Tess looked stunned. "Girlfriend? Well Peter, I'm happy for her. You are a piece of work, you know that? I didn't know you had a girlfriend! All this time leading me on and making me think something else. You tried to play me. You nutty! Also you tried to be with me. You and your grandfather's wallet ol' condom. Oh, you are so lucky that we didn't hook up the other night. You're corny! Oh my God, you so lame? I hate whack negros, playing themselves!!" Fortunately, for him they were in a museum, otherwise, she really would have lost her cool.

"Nah, Tess be cool." He held up his hands stopping her rant. "Hold up, wait here, I see someone I know." He walked away to go chat with someone he knew from the force. Tess just stood there talking to herself about how this bum dude was trying to play her like he all fly or something.

Petey walked up to his friend, thankful for a minute to think about how to correct his little error, "Hey Sam, what's up guy? What are you doing here?"

Sam, totally ignoring Petey's questions asked, "Dang Petey, who is the hot chick? Yo dude! Dang, she is fine," Sam couldn't help but stare.

"It's a girl from my current undercover," Petey replied.

"Oh really? I heard about that big bust you're trying

"Pleasure without conscience
Knowledge without character
Life can change with a single drop."

to make. Speaking of big bust, dang, Petey," Sam was not a ladies' man, nor was he subtle. When he saw someone as hot as Tess, he just couldn't help himself.

"She's associated with the suspect in the case," Petey answered, trying to sound very official until he added, "but she is mighty fine alright."

"Whew, I would sell my soul to the devil to get some of that," remarked Sam.

Petey laughed. "You mad funny." Changing his tone, he said, "I just told her I have a chick, though."

"Why in God's name would you do some dumb thing like that?" Asked Sam incredulously.

Knowing he had made a mistake but wanting Sam to think otherwise, Petey said, "Relax Sam. Women want what other women have. A purse, jewelry or a man, doesn't matter. If one woman has it, there's another woman that wants it. Trust me."

Sam skeptically shook his head. "Ok whatever, dude. Have a good one. I'll see you later."

"Thanks, same to you," Petey replied.

As Petey walked back to the entrance, Tess sat there angry and ready for the night to end. She did, however, consider letting the night continue just long enough to get a free meal off this burger and turn it into a little game of who plays who. She took a deep breath as he sat down.

"Sorry 'bout that. He's an old neighbor of mine. I had to say hi." He looked at her choosing his next words carefully, "Wow, you look extra stunning tonight."

She swallowed. "Thanks. You look ok...I guess," she said with indifference.

He smiled. "Thanks beautiful. You want to walk around the museum for a bit then we can go and get

"Pleasure without conscience
Knowledge without character
Life can change with a single drop."

something to eat?" he suggested.

"Sure," she replied coldly.

Struggling between wanting to get away from this lame dude and keeping her word to Michaela and Mizz, Tess continued to walk around the museum contemplating her next move. They came to a piece of art that they both appreciated.

"Wow this stuff is amazing and wild," Petey said standing just a little too close for Tess's comfort.

"Some people think that this stuff isn't ordinary. Basically, they don't understand it. But it's our culture," she replied, taking a step closer to the exhibit and a step further from him.

"Wow this is awesome, very unusual," Petey said walking up to another exhibit.

"It's an elephant tusk," Tess said sounding annoyed. 'Who says that? Who thinks an elephant tusk is unusual? He's really irritating me now' Tess thought to herself.

"That's weird, I didn't know that Africans were into baseball?" Petey said, trying to be funny.

"What? No, it's an elephant tusk. Yeah, yeah, you real funny now," she said not sure what he was saying.

"I know. It was a joke," he explained.

"Please, that was dumb corny, Peter," she was feeling this burger less and less as the night continued, if that was possible. Finally, she had had enough and wanted the night to end as quickly as possible but she was hungry. "Can we get something to eat Peter? I'm hungry," she asked figuring she was due a free meal for putting up with this nutt.

"Sure, great idea babe. I know an excellent place not far from here. I'll drive and we can come back and get

"Pleasure without conscience
Knowledge without character
Life can change with a single drop."

your car after," he suggested.

Thinking there was no way in the world that was going to happen, she said, "No, that's ok, I'll just follow you. I don't want to leave my car here."

Disappointed at not being able to spend some alone time with Tess, but not wanting to upset her anymore, he relented. He carefully drove to the restaurant making sure she was able to stay close.

Meanwhile, Tess kept battling her angel and devil the whole way as there were a couple of instances where she was ready to turn and simply drive away.

They pulled into the parking lot and Petey met Tess at her car. "I come here quite often to clear my head," Petey said as they walked into the restaurant.

Once seated, they both began perusing the menu. Petey offering his opinion said, "The shrimp alfredo is the best on the menu as far as I'm concerned, but get whatever you want."

"I'm sorry, what were you saying?" Tess said distracted by her overwhelming desire not to be there anymore.

"I was saying I eat here a lot and I know you can't stop thinking about me," he smiled as he slipped that last part in.

She was reaching her breaking point. She sighed and said, "Again, Peter my bad. I'm not focused right now. My mind is elsewhere. Did you just say I can't stop thinking about you?" A look of disgust washed over her face as she added, "Never mind, can we just order?"

As the server approached their table, Petey's face brightened and he smiled. "Hi. How are you? I'll have the shrimp al...," Petey began.

"Pleasure without conscience
Knowledge without character
Life can change with a single drop."

"Oh no, not today, clown," Tess interrupted. She apologized to the server and asked her to come back in a few minutes.

Petey confused but still trying to make the best of an obviously souring situation, looked at Tess, "Ok baby, whatever you say," he said calmly. Stupidly, he asked, "Let me ask you something. Why do you think I'm so hot?"

Her eyes almost bugged out of her head. She was shocked that someone as corny as Petey could exist. She was convinced that sitting across from her was a true bozo. She had had enough. She was going to take the free meal but she was going to enjoy herself too.

"Peter," she began, "the only thing that's hot about you is your breath. For real, I think you swallowed a dead moth on the way over here. Did you have your window open?"

Embarrassed, he put his hand up to his mouth, breathed into it and took a whiff. "Dang, you can smell that? I was supposed to get my tooth fixed but they faking on the insurance," he hoped she hadn't heard that last part.

"They better hurry up before your tongue falls out your mouth," She said covering her nose.

Petey stood up. He needed to compose himself from the embarrassment and see if he could find some mints. "I'm sorry, Tess. I'm ahhh, ummm, I'm going to the bathroom to wash my hands. Don't miss me too much."

"I won't be missing that breath, that's for sure. And don't forget to brush that dead tongue of yours negro!!" She was laughing hard. "Oh and can you get the waitress back here too, thanks?" Tess was still chuckling as Petey walked away.

He was thinking that perhaps her laughing was just

"Pleasure without conscience
Knowledge without character
Life can change with a single drop."

teasing and everything was good. 'Wishful thinking,' he thought.

They ate their dinner in relative silence. Well Tess was silent as she just sat there dumbfounded at every word that came out of Petey's mouth. She had stopped listening to him a while ago but thought to herself how much he could talk. She was thinking how he must love to hear the sound of his voice. Amazing, since she couldn't stand hearing it. She kept looking at her phone, praying it would ring. Didn't matter who, just ring. It never did. Finally, the longest dinner in recorded history, at least in Tess's mind, had ended.

As they walked out to the parking lot, Petey remembered that Tess's car was here. He didn't want the evening to end so he suggested they go for a little drive. Once again, Tess was flabbergasted. 'How could this dude not get it?' she was asking herself. She not so politely declined his suggestion.

"I had a great time tonight and the food was delicious. I bet you taste that good, too. How about a lil' dessert?" Petey playfully asked, clearly not getting the strong 'not on your life' vibe that Tess had been sending out all evening.

Tess laughed at the ridiculous comment. "Petey, maybe you are being unrealistic about what's really in your pants other than your wallet. You a clown. Next time, I will make the reservations and don't forget to bring the breath mints."

"Why do you keep on dissing me with the breath jokes? I swear, I brushed my teeth today. It's this one bad tooth. I'm gonna get it fixed," he defended. Not one to give up, he asked, "Anyway can I get a kiss, a hug, some kind

"Pleasure without conscience
Knowledge without character
Life can change with a single drop."

affection?"

Was he for real, she thought? "You tripping. You
wanna be a player, go be with your bum girlfriend," Tess
snapped, exaggerating the word 'girlfriend' as sarcastically
as she could. "Here's a tip for you, though, gargle before
you come again wit' your all day morning breath, skunk
mouth," she said angrily as she turned and headed toward
her car.

"You want me to walk you to the car?" He asked
trying to extend the evening as much as possible.

"No no, like for real dude...I'm fine stinky mouth.
You can do me a favor, though," she said, setting Petey up
for a parting shot.

"Oh? What's that?" he asked excitedly.

"Take your fake Denzel wanna-be butt home and
brush that dead tooth," and with that she got into her car.

Petey laughed. "You love me, girl, hush up," he
said watching her hot body slink behind the wheel of her
car. He sighed, wishing that the night had gone better.
Replaying what she said, Petey's face lit up. 'Hey, wait a
minute,' he thought to himself, she said, "Next time, I will
make the reservations..." Smiling, Petey thought, 'Ohh so
there's going to be a next time.'

Unfortunately, his smile was short lived as he
realized that he had to report to the lieutenant about the
evening's events. He felt his stomach turn a little. He was
hoping it wasn't the alfredo sauce.

Tess got into her car. She couldn't wait to tell
Michaela all about the date from hell, but she had to get out
of the parking lot, as Petey was still hovering nearby. She
started the car and drove to a nearby gas station where she
pulled in and parked. Taking her phone out of her purse she

"Pleasure without conscience
Knowledge without character
Life can change with a single drop."

dialed Michaela's number. She still couldn't believe how bad it really had been. If it weren't for Michaela and Mizz, she would have walked out on that clown before dinner. The food wasn't even that good either. Finally, Michaela answered on the third ring.

"Hello, hey girl, you know I can't wait to hear the scoop," Michaela answered with devilish curiosity in her voice.

"Well booboo, only scoop you going to hear is that I'm not faking wit' that clown anymore. I love you and Mizz but girl, I just can't! I'm dead serious, for real," Tess said, the pain of the night still fresh in her mind.

"What that fool do to you? What happened?" Michaela sounded upset and she wanted details.

"No, nothing like that but girl, that dude is too corny, I swear. That negro tried to play me like I was some non-street educated chick or something, telling me 'bout how he got a girlfriend, like he fly or something."

"What! Get outta here. Now I'm heated. That bum got some nerve. He got a girlfriend? For real?" Michaela was absolutely surprised figuring Petey was too nice to be nutty like that.

"Girl, I wanted to smack that bum around. Then he stayed playing himself, acting like I wanted him. I regret even dealing wit' him! I love your boy Mizz, but this dude got it twisted. I can't. I'm sorry," Tess said apologetically.

"It's ok girl. That dude is mad nutty and dumb corny for playing you like that," Michaela said trying to console her friend.

"Girl, for real, he is a clown I swear! But girl listen, this is the ultimate. Oh my god, this joker's breath smelled like chitlens and project hallway piss," Tess said with a

"Pleasure without conscience
Knowledge without character
Life can change with a single drop."

wince, recalling how bad the smell had been.

Michaela laughed hard. "You crazy, what??? Breath smelled like that?" Michaela couldn't believe what she was hearing. "Y'know," Michaela began recalling, "something must be wrong wit' his stomach, for real. I knew a dude named Eric that used to pick me and my girls up. He was my flunky. Girl, it would be below zero and you still had to let the car windows down. I swear, he had dead worms or maggots in his stomach!!! Tess, this dude would yawn and flies would come out his mouth. Now you know he too old to have his mouth smelling like that."

Tess's stomach started turning from Michaela's story and Petey's breath. "You know what girl, you need to stop," Tess requested as she put a hand on her stomach. "Listen, I'm at a gas station and I need to get home," Tess said.

"Ok then, let me break the news to Mizz. I'll call you lata girlfriend," Michaela said.

"Ok girl, lata," Tess replied. She hung up the phone and headed home. She couldn't wait to be in her bed sound asleep and at last be able to forget about this disastrous night.

Still thinking about poor Tess, Michaela was dreading the call to Mizz that she knew she had to make. She dialed and waited for an answer.

"Hello, what's good girl? How are you doing tonight?" Mizz asked politely.

Michaela paused, noting that Mizz didn't jump right into the Tess-Petey situation like he had done in the past. She appreciated a man that actually listened.

"I'm good Mizz," she said with a smile. "How about yourself?" She figured she'd practice what she

"Pleasure without conscience
Knowledge without character
Life can change with a single drop."

preached.

"Good now that I'm talking to you," came the smooth response.

Michaela took a deep breath before continuing, "I hope you still feel that way after I tell you what I have to tell you. Bad news, babe, bad news," she said, awaiting an outburst.

"Aw man, dang what the…" Mizz did not like the sound of that.

"Babe, I'm just going to give it to you straight. Tess said the dude was mad corny and his breath smelled like 'Sugar Honey Ice Tea' and project hallway piss," explained Michaela. She painted a nasty mental picture.

"Dang, that's crazy, girl! Ewhhhh, that's nasty! But, for real, he does look like his face stinks," Mizz said with a chuckle. His tone turned serious as he continued, "Michaela, baby, is there any way she would keep talking to 'ol stank breath until we resolve the problem?"

"Babe, I'd rather not have to ask her to do that," Michaela said not wanting to put her friend through another hellish evening.

Mizz understandingly said, "It's cool. Stink breath? That's crazy. I guess we onto plan B then."

"Plan B Mizz?" she was confused. 'Was this some kind of military operation,' she thought to herself.

"Yeah Plan B. Long story," Mizz quietly responded. "Tell Tess good looks but the show must go on. It ain't over 'til the fire is put out."

"The fire is put out? Don't you mean until the fat lady sings?" she asked, not understanding what Mizz was saying.

"No, in this case, it's not over 'til the fire is put out,

"Pleasure without conscience
Knowledge without character
Life can change with a single drop."

and I mean the fire in his stank mouth," He laughed, trying to redirect his comment and keep Michaela from asking more questions.

Michaela laughed but it was a nervous laugh because she was kind of confused.

"It's all good. Tell Tess good looks. Send your girl my sincerest thanks and the job will get done. Babe, I gotta meet up with Razah. Baby, I'll holla at you later," Mizz said, trying to end the conversation to avoid more questions and to start work on Plan B with Razah.

"Ok babe," Michaela said, still very confused. "Hey Mizz, is everything ok with you?" she asked, her voice filled with concern.

"Everything is the way it's supposed to be," he responded, sounding as if he didn't have a care in the world. "I'm out babe, I'll hit you later, girl."

"Ok, baby." Michaela hung up feeling unsure about how the call had gone. She needed to talk to Tess. She was unsure what to think with what Mizz had said and she didn't know what Tess would think, either. It was still early so she called Tess to talk about her conversation with Mizz.

"Hey girl. What's up?" Tess answered, sounding wide-awake and much better since the previous conversation.

"Girl, for real, I'm feeling like I'm right in the middle of this with you, Petey and Mizz. Check it out," Michaela recounted the conversation to Tess, "When I told Mizz what was going on, he was like 'Tess can't stop talking to Petey 'cuz they have to resolve our problem'. And I said I didn't want to put you through that so he was like, 'No matter, the job will get done. Tell Tess good looks and thanks.' He was all cool and I still don't know

"Pleasure without conscience
Knowledge without character
Life can change with a single drop."

why he wanted you getting with Petey anyway. Tess, what the heck is going on?"

Tess sensed the worry in her friend's voice, and frankly she didn't know what to say, "For real, I'd say it's nothing to worry about so if I were you I wouldn't worry about it. You thinking too much and reading into something that don't need to be read into."

"Maybe you're right, Tess. Sorry to say, but he is a genius and he doesn't make mistakes. That's what scares me 'cuz I don't know what any of this is about. Dude doesn't like Petey, so what? So don't associate with him. Instead, he goes after the dude. But sorry to say Tess, he is a genius and he is never wrong. It's better to say he doesn't make mistakes. That's what scares me period!! A chocolate brother like Mizz always seems to have an objective and a target for his mastermind self. He even said something about having a Plan B. It's crazy. Mizz always gets what he wants, when and where he wants it, even who he wants. He conquers it all. Look he got me!"

"You complaining?" Tess asked, knowing the answer.

Sheepishly Michaela said, "No," as a smile crossed her lips. Tess always knew what to say to make her feel better. They chatted for a few more minutes, said their goodbyes and went to bed. Neither of them slept very well thinking about Mizz, Petey and the so-called problem.

The Next King

The next morning, after doing some soul searching, Petey concluded that his chances with Tess were pretty much zero. Between his screw up mentioning his girlfriend and his dead tooth breath, he realized there was no

"Pleasure without conscience
Knowledge without character
Life can change with a single drop."

recovering from the evening. Even *he* wasn't *that* good. No, he needed to find another avenue to get to Mizz and his fam.

Reviewing his options, Petey suddenly remembered meeting one of the crew at Mizz's birthday party. He recalled that the guy had given him a business card. He called himself an entrepreneur, if Petey recalled correctly. Who in their right mind calls themselves an entrepreneur when you're in the narcotics business? He remembered thinking the guy thought very highly of himself. Someone like that doesn't want to always be a worker bee. Someone like that wants to be the boss. Someone like that was someone that Petey could probably exploit.

He went to his desk and started going through his contacts file for this case. He pulled the card out of the file labeled, "Crew" and looked at the name on the card, Meneto. He remembered him now, a taller dude with a baldhead and a goatee. Definitely not one of the leaders but he seemed like a good option.

He had been putting off calling the lieutenant so far this morning. He figured that if he could work another angle, Lou would be impressed that he had a backup plan. He took a few minutes to figure out his angle with Meneto. Once he came up with an outline for a plan, he ran some dialogue through his mind. Satisfied, he dialed Meneto's number. When Meneto answered, Petey wasted no time. Meneto had recalled meeting Petey at the party. Petey simply told Meneto that he was impressed with him. He knew Meneto was a true businessman. He told him how he loved the idea of the entrepreneur business cards and quite simply, he wanted to discuss a potential business opportunity with Meneto. Petey pushed all the right buttons because Meneto agreed to a meeting without hesitation.

"Pleasure without conscience
Knowledge without character
Life can change with a single drop."

They met up a couple of hours later at a local park. As Petey approached the park, he saw Meneto waiting for him on one of the basketball courts. "It's nice to see you again Meneto." Petey said, walking up. "You're a busy man and I'm a busy man so let me get right to the point. I've talked to Mizz and he told me that you are in the inside but you not family. He made it perfectly clear that you are not family. Almost like he was playin' you. Listen, not to be in your business but I see how those dudes are living and you should be living the same way. Am I right?" Petey was on a roll and Meneto was listening to every word.

"Meneto, something ain't right wit' the picture. They're clocking paper, getting that money but, my 'G,' how you living? What if I told you that I can cut you a sweeter deal than them tight lame negros will ever give you. Enough where you can expand and start your own business, Petey said trying to play mind games.

Meneto's eyes widened, "Where did you just come from? I need this in my life rite now!! Trust, them jokers getting that bread you feel me. You're the dude with the business cards, Mr. Entrepreneur. You know what the score is and you're the dude I want to be in business wit'."

"I can guarantee you be living like Mizz and his fam. Making so much you could build your own empire. I'm not greedy. I take my lil' bit and you just roll with what you do, how you do," Petey could see by the look in Meneto's eyes that he had him. He hadn't let Meneto speak with the purpose of filling his head with big gold plated dollar signs. Now, Petey thought, let's see what he's got to say.

Meneto was definitely excited. "Dios Mio, where the freak did you just come from? This is just what I was

"Pleasure without conscience
Knowledge without character
Life can change with a single drop."

looking for, ése. Yeah, they getting the mucho dinero, feel me. They paying me straight but I know I ain't family but these dudes could be paying me more, comprende? You know how much a week those dudes pullin' down? Dios Mio. Trust, Petey that mastermind Mizz is a genius. That young dude smarter than Bill Gates. He like that Facebook dude smart!!" Petey just stood there taking mental notes.

Meneto looked around then continued, "Yo holmes, check this, last week they clocked 15 million," he paused for effect, "in...one...week. Mizz is a ghetto superstar, for real, and his way of thinking is so tight, he will never get caught. I swear he is an irregular hombre," Meneto said with a hint of admiration.

Petey had the information he needed. Now he just had to close the deal. "Meneto, forget those boys but if you wanna do business wit' me it's a 70/30 split. Oh an' you get the 70," Petey informed him, knowing that 70/30 would probably get Meneto doing backflips. "But you will only report to me and me only, you dig?" he instructed.

Smiling a sly smile, Meneto said, "Done deal, Holmes, give me a number." Meneto saw dollar signs in his head.

"Here you go," Petey scribbled his number on a scrap of paper.

"Oh yeah," Meneto said, taking the paper. "I will be in touch. Be cool," he said as he turned and walked away. Petey watched him leave, then headed to his car and called the lieutenant. Petey couldn't believe how easy this had been.

"Hello?" the lieutenant answered.

"These wanna be thug slick drug dealers are going down." Petey said proudly.

"Pleasure without conscience
Knowledge without character
Life can change with a single drop."

"Oh? What you got Petey?" asked the lieutenant, his interest definitely piqued.

"Lou, I'll email an update later. I gotta stay low so there will be no station visits for a while. Gotta go, check your email later," Petey hung up and smiled. He was getting so close that he could taste it.

After school and practice, Mizz met up with Razah at the pizza shop, to give him the lowdown on the Tess and Petey situation and discuss their next steps.

"What's good?" Razah said as Mizz entered the shop.

"Raz, same ol' same ol," Mizz said as they dapped each other.

"So what's poppin' with the situation?" Razah asked, not needing to explain what he meant by the 'situation.'

Chuckling, Mizz said, "Tess said the dude was whack, trying to act like a playa, G. Yo, the best part though was she said he had potty breath like baby dookie!!" Mizz was laughing now.

"Ewwhhh, cuz'," Razah winced at the thought. "No doubt 'cuz every time I see that nutt, he got that white stuff in the corners of his mouth. Dried up nasty saliva," Razah laughed.

They both laughed out loud.

Mizz, turning serious leaned forward toward Razah and started whispering, "Plan B. Tell Leak's girl, Chantress, I need to holla at her, for real. I don't like or trust Mr. Dookie Breath. Now this joker is priority, fam, feel me. I swear on everything, something is up wit' this clown. I have that gut feeling, dig? This is what I need, all access to his phones, crib, whip, bank accounts an' all that. All his

"Pleasure without conscience
Knowledge without character
Life can change with a single drop."

B.I., Razah. I'm getting to the bottom of this. I'm tired of playin'." Mizz had already formed the plan in his mind.

"I got you, don't worry," Razah replied, knowing that he didn't have to say it. It was understood that they had each other's backs at any time and through anything. "I'll get Jesse on that. It's his tech thing," informed Razah. "I'll holla at Chantress to be waitin' for your call, too."

"All good," Mizz replied, just as their pizza arrived. While enjoying their slices, they talked sports and enjoyed a break from business.

Meanwhile, Meneto spent the day thinking about Petey's earlier offer. He was very eager to get things started. Even though it had only been hours since his conversation with Petey, he could smell the paper and was getting hungrier and hungrier for it. He didn't want to seem too anxious, lest Petey think he's not cool, but Meneto took out Petey's number and dialed his cell anyway.

"Yo, what's good Meneto? How you?" Petey asked. He knew he had Meneto hooked but he hadn't expected a call this quickly.

"I'm cool, ése. I been thinking about what we talked about. I'm definitely going to be next king, feel me? I am in, so how soon can we get started? 'Cuz each day that goes by is a day we not making real money," Meneto tried to sound cool but Petey could tell he was thirsty.

"Soon, Meneto, soon. I need to set up a couple of things now that I know you're good. Just trust me and we'll be good." Petey reassured him. 'Like taking candy from a baby,' he thought to himself as he snapped his phone closed.

Later that evening, Petey sent an email to the lieutenant explaining the overall situation. He explained

"Pleasure without conscience
Knowledge without character
Life can change with a single drop."

how Tess was a dead end, without going into detail. He couldn't help but think that the lieutenant would probably read that and figure he had messed up somehow with Tess. This, of course was true. There were no worries for Petey as he outlined his plans for his new contact, Meneto. He was going to bust this case wide open. In the outline Petey explained Meneto, his role and how he'd get Meneto to fill in all of the details. He explained that he'd be off the grid for a couple of weeks but would email reports in when he could.

Plan

A couple of days had passed. Mizz was busy with his things and Razah with his. They'd text each other but weren't able to have any real conversations about the situation at hand. Mizz had spoken briefly with Chantress but just to quickly touch base. He needed the last couple of days to work through some ideas. As was obvious to everyone who knew him, Mizz was very thorough in his thought processes.

The next day on their way to school, Mizz and Razah were discussing their current situation. Nothing much had changed in the last couple of days as everyone was in a holding pattern until Mizz's plan could be finalized. One thing was for certain, with the recent chain of events, Mizz's thinking was beyond the present day situations. He felt it was time to discuss things beyond today.

"What's good wit' you this a.m.?" Mizz asked as they walked.

"Oh y'know, I'm chilling B. Just a lil' tired, that's all," Razah responded.

"Pleasure without conscience
Knowledge without character
Life can change with a single drop."

"Yeah, I feel ya. Listen up. I've been thinking, Bro. We've made millions. I mean serious, serious paper. Not like we ever gotta do anything again in our lifetime for money," Mizz said having been thinking about it all night.

"Yeah, Mizz, you right brotha. I was thinking the same the other day," Razah agreed.

Mizz continued, "I'm thinking about getting out the game and focusing on my career as a basketball player. You feel me? I think it's getting time to leave this other stuff alone. We only did it to get paper to hold us over 'til we get paid for what we really love to do."

Razah was nodding in agreement. "Word, brotha, I'm feeling you right now."

"Bro, for real what else do we have to prove especially while we on top? Let's not be like these other hustlers before us, Rayful Edmonds, Frank Lucas. You know, on and on the list goes. They wanted to wait and wait, then something popped off and then they were finished. All that's left is documentaries and stuff. We don't need to be like, or go out like that, feel me? We straight now," explained Mizz.

"I'm definitely feeling you. Mizz, what made you thinkin' like that?" asked Razah.

"Let me ask you, what's the difference between a winner and a loser?"

"This a trick question, Mizz? I dunno, what?" Razah laughed as he tried to think of the answer.

Mizz explained, "The loser will continue to hustle when he is on top 'til he gets caught. We are not losers. You know if you're up by a touchdown wit' a minute left in the game, why would you run or throw the ball to risk a fumble or interception? You just take a knee, right? Run

"Pleasure without conscience
Knowledge without character
Life can change with a single drop."

the clock out and secure the win. It's the same situation with us. Why risk it? We on top."

"Gotcha, gotcha," Razah nodded

"Just giving you something to think about. I'll holla at you after practice. In the meantime, hit Chantress up. See what's good wit' her,"

"No doubt, B. Holla at you later, word," confirmed Razah. As they walked into the school building, their guidance counselor and their respective coaches greeted them. Mizz and Razah gave a quick glance toward each other and swallowed hard as if thinking, "Oh oh."

"Gentlemen, we just wanted to touch base with the two of you since the school year will be over in a couple of months. We wanted to see what your plans were for the summer and if you needed any assistance in getting into any academic or sport programs that you may have interest in," the guidance counselor offered.

"Both of you will be juniors next year and as you know, the scouts have been hustling. Every scout I've spoken to has been asking questions about you both as in a package deal," Razah's football coach said excitedly.

"Yes, I've never seen anything like this before and I doubt many coaches have been approached about such a thing. We all just want to make sure that the both of you are focused, that's all. We are here to help you boys succeed in any way we can. Plus, in case you haven't noticed, we are very proud of the both of you," Mizz's basketball coach added.

Mizz spoke first. "We wanna succeed just as much as you want us to, please believe," he said with sincerity.

"We especially appreciate the support that you have for us. You are all a really big part of our success," Razah

"Pleasure without conscience
Knowledge without character
Life can change with a single drop."

added.

"Well boys, just so you know that you can come to us at any time. Seriously, consider your summer plans and come to any of us if you need assistance. Now, get a move on to class before you two are late," the guidance counselor said, reassured that the biggest names in the school's history were focused in the right direction for the present and their futures.

The boys headed down the hall and turned the corner out of sight of the counselor and coaches. Before parting ways and heading to class, they stopped. They both felt their hearts beating a little too fast.

"Yo! For sure, when I saw them all standing there I felt they was on to us B, word," Mizz whispered.

"I thought it was over for us, real talk." Razah agreed, his eyes still wide open.

Mizz took a deep breath. "Dang, we going to get wit' Chantress tonight and see what's really good. I can't be trippin' like this and don't know what's up, Dooke. I will holla lata." They heard the bell ring and they headed off to class. After an uneventful day and after practice Mizz and Razah met up with Chantress at their pizza joint. They gave her the 411 on the Petey situation and what they needed her to do. They felt like time was running out and they needed to get a handle on things sooner than later.

"Hey babygirl," Mizz said as he hugged Chantress.

"How you?" Razah asked as he hugged her next.

Mizz began, "Glad you could come out tonight. Here's the scoop. You know that Tess was chilling wit' Petey."

"Yeah, I seen that clown around. Why is she chilling wit' him?" she asked. "She too fly for him. She

"Pleasure without conscience
Knowledge without character
Life can change with a single drop."

need to be wit' me," She said with a wink and a smile. Chantress always had a thing for Tess and that was no secret. "I don't trust that cat for some reason," she added, her tone oozing with suspicion.

"So it ain't new news that she chilling wit' him. You seen them, right?" Mizz continued.

"Nah, it ain't new news. I seen them a few times," she responded.

"That's why we need your help," Razah said. "Something ain't right wit' that dude and we trying to figure it out."

"Yo, Chantress, I think he police," Mizz said hoping that she got his point. "I don't know why, I just do. Something about his walk, he walk like he gotta take a dookie. You know that police walk," Mizz joked.

Chantress laughed. "You mad stupid. So what you want me to do? Consider it done," she said without hesitation.

"Well like I said before, Tess was chilling wit' him. We asked Tess to chill wit' him so we could see what he is about. Like you, Tess is extra fly. What dude won't tell Tess his busi….Feel me," Mizz was saying as Chantress interrupted him.

"Ohhh, I knew there was a reason why she was chilling wit' a clown like that. It's all coming clear now. I'm sorry Mizz, go 'head and finish what you was saying."

Mizz continued. "Well she said she can't mess wit' the dude no more 'cuz he's unbearably extra corny. This is where you come in. We need you to just go wit' the flow and flirt wit' the dude. You need to make the clown feel wanted and seduce him. Get all the information you can. If it's none then it's none, but I know I'm right wit' my

"Pleasure without conscience
Knowledge without character
Life can change with a single drop."

instinct."

"I'm down," she said looking a little confused, "but one problem, I'm not Tess?"

"Aha!" Mizz said like the light bulb went on in his head, "Yes, you are Tess. Check it, body wise you two are practically twins, both fly and curvy in all the right places, 'bout the same height too. We doing the mask joint."

"The what?" Chantress asked, looking very confused.

"Little trick we learned when we were in California. Michaela is going to take pics of Tess from every angle. Razah will upload the photos on the pc and with the help of a little Hollywood magic, we are going to make a mask. We picked up some special effects details from that director dude, Chase."

"For real?" Chantress wasn't sure if she should be concerned or impressed. She knew Mizz well, so she was leaning toward impressed.

Mizz added, "I almost forgot, we need Michaela to record Tess speaking so we can get the audio of her. You two sound alike but with practice you'll sound just like her."

Definitely impressed, Chantress agreed with the plan, "Ok Mizz, whenever you ready I'll do it. I'm really curious too, now. I wanna know what's really good wit' the fool."

"No doubt sweetheart, it will be sooner than you think. Believe that, sooner than you think," Mizz said with determination.

The next day was a busy one for everyone involved in the plan. Michaela had taken all the photos of Tess as Mizz had requested and sent them to Razah. He in turn had located a local Hollywood-quality mask maker that

"Pleasure without conscience
Knowledge without character
Life can change with a single drop."

promised a twenty-four hour turn around once they received Tess's photos. He made sure they received the photos within a few minutes.

Next, Mizz hooked up her voice to the voice synthesizer, just like he had been shown by the director while out in Cali.

Then Chantress went to Tess's house so Tess could give Chantress the low down on Petey. They also went through Tess's closet since their tastes in clothes were radically different. Chantress had to borrow a few things. They both were laughing hysterically as Tess recounted the story of 'ol' stank breath' on their last date. Every now and again, Chantress thought to herself, 'Oh no, man. Why his breath stink like that?'

They all decided that they'd be ready for Thursday which gave them a couple of days more to prepare. Chantress was doing a fantastic job with getting Tess's voice and mannerisms down. If the mask was as good as what the company promised then there would be two Tess's running around the city.

Mizz decided that Chantress would call Petey on Wednesday to set up a date for Thursday. He wanted her to control the conversation including making the plans with him. That way, should anything go wrong, they could all be ready and in position to bail Chantress out if, she needed help.

When the mask arrived they did a fitting. Tess did Chantress's hair and makeup after Razah fit the mask on. Once she was made up and dressed, she practiced some lines mimicking Tess's voice. More than once during the process everyone stopped in amazement as they marveled at how Chantress had eerily become Tess.

"Pleasure without conscience
Knowledge without character
Life can change with a single drop."

After all of their preparation, Wednesday finally arrived and it was time to make the phone call. Surprisingly, Chantress seemed the least nervous of all. She was ready. Mizz compared Chantress's calmness to his on a game day. He was impressed. He and Razah listened as she called Petey to ask him out to chill on her cell's speaker phone.

Petey, looking at his phone was surprised to see whom it was calling him. He smiled and quickly answered in his playa voice, "Hey, what's up girl?"

"How you doing boy?" Chantress hoped she sounded just like Tess. "I was thinking about you and was just wondering if we can get together to catch up. I really miss you."

"Yeah girl, I know you miss me. I know you can't stop thinking about me either. I tell you what, I'll do you a favor. Meet me tomorrow night at seven at the mall in the food court. Don't be late, my time is limited," Petey's cockiness was over the top. The fact that 'Tess' called him blew up his ego to intolerable proportions.

"Ok, I would never be late for you boy. I can't wait to see you," she answered sweetly. "See you tomorrow night. Wear something loud so you stand out. I wouldn't want to go home with the wrong man by mistake, now would I? Like when you go to a masked ball and we all go as someone else..." and with that she hung up.

After she hung up, the room was silent for a moment as Mizz and Razah looked at each other, not believing what they just heard. Even though it didn't go exactly as planned with Petey choosing the location, it worked out because the mall was where Chantress was going to suggest for the meeting anyway. Aside from that, they were in business.

"Pleasure without conscience
Knowledge without character
Life can change with a single drop."

"Word! That fool is dumb corny," Mizz laughed. "Is he serious? Wow, he really needs to knock it off." He playing himself!!

"Ewhhhhh, word B, I see why Tess ain't wanna chill wit' him. He's a herb," agreed Razah.

"He is dumb lame, fake Don Juan, for real. Oh my God! Dang, he is loc (lack of class)." Chantress said.

"Step one is complete. Chantress, get a good night sleep 'cuz I think tomorrow night's gonna be whack," advised Mizz. They all said their goodbyes and each tried to get sleep. None were successful as they all fidgeted from excitement and nervousness.

Thursday afternoon was spent getting Chantress ready as they had practiced the day before. She had remarked how she now knew what it was like to be an actress getting ready for a role with the costume, hair and makeup. The group as a whole seemed relaxed, as they were all confident in what had to be done.

Mizz offered some last minute instructions, "Chantress, make this dumb dude feel wanted and boost his ego more 'cuz the nutt is really feeling himself. I hope he can walk through the door."

"I got you baby. Trust me," She looked in the mirror and could not believe how good she looked.

That night, Chantress found Petey waiting for her at the mall food court as planned. Immediately she started gaming him, "Hey Petey, good to see you. Wow boy, you look causally fine tonight. How have you been?" she said trying to act as she thought Tess would.

Upon seeing her, his face lit up, but his words tried to play off his excitement, "Well you look different, in a good way. You, of course had to step your game up being

"Pleasure without conscience
Knowledge without character
Life can change with a single drop."

next to me."

"I know, right." Chantress agreed while thinking how much of a clown this dude was.

Sitting in their car outside, Razah and Mizz listened in on the wire they had planted on Chantress. "You hear this dooke? Do you actually hear this nuttiness, B?" Mizz shook his head in disbelief.

"Mizz, word! It's a dang shame lame cats like him exist," Razah agreed nodding his head.

"Word that mutha ..." Mizz stopped short as they heard Chantress's voice coming through the speakers again.

"I always wanted to tell you this. When I first saw you, did you see me staring at you?" She said touching his arm.

"I can't say I did," Petey said honestly.

"Well I was. I knew you were new in school and you didn't have any friends." Chantress looked up at him playfully exuding as much sexiness as she could. "I knew I wanted to be your friend, from that moment on," she purred.

Petey smiled. "Well let's make up for lost time. You can definitely be my friend!" He said grinning like a chess cat.

Suddenly, Chantress's phone rang as planned. It was Mizz on the line pretending to be Tess's father. Chantress was to answer the phone and act startled by what she heard so that she could excuse herself. The thought being it would make Petey even more desirous and anxious to agree to see her again.

"Hello," she said answering the phone. After a brief pause she said, "Hi Daddy, what? ... Oh no! ... Is she OK?" Her facial expression was matching the tone of her voice. Petey looked at her intently showing equal concern.

"Pleasure without conscience
Knowledge without character
Life can change with a single drop."

"Oh, ok Daddy. I'll be right there," she said before hanging up.

"Oh Peter, I'm so sorry." Chantress sounded truly worried. "That was my pops. He says my moms is really sick and I need to get home to help him look after her," she said, lying through her teeth.

Disappointed, but understanding, Petey asked if she'd be alright and if she wanted him to drive her home. He didn't want her driving recklessly.

She smiled, "That's so sweet, no, I'll be fine but I have to go. Let's go to Mizz's game tomorrow night," she suggested. "I have two tickets, I know you're a fan. Let me make it up to you."

"Oh that would be great and the best part is I get to see you again," he smiled his corny playa smile. Just then he leaned in for a kiss but it was too late as she had already turned and was walking away.

"Bye, I'll see you tomorrow." she said while waving to him.

Like a sad puppy, he waved back and muttered, "Bye."

Dang! Mmm, mmm, mmm!

The season was almost finished with just one more conference game left before the state tournament started. If Mizz and his team finished strong with one last win, for the first time in the school's history, they would be a number one seed in the tournament.

It was early morning on game day and Mizz was going through his standard game day routine, which included a big breakfast. His phone began to ring. He

"Pleasure without conscience
Knowledge without character
Life can change with a single drop."

looked at the caller id and saw that it was Michaela. 'Wonder why she's calling so early in the morning?' he thought to himself before answering it. "Dang girl, you calling mad early. You thinking about me that much?"

"Hey baby, you know I was thinking about you. How can I not?" she said softly.

"All jokes aside. It's dumb early. You never call this early. You ok?" he asked with concern.

She swallowed hard. "I know you got a big game today and I really didn't wanna bother you wit' it right now, but I have to. Baby, I haven't gotten my period yet and I'm scared. I don't know what to do." Her voice quivering as she spoke.

Without thinking, Mizz exploded, "Word! Say Word! Michaela you know we used protection, feel me. Wow, you like all the rest of these gold diggers. Got your freaking hand out 'cuz you see a successful G and seeing dollars signs, ain't that some bull."

Shocked and hurt by his reaction, Michaela shot back, "Really Mizz, I wasn't saying anything. I was just letting you know I didn't get my period and I'm scared, I wasn't saying anything else," she said fighting back her tears, "Oh, but I see you insensitive to my feelings. You only care about Mizz. It's all good. I see a so-called G's real colors. You a black rotten... I'm not gonna go there but you know what? You are one sorry brother. You going to lay down wit' me, but you a selfish negro and don't wanna take care of your responsibility if you need to? I'm good enough to have sex wit' but not good enough to maybe have a family wit'. You're a black ignorant dirtball. Kick rocks Mizz! Kick rocks! You're a poor excuse for a brother." She yelled into the phone before hanging up.

"Pleasure without conscience
Knowledge without character
Life can change with a single drop."

During Michaela's tirade, Mizz realized he had reacted all wrong but was unable to interrupt her. As she finished he pleaded, "Nah, hold on baby Michaela! Michaela!" But it was too late, she was gone.

Michaela sat on her bed just staring at her phone and trying not to cry. She was in shock as to how Mizz had just spoken to her. She felt disrespected, used, abused, and violated. 'How could he be so insensitive?' She thought to herself as she buried her face into her pillow and began to sob.

A short time later, Razah looked at Mizz as they walked to school. He sensed by Mizz's body language that something was up.

"What's good? You got your head down, moping like your dog died or something. You nervous about the big game tonight? Dude, last conference game for the one seed, playing against that dude going to Georgia Tech? What's really good?" Razah commented, seemingly more excited than Mizz appeared to be.

"I know B, I know," Mizz responded not looking up.

"You don't seem into it at all today. You straight?" Razah was concerned now.

Mizz sighed. "I'm straight cuz'. I just got a lot on my mind, but I'm good. What's poppin' wit' Chantress?"

Razah responded flatly, "We know that they both coming to the game tonight." Razah peered at Mizz looking for some reaction.

"Word, word, ok, ok. Does she think he's opening up to her yet?" Mizz asked.

"Word, she's bad as a mutha. If I were him, I wouldn't tell her I'm too busy to get some of that." Razah laughed. "Real talk, tell her something. Anyway, you gotta

"Pleasure without conscience
Knowledge without character
Life can change with a single drop."

focus. Forget the business. You got a big game tonight," Razah suggested.

"True, true, you right," Mizz agreed. He paused, looked at Razah and with sincerity, he said, "My man, Razah! You keepin' my head leveled, no doubt Bro."

As the day progressed, Mizz was starting to feel better. He decided that he would deal with the Michaela situation after he took care of business on the court. After pregame warm-ups and just a few minutes before the tip off, he was sitting on the bench. He found himself unable to stop thinking about Michaela.

Razah, like every game time ritual, sat behind him on the bench so that they could chat, but this time Mizz still had the same grim look on his face from earlier today and wasn't talking.

Razah noticed the crew in the stands and pointed them out to Mizz. "There goes the crew as usual. And look, its Chantress and ol' doo doo mouth over there," Razah said with a smile, hoping he could get Mizz to smile too.

"I told you she is going hard B, word. Dang, where's Michaela?" Mizz asked looking all around the stands. Deep down inside he realized that she probably wouldn't be coming but he was holding onto hope.

Razah hesitated before answering, "Mizz, I haven't seen her. I haven't seen her B." Razah then realized that Mizz's down mood wasn't because he was nervous about the game but apparently something was up with Michaela. For a quick moment, Razah thought about calling her but then thought better of it. After all, he could be totally wrong and cause even more problems.

As the game began, Mizz continued looking around but there was still no sign of Michaela. He was unable to

"Pleasure without conscience
Knowledge without character
Life can change with a single drop."

focus on the game. Mizz was totally out of sync. He began yelling at his teammates, forcing shots and even turning the ball over. The coach, seeing that something was wrong with his star player, called a timeout.

"Timeout, please," the coach signaled to the ref. As the team approached the bench, he pulled Mizz towards him. "Mizz, what's wrong? Have a seat and just relax. You're trying to do too much and you're forcing plays. Sit here for a minute and get your mind right."

Mizz sat there with his head between his legs and his hands on his head. He knew what Michaela told him this morning was having a major effect upon him and his play. It's nothing the other team was doing, it was all him. After about five minutes, Mizz got his head together. He told the coach he was straight and got back into the game. He pushed his thoughts about Michaela, their situation and business to the back burners and he let the game come to him. It worked as he ended up with the game high forty-two points, twelve assists and seven rebounds. Even more important was that they won the game and for the first time in the school's history, secured a number one seed in the state tournament. The team, the coach and their fans went crazy as the final buzzer sounded. It was all-surreal to Mizz because even though they had won, he felt nothing. It was as if he was a spectator looking in from the outside. Michaela had returned to his front burner. Mizz decided to call Michaela. Not surprisingly, there was no answer.

Meanwhile, following the game, Petey and Chantress, as Tess, stood in the parking lot chatting about their friendship.

"Hey Peter, we've been chilling for a while now, I'm really feeling you." Chantress started to move in for the kill. "I just hope you feeling the same way about me, 'cuz it

"Pleasure without conscience
Knowledge without character
Life can change with a single drop."

won't be a good look if you not. I don't wanna get hurt," she said with sincerity.

"No, no, I understand baby. I don't wanna be deceitful. I've been thinking for a while especially since you and I been chilling real hard. I wanna be completely honest wit' you. I think I'm falling in love wit' you. It's crazy for a G like me to do that but it can be done." Petey said, caught up in what he thought was a score with Tess.

Chantress looked at him and smiled, thinking to herself that this lame dude should sit his corny butt down somewhere. Saying what she was thinking would not be a good idea, so she refrained and instead said, "Oh my God, really? I was hopin' you felt the same. Tell me more about yourself. Like, do you have any secrets or something that you want to trust me wit?" She had him hooked and knew that anything he had to hide he would tell her now. "I have a question for you since you know I'm giving you my heart," buttering him up she asked, "Like, I was wondering, how do you have a really hot whip and fly gear? I mean, you have no job."

He thought for a moment. "Ok, ok," he said, throwing all pretense out the door, "I have to confess something to you, only 'cuz you are right. I owe you at least some honesty from me, but, you have to always keep it real wit' me, Tess. I see a big future with us and I'm feeling you hard."

He paused and took a breath. He looked around the parking lot to make sure no one was within earshot. Quietly he bluntly said, "Tess, I'm an undercover cop. I'm telling you this 'cuz I don't want you to get caught up wit' Mizz, Razah and their goons. They're going down."

Mizz's instincts were on point, so, when Mizz said this

"Pleasure without conscience
Knowledge without character
Life can change with a single drop."

dude was sheisty, she believed it. The shock wasn't that he was a cop, the shock was the fact that this clown was just blurting it out. "What! Are you serious?" she laughed, "You're crazy, Peter! Mizz? Razah? Their goons? What does that mean?"

Undeterred by her laughter, he continued, "Tess, those two so-called role models are the biggest drug dealers in the tri-state, maybe the east coast. I have folders of their operation at my crib in a safe."

Still disbelieving what she was hearing, she challenged him, "You do not!"

"I most certainly do," he shot back, "For real, I'll even show you."

"Please do!" She said excitedly. "I gotta see this. This is too much, baby," she said, still in shock that this was going so easily. She wanted more information and figuring that while she was on a roll, she would just keep asking questions, "So, if you a cop, who do you live with?"

"Baby, I'm 22 years old. I have my own crib," he replied.

She couldn't believe he wasn't holding anything back. "Word, your secret is secure wit' me, trust!"

"I knew it would be, that's why I told you. So tell me about you?" he asked looking into her eyes.

Chantress thought she'd have a little more fun with him. "What? Don't you have a 'lil file on me?" she asked, pretending to sound insulted.

"The only file I have on you is right here," he replied, tapping his temple with his index finger.

She smiled. "Ok Peter," she began, "If you must know. Well, I'm a drug dealer and I help Mizz and Razah get money. I'm a runner." She answered honestly,

"Pleasure without conscience
Knowledge without character
Life can change with a single drop."

knowing that he wouldn't believe her, especially as Tess.

He laughed, "You silly, girl. They ain't smart enough to have a sweet girl like you selling no drugs for them. Nice try, I'm not that dumb."

'Oh, yes you are,' she thought to herself while smiling sweetly. Out loud she said, "Aww, I know baby, I was just playing," she laughed, "I'm just a student and not half as interesting as you. You a renegade. Smh, I'm really falling in love wit' you."

He opened the passenger door and motioned for her to get in. "Come on, I'll show you, then you'll believe me," he said.

"But my car?" she protested.

"It's ok, I'll bring you back, "he assured her. So she got in his car. Twenty minutes later they arrived at his crib.

"You have a nice place, booboo," Chantress said as she walked through the front door.

"Thanks sweetheart, maybe someday you can move in," he said as he took her hand and led her into his bedroom.

"Petey, nice bedroom but…" she began to say.

Sensing where she was going with what she was saying, he smiled and said, "Oh no baby, I'm not thinking like that. Relax and watch." He then reached under the bed and pulled out a safe, typed in a password and said his full name unlocking the voice-activated lock. The safe opened and Petey pulled out the folders he had mentioned earlier.

Impressed, Chantress said, "Man baby, that safe is banging. I know you get money, real money."

Cockily, Petey responded, "I do my best. Here are the folders I was telling you about. Look at all these people. You probably know most of them."

"Pleasure without conscience
Knowledge without character
Life can change with a single drop."

Chantress was making a mental list of all the folders labeled with the names of all of Mizz and Razah's people. He even had various photos of each individual as well. She was dumbfounded when Petey handed her a folder labeled 'Chantress.'

"Check her out. She is beautiful. Best as I can tell, she's a runner for those scumbags, stupid chick," Petey commented.

She held back her impulse to slap him upside his head. "Oh yeah, I do know her," she said after she gathered herself.

"All these people are going down," Petey informed her.

"Trust, Peter you really did your homework. Looks like you got everyone. I feel your gangsta for real," Chantress still was stroking his ego.

Looking at her he said, "See, so that's why I don't want you around with these wanna-be kingpins 'cuz when we come, trust me, we coming correct. All the evidence is right here and I'm the only one that has it. This is my case. This will be my promotion. Then you and me will be set for the future."

"Baby, thank you. I know you have concern for me. That's why I'm really feeling you. Oh booboo, it's late and I have a test in the morning. I don't want to go but can you bring me back to my car, please?" She had accomplished her mission and knew she had to get this info back to Mizz, pronto.

With an obvious look of disappointment on his face, he said, "Sure, anything for you baby." He didn't want to push her too fast.

As they were leaving, Chantress went for one last

"Pleasure without conscience
Knowledge without character
Life can change with a single drop."

bit of information. "I see you got two phones, "she remarked. "You definitely balling. I only have one number for you."

He got the hint, "That's my work phone. Of course, you can have the number. I know you won't give it out."

They left his crib and headed back to her car. As they pulled up next to her car in the now empty parking lot, Petey put his car in park. Chantress immediately opened the door and looked back at Petey. "Hey Peter, I had an amazing night, very unforgettable," she said with a knowing smile. "Can I call you tomorrow?"

"The pleasure was all mine and I'd be sad if you didn't call. Hold up Tess, before you leave, can I get a kiss or some kind of form of affection?" He sounded all thirsty.

"I really want to, really I do, but Peter, I am feeling you on a level I can't explain. I wanna make sure that this is right," Chantress said, trying not to gag at the thought of kissing him. "So I just wanna take things slow and do it the right way. You understand, don't you?" she asked, hoping he wouldn't push the issue. Her game was tight. She was playing him like Xbox!!

"I respect that, babe. I'll wait for your call tomorrow. Don't make me wait too long, though," he said with a smile.

"Thanks again for tonight and please believe you will be on my mind. Don't worry, I won't make you wait too long...for anything. Goodnight, babe," she said smiling as she was getting out of the car. She knew he'd wait until she drove off before he'd leave so she decided to drive to the nearest gas station. She couldn't wait to talk to Mizz and Razah. She waved as she pulled away and as she suspected, that's when he pulled away as well. She thought

"Pleasure without conscience
Knowledge without character
Life can change with a single drop."

that overall, even as corny as he was, Petey did act like a gentleman, even asking about her Mom when they first got to the game.

As soon as she was sure he wasn't following her, Chantress pulled into the first gas station she came across. Anxiously she called Razah. They needed to meet. He told her that he'd call Mizz and get back to her in minute. True to his word, Razah called her back. He told her to meet them at the spot.

She almost immediately agreed then she had a thought, "Razah, no, we need to meet someplace new. I'll explain later but let's meet at the diner by the train station, you know Tower Grill?"

"Yeah, I know it. Ok, we'll meet you there," he agreed.

Chantress arrived at the diner a short while later. She saw Mizz and Razah on the side of the road, both sporting looks of concern as they turned when they heard the car pull up. When she opened the door, Mizz said, "There are cameras in this diner. Let's walk to the park up the block." Mizz was always cautious. "We don't know if you were followed here."

The evening's events had caught up to her and she was starting to freak out a little. She took out a bottle of water she had in her purse and took a couple of sips and said, "Yo, you won't believe this." She was breathing hard. "Yo, I'm messed up right now." She had a little more water.

"What up?" Mizz asked in an obviously worried tone, looking all scary.

"Mizz you were right. That sneaky black snake is undercover," Chantress said as her eyes opened wide as if glaring at someone.

"Pleasure without conscience
Knowledge without character
Life can change with a single drop."

Mizz shook his head. He whistled and then mustered a "Mutha!" He knew something all along but to have it confirmed really brought it home.

"Mizz, ain't that crazy? What do we do now?" Razah asked shaking his head.

"I knew he was something. Smh! That is crazy. That cat was trying to infiltrate. Wow!" Mizz's mind was reeling. "Yo, like Santana said, 'I tried to be easy, I tried to be calm, breathe easy and don't seem easy.' That's why I'm always on top of my game ducking and weaving. But, this wall ain't coming down. Trust, we built this empire. Either lay or get laid down, ain't happening! Wow, if I was on some nutty stuff like Cam said, "I don't need a gun just a screw driver, two tires, two pliers, a wrench and a few wires." Mizz was listening to Dipset on the way over. He was talking crazy and thinking crazy. Quickly he was out of that mind set. "This is war now, get played or get taken down. Losing isn't an option!!"

Chantress said, "That clown knows everything, well almost. Get this though, crazy boy thinks we selling drugs, not the legit stuff we dealing," Chantress said.

Mizz held up his hand pausing Chantress in her tracks. He needed a quiet moment to wrap his head around the situation. After a minute, he looked at Chantress and asked her to recount for them everything that Petey and she did during and after the game, everything she saw and everything he said. Both he and Razah wanted every word, making mental notes of every detail Chantress described.

Chantress began with during the game. Nothing much, they exchanged idle chitchat but she was extra charming. She did comment to Mizz about his sloppy play in the first half. Mizz brushed it off saying it happens and

"Pleasure without conscience
Knowledge without character
Life can change with a single drop."

asked her to continue. She told them about Petey admitting he was undercover, he's twenty-two, has his own crib and a fly high-tech safe. Mizz and Razah were both intrigued about the safe.

"Too bad we don't know what's in the safe," Razah thought aloud.

Chantress looked at him and smiled, "Patience Homie, patience. I haven't gotten to the good parts yet."

Both leaned in closer as Chantress continued. She told them about the files on everyone, including the photos. That was the reason why she didn't want to meet at the spot, "...just in case ol' stinky breath undercover was staking out the joint."

"Good thinking," complimented Mizz.

Once she was done detailing the evening, they all realized that everyone wants a piece of what you have. Mizz had a certain sense of calm about everything. Razah knew this was a good sign, it meant that they would have a plan soon.

Chantress looked at her watch. It was mad late and she really did have to leave as she did have a test. She swore she would never take a Saturday morning class again. She apologized for having to leave but after the excellent job she had done, the boys would have none of her apologizing. They all agreed that Chantress would still chill with Petey until Petey was out of the picture. They all stood and Mizz and Razah each gave her a hug and complimented her on what she accomplished. They told her good night and in the ABC Park began formulating a plan.

"We're going to maneuver it, flip it and bounce it," Mizz said after Chantress left. Like Razah, his mind was already working on a plan. "That ignorant dude thinks he

"Pleasure without conscience
Knowledge without character
Life can change with a single drop."

smarter than us. He violated and tried to come into our circle." "That is crazy. Soon, he will feel me!! Trust Bro, don't worry I got this. This is personal! How can roaches live wit' themselves doing dirty stuff like that? That is unbelievable to me." Razah said. "I mean, I know he thinks he's doing his job but he playing himself. Dude needs to do his homework."

"Bro, don't be surprised. That's just how some people live, no loyalty to nothing. I bet he Republican," Mizz commented.

"Mizz, I know how you get down," Razah said, "Just so you know, I'm down for whatever we need to do."

"Word, that goes both ways, I got your back," Mizz returned the comment. "Listen, I'm not going to school tomorrow. I'm going to get one of Leak's girl's cars and follow the clown. Gonna do a little recon work. It's on now, for real. I'm dumb tired. I'll holla at you in the a.m."

"Yeah me too," They dapped each other up and headed home.

Mizz and Razah lay on their beds looking at the ceiling, wondering what had just happened. They were both disgusted at the recent turn of events. Both unable to sleep, they thought about their next moves and confident they would succeed.

Caught Slippin'

Early the next morning, Mizz set himself up on the roof of an abandoned building across the street from Petey's crib. He watched him through a telescope, focusing in on Petey's bedroom. He caught him opening the safe and pulling the paperwork out. He looked it over for a moment and put it back. Mizz was still in disbelief at

"Pleasure without conscience
Knowledge without character
Life can change with a single drop."

what was happening, but he had seen what he needed to see and bounced.

He went downstairs to the loaner car that Leak had lent him. It was an old beat up ragged thing, which fit Mizz's needs perfectly as it blended into the neighborhood like a chameleon. He was going to follow Petey for a while and see what was up with him. He slinked down in the seat and waited for Petey to come out.

This down time allowed him to reflect on the past couple of days. Crazy days they had been. His mind was a real mess and it felt like it was going a hundred miles an hour. Starting with how he screwed up Michaela's phone call, to the championship game and finally, this mess with Petey. It was at this precise moment he realized his one true passion of basketball was being neglected. His team won the league championship and he hadn't even had an opportunity to celebrate. He decided that things had to change but he had to take care of business first.

With that, and almost on cue, Petey exited from his building and got into his car. 'Ok negro, let's see what you're up to,' Mizz thought to himself as both cars eased into traffic. They traveled around the neighborhood with Mizz making mental notes of the locations that Petey slowed down and showed interest in. Just so happened those were the spots where The Black Enterprise did most of their local business. Mizz realized Chantress was right, Petey was following the money knowing more about the business than Mizz was comfortable with.

They headed up Fulton a ways to an area Mizz didn't know when Petey pulled over again. Mizz looked at the unfamiliar buildings and realized that one of them was a Police Precinct house. Mizz put a hand to the side of his

"Pleasure without conscience
Knowledge without character
Life can change with a single drop."

face as he passed Petey's car and carefully watched in his rearview mirror as he saw Petey exit his car and head toward the station. He had seen enough and headed back to the 'hood.

When he returned home Mizz went to his room and continued working on the 'Get Rich or Die Trying' operation, the 50 Cent motto. He came up with this motto because Mizz was fortunate enough to meet 50 at a boxing event he was promoting in Hartford, CT at the Convention Center. Since then, his level of respect for 50 had intensified with his presence and the way the homies and females from the hood embraced him. 50 was about the paper and so was Mizz. But thoughts of Michaela kept creeping in. He thought about calling her. He decided it wouldn't be a good idea, but he called her anyway.

"Hi Mizz," Her voice always sounded so sweet.

"Hello Michaela, what's up? How are you?" He said in an almost apologetic voice. He was more nervous now than in any basketball game he played.

"I have to let you know before you go any further. I'm not in the talking mood. I'm working on my speech for the conference."

"Dang, the speech ain't for a couple of weeks, why you doing that now? Anyway, look babe, I am so sorry I was being so unreasonable. No excuses, but I did have a lot on my mind so I wasn't being considerate of your feelings, belie..."

"...Mizz, thanks but for real, and I mean for real," she cut him off as she wanted the conversation to end, "for real Mizz, it's just that I'm not feeling you. Listen, I'm a just fall back for a minute. I will never forget you but I need my space. You play on a basketball team and there is

"Pleasure without conscience
Knowledge without character
Life can change with a single drop."

no 'I' in team, right? Take your own advice. It ain't always about Mizz. Hey, you took up enough of my time. Good luck on Saturday. Please do not call me, I'll call you. Have a wonderful day," Michaela hung up the phone feeling no remorse, leaving Mizz in definite 'wow' form and thinking to himself that this really wasn't his week. Then he caught himself. Instead of thinking how she was, he made it about him again. She was right, it's not always about Mizz. He was determined to work on that.

The rest of the day was a blur. Coach had given the team the day off from practice, which Mizz was regretting now. He needed something to distract him, if even for only a couple of hours. Instead, he locked himself up in his room and worked on what he was calling 'The 50 Plan.' He spoke with Razah about a couple of ideas but none of them seemed to be the right answer. It was getting late. Maybe a good night's sleep would help.

The next morning Mizz was still moping around. His sleep was fitful at best. He met up with Razah and Razah could tell Mizz was still down. With Michaela not at the game, Razah felt it was a safe assumption that there was trouble between Michaela and Mizz. He knew him well enough to know that when Mizz wanted to speak about it, he would. Razah wouldn't push the issue. Razah thought that maybe an alternate route to school would help, so he suggested it. Mizz half-heartedly agreed and off they went. They'd do that sometimes figuring a change of scenery might be helpful. Oddly enough, it was helpful, as they spotted Meneto and Petey walking into one of the project buildings. They looked at each other not believing what they just saw.

"Mizz, did you see that?" Razah asked. It was

"Pleasure without conscience
Knowledge without character
Life can change with a single drop."

rhetorical because Razah was fully aware Mizz saw what he saw.

"Yeah, what's really good wit' that, B?" Mizz thought aloud. "For now let's not worry about it. After school have Jesse tap his phone. Then we will see what's good," Mizz sounded more together than he felt.

"Bro, I see why you never trusted that bean Meneto anyway. Something is up for real. Something's gotta give," commented a determined Razah.

"Dude, they doing something," Mizz agreed. "They cutting some type of deal 'cuz Meneto thinks there's no bugs or anything inside there. What he don't know is that on the table there's a wireless camera with audio in the clock. Bust it. Call a meeting at the ABC Park. We will go in the back where the picnic tables are. No one knows about them unless you hustle. I will be there after practice. Holla back to confirm, and hey," Mizz snapped his fingers, "just family."

For the first time in a few days, Mizz was feeling it. Sure the problem with Michaela was there and yeah, Petey was still there, but Mizz was back, like the 4-5. To quote JayZ, "Back like Jordan wearing the 4-5. It ain't to play games wit you 'Jordan'." With Mizz being Mizz, those problems would be corrected. After practice Mizz headed straight to the park. Leak and the rest of the fam was already there waiting for him.

After Chantress's spy mission, Mizz and Razah had filled in the fam about Petey's undercover police activities with strict instructions not to tell anyone. So they proceeded to fill in some details. In Petey's presence, no one was to do any business and everyone had to be good about that. They saved the news about spotting Petey and

"Pleasure without conscience
Knowledge without character
Life can change with a single drop."

Meneto for last because that was the last piece they needed for 'The 50 Plan.'

"I won't keep you much longer. I know time is money and we all gotta jet, so here's the scenario. This weekend is a big weekend, especially for me. It's like an NBA all-star weekend, in case you didn't know the festivities, the championship game, everything that goes wit' it." He lowered his voice while looking right at Leak. Leak was like a father figure to Mizz, like Lil Wayne and Baby, Mizz spoke "Bro, yo, I know you didn't know this, your boy Meneto is infiltrated."

Leak's head snapped as he looked at Mizz, "He what?"

"Yeah, that slithery snake is in the process of cutting a side deal wit' that pig Petey and he think they going to get away wit' it. But Meneto don't know Petey is 5-0."

"I will never do anything to hurt you Bro, B. I brought the joker in and he treating me likes a two-dollar hooker. Yo, you know she ain't got no limits! My bad. I swear I gotta make this right. I'm going to smack that scumbag wit' a raw steak. He won't even be able to use ice cubes. He going to need a big piece of ham hock to put on this face, word," Leak said pounding his fist into his hand.

"Ewwh cuz', dang that sound like it going to hurt," Razah said cringing.

"Why? Why would you do some ghetto mess like that? Man, you ghetto Leak but all you going to do is bring more heat to us," Mizz cautioned. "Come on Leak, we business men. We off that gangster mess, B. We on that paper chase. Everyone is on the low for a while, so no dealing, no nothing. Say we dry 'cuz I'm focused on the

"Pleasure without conscience
Knowledge without character
Life can change with a single drop."

tournament and we ran out. We gotta wait. Then tell him the other connect you got is the white girl, feel me. You'll check things out, then if he bites, that's how we gonna get that trick."

"No doubt, I will tell him that 'cuz he know how I used to hustle and get it in," Leak said.

"Yeah no doubt and wit' Meneto knowing that I don't deal wit' that white girl, he'll feel that you and him are down. He'll just think you're making a side deal wit' him. Sell him two keys. No wait, better still, front him the stuff so there's no trace back to you. Then, outta respect, he'll tell you who he selling to. He is your man. I saw on the video feed from the hidden camera that Petey and Meneto talking about being the next king. Wait a couple days then he will come to you on the re-up and hit him wit' that."

"This dude is crazy. I can't believe this. He going to pay," Leak said, feeling Mizz's plan.

"What you can't believe? That he ain't family and you can't gratify insanity. He's a fool. You can't control what someone else thinks or do. You can only control yourself. What do you expect from a suburban Uncle Tom Republican tea party member? That type will tell his own mother to shut up, so why you think that grimy scum will respect you? He don't even respect his self. Bump it, everything is everything, just no sells. We all good on the plan. I gotta be out. With all this, I'm also working on my speech for the convention on Sunday. See y'all later," Mizz had other things on his mind. He headed home to work on his speech.

In his crib Petey was just chillin' but getting a little frustrated. He grabbed his cell and dialed Chantress'

"Pleasure without conscience
Knowledge without character
Life can change with a single drop."

number for the fifteenth time in two days. She had been ignoring his calls, but not wanting him to get suspicious, she finally picked up.

"Hi baby," she answered in her best Halle Berry impression 'Tess' voice.

"Oh hey," he said, actually surprised to hear her voice. "Wow, you finally answered my call. I don't get no calls from you or nothing, huh? Babe, you forgot about me? Dang," Petey said practically whining.

Although she eye rolled at his whiny comments sounding like Keith Sweat begging. She answered sweetly, "Babe, how can I forget you? What you think, I just say things 'cuz it sounds good. For real, I've been mad busy wit' a lot of homework. How you doin'? How's your investigation going, baby?"

"The investigation is crazy. I haven't seen anyone in the street or even heard anything. I know you didn't, but I gotta ask, did you say anything to anyone?" He asked reluctantly.

"Oh baby, I'm shocked you'd ask me something like that," Chantress said, pretending to be hurt.

"Oh no Tess, I knew you didn't but I just had to ask, y'know makin' sure you accidently didn't let something like that slip out," he said, regretting he even mentioned it. This woman loved him, she would never do anything like that.

"Baby, you're my 007, or should I say 00 negro, my undercover man. I'd never do anything to put you in a bad situation. Honestly, I thought it came to an end 'cuz I haven't seen or heard from them either. Even Michaela hasn't spoken about them. Plus you said you wanted me to stay away from them anyway, so I was listening to you,"

"Pleasure without conscience
Knowledge without character
Life can change with a single drop."

her stomach was almost turning at the thought of actually following this no backbone punk's instructions.

"That's what I'm talking about, a woman that's submissive," he commented. She could almost hear him grinning and nodding his big ol 'chauvinist head. "That's right though," he laughed. "Hold on babe, I gotta handle something. I will give you a call back," he said suddenly as he had an idea.

"Oh boo," she said pretending to be disappointed. "Ok, call me back. I'll miss you," she added as she hung up the phone. She could still not believe how corny he really was. She couldn't wait for his sorry butt to be out of the picture. Petey hung up and immediately called Meneto on the phone that Mizz and Razah had got tapped earlier.

"Yo Meneto," Petey said slightly anxious as Meneto answered.

"What's up amigo?" Meneto responded coolly.

"What the heck is going on? Where you dudes been hiding? I have been driving by the block, the spot and no one is around. What's good?" Petey asked in rapid fire.

"Yo, Petey, chill with the questions, dude. I know, I know. I'm not really sure. I was wondering the same thing. What I'm gonna do though is touch Leak. I wanna meet up wit' the dude," Meneto figured he'd clue Petey in on his plans. Petey sounded a little rattled and figured he didn't need his partner coming apart.

"Ok, holla at me after you get up wit' him, ASAP," instructed Petey. Meneto was right. Petey was getting nervous that something might be up but for totally different reasons than Meneto suspected. Petey had a Captain and a Lieutenant that were breathing down his neck. Petey wasn't sure how much longer he could stall them before they

"Pleasure without conscience
Knowledge without character
Life can change with a single drop."

pulled the plug on the whole operation or worse yet, send in someone else. If that happened, Petey would get no credit. He could say goodbye to any promotions he was hoping to get out of this.

"Relax amigo, I got you," Meneto hung up and immediately texted Leak. The text said that he wanted to meet Leak up by Tiny's in thirty minutes. Leak got the text and replied that it was cool and he would meet him there. Leak looked at his cell and read the text again. He smiled to himself. He had been waiting for this text. He sent a text to Mizz to give him a heads up that he was meeting Meneto and the plan was on. He'd give an update when he had something. Twenty minutes later, Leak sat in his car waiting for Meneto to arrive.

Meneto drove past Leak's car and pulled into a spot a few car lengths in front. As he got out of his car, he looked around making sure no one suspicious was lurking. Leak was watching him the whole time. He wanted to beat up this double crossing scumbag but he knew Mizz would be dumb mad. He took a deep breath to chill. Then he got out of his car and directed Meneto off to the side to meet.

Meneto quietly pounced, "Yo! Where y'all been at? Man, I'm hit. I need paper bad! The mortgage, cars, kids, school, all that. What's up mi amigo?"

"Bro, bro, chill, I know, I know. The last batch is gone and the only one that knows how to make it is you know who. He's mad busy right now and that ain't his focus," Leak said calmly. "All the paper you been makin' and you got nothin' stashed for a rainy day?"

"Rainy day? What? Yeah really, all my money is tied up in mutual funds and I'm waiting for the market to go up before I unload my stock portfolio," Meneto said

"Pleasure without conscience
Knowledge without character
Life can change with a single drop."

sarcastically. "Man, I've got obligations, like I told you. Leak, my friend, I knew this would happen! What am I going to do? I'm so hit. I'm dying over here," he said sounding sincere.

"You worry too much. You know I'm a hustler. I always got something poppin'. The question is, if you want in?" Leak had the baited hook right in front of the fish's mouth.

Meneto's eyes popped open, "Leak I told you I was hit. I will do anything. We straight."

Leak glared at him and shot back, "We? What you mean we? You got a buyer? You don't even know what's for sale. You doing side deals?" He asked suspiciously knowing the answer was yes.

"I have to. We have nothing," Meneto admitted.

Leak knew who that 'buyer' was but he had to ask, "It's cool, I understand. Anyway, who's your buyer? Can you trust him?"

"Petey is my buyer," Meneto answered.

"Word? That young dude got bread like that? Well bust it. I got that white girl, two keys, 28 a key. Can you dig it?" Leak saw by Meneto's expression that he was itching to deal. "Meneto, better yet brother, I'll front you the keys 'cuz we in a drought. You just hit me off when we back on. Cool?"

Meneto couldn't believe his ears, "You serious? I swear Leak, you my man. We be straight."

They dapped each other up and broke out. When he got to his car, Meneto called Petey and told him what's good and that they needed to meet. They agreed to meet on the track at the high school. Fifteen minutes later, Meneto stood anxiously waiting for Petey to arrive. He still

"Pleasure without conscience
Knowledge without character
Life can change with a single drop."

couldn't believe how cool Leak had been. He was sure Petey would feel the same.

"What's up Petey? How you amigo?" Meneto asked as Petey approached.

"Well it depends what you tell me first, then I can tell you how I'm feeling," Petey responded.

"Well that's on you and how you take it. Bottom line, it's getting the paper," Meneto winked as he rubbed his fingers together.

"You got that right. So what's the deal?" Petey was anxious to hear some details.

"Ok, this is the deal dude. It's drought you know, that's why you haven't seen them around in case you didn't know that. Dude mad busy and can't do anything and he is the only one that knows how to make it. You know who I'm talking 'bout. But here's the other option, Leak got two keys of that white girl, 28 a key," explained Meneto.

Petey's mind was racing. Without knowing it, Meneto had given him two big clues. Clues he needed. He had assumed that Mizz was the man but he had always thought he had some major supplier. From what Meneto was saying, Mizz was making the stuff. Until now he thought they were dealing coke or heroin. But when he said he's the only one that knows how to make it, made him wonder. So, he figured they were dealing in pills, but what kind, if pills at all? He was anxious to find out.

"Dang, that's high for each one," Petey said pretending to know what they were talking about.

"I told you it's a drought. Besides we flip it and make triple from that. Amigo, that's a quarter mill profit," Meneto said with a big grin.

Not believing what he was hearing and not

"Pleasure without conscience
Knowledge without character
Life can change with a single drop."

believing his luck, Petey returning the grin and said, "Whatever, I'm in. I'll get the money. Just tell me where and when you want to do this."

Meneto had bad intentions as he was planning to keep the money and the product. He was just beating Petey in the head with the price and was already working on a plan to eliminate him. He was a real dirtball ghetto crime lord, the kind that Mizz was trying to do away with. "Let's do it the night of the state championship game. No one will be around and we can swap out. We will be the next kings, understand Holmes? We will be getting that money and start our own real estate."

"You right, we will start wit' this. Where do you have in mind to swap?" Petey asked.

"Let me think a sec," Meneto answered, thinking of a secluded spot where no one would pay attention. "I got it. They was building a new lab off Burton Street. I'm running some wiring with Jesse for the computer system. I got the key to the joint."

"Cool, that's what it is then. We will holla later," They dapped each other up and headed their separate ways. Petey was already imagining the press conference with the Mayor and Police Commissioner awarding him with his promotion. He was thinking that a promotion to Lieutenant was not out of the question.

Meneto called Leak to tell him it's a done deal.

"What's good? Why you calling me? You know to text me," Leak answered sounding annoyed.

"I'm just letting you know it's a go. I told him to meet me at the new lab where I'm doing the wiring with Jesse. It's going down the night of the game."

"I can't meet you 'cuz I'll be at the game. I'll make

"Pleasure without conscience
Knowledge without character
Life can change with a single drop."

arrangements to have it there for you though," said Leak, "I'll call you that night at 6:45 and I'll tell you where to look."

"6:45? Ok, got it, I'll wait for your call. Leak, again, I got you. I really owe you," Meneto said almost with sincerity. He planned to repay Leak 'cuz as they say, (Maino) 'Hustle hard, death before dishonor.' That and if he didn't, Leak would take him out. "Amigo, you gotta take care of your bills. Handle that and when you on your feet, I know you got me. We straight. Holla at me. I'm out," and with that, Leak hung up. "Lata G," Meneto said as he hung up.

Leak called up Mizz after hanging up with Meneto and asked if they could meet as soon as possible. Leak was happy to be working under Mizz. Anyone else wouldn't have seen Petey coming and they would have all been facing serious charges. Looking at his watch, he realized he only had a short time before it was time to meet up with Mizz. As he arrived at the park, Mizz was already there eager to hear what Leak had to say. He could tell from Leak's smile that it was all good.

"Really Bro, what you all smiling about cuz'? It's all good?" asked Mizz.

"It's about to be a wrap. That clown ready. He is working wit' it hard body," Leak said sounding like his usual gangster self. "Trust, he mad thirsty!!"

"You told him to go to the fake drug lab, right?" Mizz confirmed.

"Yo Mizz, for real, *he* told *me* 'cuz he has the key to the lab already and it was secure. Remember he working with Jesse runnin' the computer wires and stuff?" Leak said.

"Heh, he think he callin' the shots. Ok, cuz', he

"Pleasure without conscience
Knowledge without character
Life can change with a single drop."

really 'bout to be dealt wit. There's scales and all types of drug paraphernalia in that spot, B. Word, they 'bout to be all set, trust that. Good for them maggots," Mizz said shaking his head and smiling.

"Everything is everything B, you can just chill now and get ready for your game cuz' and be focused. We got it over here. Family trust B, word. We will never let anything happen to you. Fam first. Should I say 'First Family' cuz we like Secret Service around you brother!" Leak said hoping to assure Mizz that he has nothing more to worry about.

"Good look, Leak! Good look. I love you fam, word, life," Mizz said as he tapped his heart with his fist.

"You and the family are my heart," Leak said returning the gesture. "Peace out cuz'." They bumped fists and left.

As he began walking home, Mizz felt revived from his talk with Leak. Even though he still had a lot on his plate, things were starting to look up. The missing pieces to his plan had just fallen into place.

He decided to call Razah and get him up to speed about the Petey situation.

"Yo Mizz, what's the good word?" Razah asked. He knew Mizz was feeling down so Razah was keeping things light trying to cheer up his best friend.

Mizz explained the conversation he just had with Leak. He gave Razah all the details about the upcoming meeting between that clown Petey and the traitor, Meneto. He then confirmed the details of the plan.

"Yeah Mizz, it all sounds good," Razah was relieved to hear that things might work themselves out.

"We good," Mizz said with a smile.

"Pleasure without conscience
Knowledge without character
Life can change with a single drop."

"No doubt," Razah agreed also smiling.

"Everything will be in place, Leak will take care of those things," Mizz confirmed.

"Leak is good fam," Razah said.

"Yeah, he get a lil' gangsta cuz he cares every now and then but you right, he is good fam. Holla lata," Mizz said as he hung up. Breathing a little easier, for the rest of the walk home he simply started to think about the upcoming championship game.

The Set Up

The night of the championship game arrived. Everything Mizz and his teammates worked for all season came down to this one game. The arena was abuzz and packed to the rafters with college scouts, NBA scouts, reporters, fans and anybody that was somebody. Razah looked up at the clock on the scoreboard as the teams came out of their locker rooms for pregame warm-ups. He got up and walked toward the back, tapped Leak and told him to make the call. Leak got up and walked out to the lobby.

"Hola," Meneto answered.

"Yo, it's me, you inside?" Leak whispered into the phone.

"Yeah," Meneto answered.

"A'ight, go to the back and look in the cabinet behind the sink. Also, Meneto, there's a briefcase wit' the joint, a little something special for you 'cuz you always looking out for me when times get rough."

Meneto followed his instructions and found the case.

Meanwhile, Razah made a call to Mizz, "Get busy. The game is starting in forty minutes. The teams just came out for warm-ups. Good luck," Razah told him, his

"Pleasure without conscience
Knowledge without character
Life can change with a single drop."

nervousness not evident.

"Thanks, B," Mizz said. "I'll be there before tip-off and make a grand entrance like Michael Jordan's comeback feel me. A'ight aha," Mizz hung up. He took a deep breath and dialed the phone.

"27th Precinct, Sergeant Wilson," Mizz heard the bored voice of a desk sergeant.

"Hello, may I please speak to Lieutenant Stevens? It's an emergency," Mizz sounded frazzled.

After a few moments he heard, "This is Lieutenant Stevens..."

Mizz cut him off and in a friendly voice he said, "Hello Lieutenant, how is your day going today?"

The lieutenant was in his office with three of his detectives. He replied, "I'm fine. Who is this?" The lieutenant then asked gruffly, "How can I help you? They told me it was an emergency." As usual, the lieutenant was short on patience. The detectives looked at the lieutenant, curious about the call.

Mizz's tone changed as he responded, "Who I am is not important. What is important, Lieutenant Stevens, is that you listen very carefully."

"This sounds like some bull," the lieutenant was not in the mood to deal with any prank calls. "You don't know who you're messing with..."

Mizz interrupted him and sternly yelled into the phone, "You need to be listening to me and stop with the tough guy act. Pay attention. You got stuff popping off and I'm gonna tell you what it is."

The lieutenant pointed to one of the other officers and told him to trace the call. A few seconds later the officer motioned to the lieutenant and then said the call was

"Pleasure without conscience
Knowledge without character
Life can change with a single drop."

coming from Petey's house. The lieutenant took a deep breath, as all of them were in suspense. His face was priceless, shaking his head "Ok, I got you. What's up? How can I be of assistance?"

"See Lieutenant, that's what I'm talkin' 'bout doggy. I knew we all can get along, just trust me! You must have traced the call and see I'm calling from one of your employee's houses. Go to your office and turn to Channel 8. I know you'll find this very interesting."

"Alright, give me a minute," Stevens responded. He quickly scribbled a note for one of the other officers to get someone from the IT department right away. He waited a moment pretending he was on his way to his desk. After a few seconds, he said, "Alright, what's the channel again?"

It's 8 dude. You'll see one of your undercovers doing a big drug transaction worth a little, no, a lot of money. And he ain't doing it for the WPD, he's doing it for himself. I'm not trying to tell you how to run your precinct but you should go down there to 34 Adam Street and handle that. Good day officer..." Mizz quickly hung up the phone and headed to his next destination.

The detectives were looking at the lieutenant and noticed that he looked as if he just saw a ghost. What the freak was that. "Lou, what's the matter?" one of them asked.

The lieutenant just pointed at the television screen on his desk. They gathered around the screen behind him.

"Is that...is that Petey?" Asked another detective as the four of them saw a nice clear picture of Petey and some other guy standing in what looked like a lab of some sort. After a few moments they realized what kind of lab it was.

"Yeah, what is that moron doing? This dude is

*"Pleasure without conscience
Knowledge without character
Life can change with a single drop."*

crazy!!! Wow, why? Man he is messed up!! He setting all of us back wit' this BS. I'm heading down there. Send a couple of units, silent, to meet me there. Abby, grab a unit and get to Petey's place. Earl, put the donut down!! Dang man, check that monitor. Hit me on my cell if you see any transaction before I get there. When the IT guy gets here, have him confirm this signal is legit and where it's originating. I don't want to be on some wild goose chase. Nobody calls Internal Affairs until we get to the bottom of this. And if any of you call Petey, your butt will be out the door. Got it?" The lieutenant barked the orders as steam was coming out of his ears. He grabbed his coat, shaking his head in disbelief that he may be on his way to arrest one of his own.

The lieutenant was on the phone with the detective watching the television screen. The detective said it seemed as if Petey knew the other guy and it looked like they were just two guys having a conversation. The detective expressed his curiosity as to what was in the briefcase that Petey was holding.

"Well if it is a drug deal, what do you think would be in the briefcase, Earl?" snapped the lieutenant. As he pulled up to the address, he saw the two police units parked out front of what looked to be an abandoned warehouse. He also saw Petey's car. There were no updates as Petey and the other guy seemed to be carrying on a conversation, reported the detective back at the station.

The lieutenant approached the four uniformed cops. He knew all four men and they knew him. He asked if anyone had gone in or out of the building since they got there. Their response was a negative. The lieutenant apprised them of the situation, stressing the fact that an

"Pleasure without conscience
Knowledge without character
Life can change with a single drop."

undercover was inside with one other man. Admitting that he wasn't totally clear on the details, he advised the officers to treat Petey as a suspect since he wasn't even sure if Petey's cover was still good with the other guy inside.

Petey had walked in just a couple of minutes or so before Mizz called the lieutenant. Obviously he hadn't seen any police units so as far as he was concerned no one was the wiser of his whereabouts or what he was about to do.

"Hola amigo," Petey said as he walked into the lab. The outside of the warehouse was a perfect cover for what obviously was a high production drug lab. Inside was well lit and everything looked so new.

"Hola Petey, what's happening?" Meneto was keeping it friendly so as not to raise Petey's suspicions.

"I couldn't help but notice that everything looks like new here. You guys must have a heckuva cleaning service," Petey chuckled.

Meneto laughed too, "No Holmes, this one isn't running yet. They expanding the operation, this is a new location." It was now time to conduct business. "So, what up Bro, you got the paper?" Meneto asked.

"Of course I do Bro," Petey answered picking up the briefcase he had brought in with him. "You got the product?"

"All here, baby." Meneto said sweeping his arm behind him showing Petey his own briefcase and setting it on the table. "Open the case," instructed Meneto.

Meneto looked at Petey, "Bro, your phone is ringing."

"What? My phone ain't ringing," he said trying to play it off. "Not ringing, it's buzzing," Meneto snapped. He was sensing something was up and told Petey, "Just answer

"Pleasure without conscience
Knowledge without character
Life can change with a single drop."

your phone."

"Ok, ok, hang on," Petey said as he dug out his phone. Without thinking, he answered, "Hello, Peter Martino."

'Who? Peter Martino? What the?' Meneto was thinking to himself. Something was definitely feeling wrong. Meneto reached into his coat and casually grabbed his piece. He had an uneasy feeling that he was being setup.

The detective monitoring the screen back at the station informed the lieutenant that Petey had opened his briefcase and the other guy was grinning. But the exchange hadn't been completed. The lieutenant was getting antsy and was about to give the signal to move in when the detective told him to hold up as it looked like Petey was now talking on his phone.

"I knew you'd call." Thinking it was Tess on the line calling him.

Mizz laughed and said, "This isn't Tess." Mizz had started recording Petey when he answered the phone. Then he said, "This is Mizzier Sanders."

Petey wasn't at all surprised, not yet realizing that he was talking to Mizz on his 'police' phone. "Hey Mizz, what's going on?"

Once Meneto heard it was Mizz, he relaxed the grip on his piece and calmed down a bit.

"Good luck at your game. I'll be there in a little while," Petey said, and he suddenly realized which phone he was holding. "Hmmm Mizz, I was wondering when you were going to make this call. How did you get this number?"

"You didn't actually think that I would let you get away wit' this, did you? Sucks huh! Emotional blackmail…She's fine isn't she?" Mizz said. "If you

"Pleasure without conscience
Knowledge without character
Life can change with a single drop."

thought I'd let you get away with it you're even stupider than I thought you were."

"If you wanna set up a meeting we can definitely do that. I got what you need," Petey said hoping Mizz would take the bait.

"Oh really? So where are you now?" Mizz asked, even though he knew exactly where the cop was.

"Oh, I'm at home chillin'. I'm leaving for the game in a few minutes," Petey said trying to sound relaxed.

"Knock it off Homie. I doubt that!!" Mizz snapped back. "If you were at home right now we'd be having this discussion face to face." With that, Mizz hung up the phone, smiling and wondering what Petey was thinking at that moment. Petey stood there in disbelief.

Meneto looked at him wondering what just happened!! He was thinking if he should just handle Petey!! "We cool, Holmes?" He asked Petey.

Just outside the door, the lieutenant was sick of waiting. 'Screw it,' he said to himself as he prepared to break down the door. The message from the precinct came over his phone, "Ok Lou, Petey's off the phone."

Mizz dug out the safe from under the bed. He typed in the passcode to the safe that Chantress spied when she was there. He then played the digital recording of Petey's voice he captured when Petey had answered his cellphone. He grabbed all the files, photos and notes that Chantress had talked about. Mizz then locked the safe and returned it to its place under the bed. As he left the apartment, he was very careful not to disturb anything else so when he closed the door behind him, the crib looked as if no one had been there.

As he exited the building to quickly make his way

"Pleasure without conscience
Knowledge without character
Life can change with a single drop."

to the game, he saw a squad car pull up in front of Petey's building. A weary smiled crossed his lips as he turned the corner and started sprinting toward the arena.

With guns drawn, the lieutenant gave the signal and one of the officers kicked the door in. Shouting, "Police, Police," the officers quickly surrounded the two men standing in the middle of the room, which appeared to be a drug factory. Both Petey and Meneto looked angry and dumbfounded. Seconds later the officers were yelling, "Freeze! Is there anyone else?"

Petey was thinking his whole undercover operation had been blown and Meneto was thinking that Petey had set him up. He almost pulled the trigger but upon seeing the blue uniforms with guns drawn, he thought better of it. Petey looked at his fellow officers and muttered, "What the…?"

'Ay Dios Mio,' Meneto said to himself as he slowly raised his hands.

"Lieutenant, the premises are secure," one of the officers informed the lieutenant.

"Thanks," he said to the officer before turning his attention to Petey. "You freeze, especially you, you dirty dirtball. I can't even put it into words, you punk. Well," the lieutenant pointed at Petey, "what you got to say for yourself? Petey, I gotta be honest with you, this doesn't look good. What are you doing with your butt in a drug lab obviously buying this crap? You didn't requisition department money so who's money is filling that briefcase?"

Petey was still confused as to how the lieutenant knew where he was, why he was here with back up and what he was being accused of. "Lou, what the heck are you doing here? I mean we got this scumbag but he's a nobody.

"Pleasure without conscience
Knowledge without character
Life can change with a single drop."

You blowin' my case over a nobody?"

Meneto just glared at him and sneered, "Petey, you two face punk! I should've capped your butt when I had the chance before. You nuthin' but a lowlife snitch? Or worse? A cop?"

The lieutenant's phone rang. He answered it and listened closely, all the while never taking his eyes off Petey.

"Lieutenant, we're here at Petey's house. It looks secure and quiet. There are no signs of forced entry. What do you want us to do?" the detective asked.

"Ok, thanks, Abby. Sit tight, I'll get back to you," the lieutenant hung up, disgusted with the situation. He then turned his attention to Petey. "Bro, you played yourself, the unit, and especially me, Petey. First, this ain't your case no more. Second, you think carefully before you say anything 'cuz I'm not sure you gonna be a cop anymore. Explain to me why I get a tip telling me you're a bad cop and then I find you in a lab with a briefcase full of money trying to buy what?" screamed the lieutenant.

"Lou," Petey wasn't sure where to start, "First, the briefcase isn't full of money, they're fake packs..."

Meneto screamed, "You loco, you wuz gonna try and rip me off???"

Petey paused to look at Meneto, then chose to ignore his comment. "Second, anybody telling you I'm a bad cop is trying to frame me," he added. Then Petey's eyes lit up, "Lou, it's Mizz Sanders. He's the one. He just called me from my place. He's there right now."

"Oh, he is, is he?" asked the lieutenant. "Just so happens that Abby is there with a couple of uniforms, so I guess you wouldn't mind if they bust the door down?"

"Pleasure without conscience
Knowledge without character
Life can change with a single drop."

"Really? Yeah Lou, then we can get that dirtball for B&E too," said Petey confidently.

"OK then," said the lieutenant as he called the detective at Petey's place. "Yeah Abby, go ahead and bust the door down. Heads up though, Petey claims Mizz Sanders is inside. I don't know if he'd be armed so proceed with caution."

"Roger that Lou," the detective responded. With that he motioned to the two cops that he was going to break the door down. One swift kick later, the three officers entered Petey's apartment, guns drawn as they proceeded to do a sweep through the residence. A minute later, Abby was back on the phone talking to the lieutenant. "Ok Lou, we did a full sweep. Nobody's here. Place was locked up and secure."

The lieutenant's furrowed brow was staring directly at Petey as he received the report from the detective. "Thanks Abby, sit tight," he ordered.

"Well Petey, seems like nobody was home," the lieutenant said sarcastically.

"Lou, I'm telling you he was there. He called me," Petey was starting to get nervous.

"Wait a minute. What time is it," the lieutenant asked rhetorically as he looked at his own watch. Realizing the time he said, "I'm pretty sure I know where Mizz Sanders is. He's not at your crib Petey. Tonight's the night of the championship game. I'm pretty sure he'd be there. Hang on."

The lieutenant called Earl, the detective watching the monitor in the lieutenant's office. "Detective Smith," the detective announced as he answered.

"Yeah Earl, it's me. Didn't Stan request tonight off

"Pleasure without conscience
Knowledge without character
Life can change with a single drop."

so he could go to the championship game?" asked the lieutenant.

"Ahhh, yeah Lou, he said something about his nephew was playing in the game," recalled Earl.

"Thanks, I'll talk to you later," said the lieutenant right before he hung up. He then went into his phonebook and dialed Detective Stan Kowalski's number.

Kowalski was just buying a soda and heading to his seat when his phone vibrated. He fished the phone out of his pocket and saw it was the lieutenant calling. 'It's my night off, what does he want?' the detective said to himself. For a brief moment he thought about not answering it but decided against that idea.

"Hey Lou, what's up?" He answered, trying to sound concerned and not irritated.

"Yeah Stan, listen, sorry to bother you. You at the championship game?" asked the lieutenant.

"Yeah, my nephew's playing...well he's riding the pine but he might get in," Stan responded, thinking the only way his nephew gets in would be if the rest of the team had a sudden case of food poisoning.

"Do me a favor Stan, you know that case that Petey's been working on?"

"Yeah, the supposed 'unknown what kind of drugs' drug case being led by Mizz Sanders?" Stan sarcastically asked, thinking back to that fiasco of a meeting Petey had pulled together.

"Yeah, Mizz Sanders, you got eyes on him?" questioned the lieutenant.

"Hang on, I'm just getting' back to my seat," as he was still shuffling with the crowd in the tunnel entrance before the Arena seating area. As he cleared the tunnel he

"Pleasure without conscience
Knowledge without character
Life can change with a single drop."

could see both teams were in the process of heading off the court after warm-ups. "No Lou, I don't see him but half the teams are back in the locker rooms," Stan reported.

"What about the other's that Petey mentioned, Razah, Leak, Chantress, Jesse, you see any of them?" pursued the lieutenant.

The detective started scanning the crowds, then he focused behind Mizz's bench. There, he spotted everyone the lieutenant had mentioned. "Yeah Lou, they're all here, behind the bench," Stan confirmed.

"Listen Stan, sorry to do this to you, but I need you to go down to the locker room and confirm Sanders is there," the lieutenant sounded apologetic.

"Sure Lou, tip-off's not for a few minutes anyway. I'll call you back," Stan replied and then hung up. He looked around at the crowd pouring in and decided to wait a minute otherwise he'd be like a salmon swimming upstream.

Turning his attention back to Petey, the lieutenant still didn't believe him. He looked at Meneto. "Ok, what's your name and what's your story?"

Meneto scowled, "My name is Meneto and I don't have to tell you pigs nuthin'. Bad 'nough I had to deal with this *fideo tonto*. I didn't do nuthin.'"

"Why are you here?" demanded the lieutenant.

Meneto had spent the last couple of minutes watching all the dynamics of what was going on. He realized Petey was an undercover cop, this suit was his boss who didn't believe anything Petey was saying and they were looking to bust Mizz for dealing drugs. All he had to do was come up with a way to walk out of here.

"Your boy here was looking to buy that," Meneto

"Pleasure without conscience
Knowledge without character
Life can change with a single drop."

said as he nodded his head in the direction of the briefcase. "I'll tell you more but we gotta talk deals," he said, playing the 'Let's-Make-A-Deal' card.

The lieutenant looked in the direction of the briefcase. He instructed one of the officers to grab it and bring it over. The officer did and placed it on the table. The lieutenant paused, looked at Petey, then he grabbed the briefcase and opened it. His face contorted into a puzzled expression.

"What the..." his voice trailed off. The officers gathered around the table as the lieutenant yelled, "Man!! Heroin, cocaine and money!! You jokers going underneath the jail for this. This whole time you were blaming the poor kids and you were the one buying and selling drugs. Petey!!!," screamed the lieutenant, "You better have darn good evidence at your house."

Stan had finally made his way down to the locker room. The crowds were unreal. Who'd think so many people would be interested in a high school basketball game. As he approached the locker room, he saw a kid standing in front of the locker room entrance door. "You one of the players?" he asked the kid.
"No, I'm one of the equipment managers," was the response.

"You know Mizz Sanders?" Stan asked.

"Well, yeah," answered the kid while thinking, 'duh, everybody knows Mizz.'

"He in there?" Stan just wanted to get confirmation and get back to his seat.

"Yeah, tip-off's in a few minutes. The whole team is in there," the kid answered sarcastically as he was starting to get annoyed with the questions.

"Pleasure without conscience
Knowledge without character
Life can change with a single drop."

"So you've seen him today, in the last few minutes?" Stan continued his line of questioning.

"Of cou..." the kid paused. He started thinking to himself. Had he seen Mizz? Now he wasn't sure. Obviously he did, didn't he? After all, it *is* the championship game. But he wasn't one hundred percent sure, so he went with a safe answer, "I think so."

Annoyed because now he'd actually have to go in and maybe miss the tip-off, Stan pulled out his badge and informed the kid he had to see Mizz Sanders. The kid wasn't sure what to do but figured he wasn't going to try and stop a cop.

"Let me get Coach," the kid said while turning to open the door.

"I'll follow you," the detective said while grabbing the door.

Mizz arrived at the arena as the crowds were entering. He dug for his student I.D. but kept his head low. He didn't want to be noticed outside just a few minutes before tip-off as that would raise some questions. Once he was inside he raced down to the locker rooms as quickly as he could. As he rounded the corner to the hallway where the locker room doors were, he spotted some guy talking to Al, one of the equipment managers. The guy looked all right until Mizz noticed his shoes. Hmmm, cop shoes. Keeping his head down and walking along the far wall, he hoped Al didn't notice him. Mizz made his way to the locker room exit door. Taking one last glance at Al and the cop, Mizz slipped inside.

Mizz noticed the coach and his assistants huddled in the office going over last minute strategy plans. His teammates were doing their normal pregame rituals,

"Pleasure without conscience
Knowledge without character
Life can change with a single drop."

whether it was listening to music, resting their eyes or reading the sports pages hoping someday they'd be in the headlines. Mizz simply pulled off the tracksuit he was wearing to reveal his uniform underneath. He quickly stashed the suit in his locker when AI came in followed by the cop.

"COACH!" Ant screamed, not realizing how much quieter it was in the locker rooms than out in the hall.

Startling everyone, they all looked up. The coach, seeing AI and some guy walking into the locker room, jumped up immediately not wanting any reporters or the like bothering his players.

Anthony Ireland, what's up and who's this?" the coach asked, calling AI by his full name outta frustration. Before Ant could answer, Stan pulled out his badge and introduced himself, "Detective Kowalski," he said, flashing his badge. "Sorry to bother you Coach, I just needed to know if Mizz Sanders was here?"

"Mizz?" asked the coach, "Why are the police looking for Mizz?" Then the coach called out, "Hey Mizz!"

Before the detective could answer, Mizz popped his head around the corner of the lockers and said, "Yeah Coach, you need me?" AI man, I'm focused, no autographs right now. Sorry, after the game I promise.

There was an awkward silence, and then the detective muttered something about a misunderstanding. He wished everyone luck, even though his nephew was playing for the other team, turned and left.

The coach, still with a puzzled expression on his face, turned to the team and said, "Alright guys, huddle up."

Once Kowalski got out of the locker room he dialed the lieutenant. After the lieutenant picked up, the detective

"Pleasure without conscience
Knowledge without character
Life can change with a single drop."

told him that he personally saw Mizz in the team's locker room getting ready for the game. "He even turned me down for an autograph," he laughed. The lieutenant thanked him, apologized for bothering him on his off time and told him to enjoy the game.

After the lieutenant hung up, he looked at Petey. He looked at the drugs and then back at Petey. "Petey, Sanders is at the game as I suspected. You're trying to buy drugs while ripping off a drug dealer and I see no end in sight to this case that you've supposedly been working on."

Petey became defensive, "Lou, I'm working this case for months now. All the evidence is safely secured at my house. I'll have this whole thing wrapped up in a couple of days now. I mean, look at where we are. This is it, Lou."

"Where we are is in a drug lab with you trying to buy... drugs? You got the evidence at your house?" asked the lieutenant.

"Yeah Lou, everything is there. We can go take a ride and I'll show you," Petey said hoping they could get out of this building.

"No Petey, Abby is there. Where's the evidence? I'll have him get it," instructed the lieutenant.

"It's in a safe under my bed. It's a combination and voice activated safe," stated Petey.

The lieutenant looked at him incredulously, "Voice activated? You think you're 007 now? This is what you're gonna do. You're gonna tell Abby the combination and then talk to your safe over my cellphone. I'm getting tired of playing around." The lieutenant looked tired. It had been a long day and he wasn't seeing it ending anytime soon.

The lieutenant called the detective at Petey's apartment. "Hey Abby, listen, Petey's got a safe under his

"Pleasure without conscience
Knowledge without character
Life can change with a single drop."

bed. He's gonna tell you the combo and then he's got to talk to it so you'll need to hold the phone to it... yeah I know, freakin' 007 spy stuff. Let me know when you find the safe." There was a short pause, and then the detective informed the lieutenant he had found it. The lieutenant handed the phone to Petey.

"Hey Abby, yeah the combo is 2216….. Ok, hold the phone to the mic pickup near the keypad….. Peter Martino," then Petey heard the familiar click of the safe opening. "Ok, grab all the stuff inside the safe. I guess we'll meet you down at the station."

"What's that Abby? The lieutenant? Sure, hang on," Petey said handing the phone to the lieutenant.

"Yeah Abby," said the lieutenant as he took the phone from Petey. After a long pause he said, "What?!? You sure? What?!?" As he listened, his stare at Petey became increasingly more intense. "Ok Abby, bag everything and cordon off the front door." Petey's head snapped up as he heard the last instruction from the lieutenant.

"Why are you taping up my house?" Petey demanded.

"Stop playing me, you bum," screamed the lieutenant. "You honestly think you were going to get away with it?"

"What are you talking about?" Petey yelled back, truly confused.

"Negro, they found your stash. Really Petey? Three keys of Heroin, two keys of Coke, three pounds of Weed, two scales. Before the lieutenant finished his phone rang again. It was Abby. "Lieutenant, that wasn't it. There is more here under the mattress. We got three silencers, two nines with

"Pleasure without conscience
Knowledge without character
Life can change with a single drop."

the serial numbers filed off, all guns loaded." Abby whistled, wondering what Petey's doing. The lieutenant hung up on Abby so disgusted that he couldn't hear anymore. He was stunned, walked up and got right in Petey's face. Looking at Petey he said, "You gotta be out your mind. Were you so far undercover that you switched sides or were you always a scumbag cop?" he asked as he motioned for the officers. "Cuff these two dirtbags and read them their rights."

"Petey, give me your badge," he said as he stepped back and put out his hand. "You going right where you belong, you sorry for nothing roach!!"

"What the? You talking about drugs at my crib? What you mean?" Petey couldn't believe that this was happening. "That ain't mine I swear!" he pleaded, "you going to do me like that."

At this moment, Meneto spoke up, "Ummm, 'scuse me, but what am I being arrested for? I didn't give him anything." Although, Meneto was well aware of what he did.

The lieutenant looked at him for a moment and then asked him, "Do you own this building?"

Meneto put his head down and mumbled, "No."

"Fine, then we'll start with trespassing and work our way from there," the lieutenant snapped. Looking at one of the other officers, he instructed him to thoroughly search Petey and Meneto's cars. Upon hearing that, the lieutenant got on the phone and called the detective monitoring the TV screen. "Earl, it's time to call Internal Affairs and Narcotics. Get them down here right away," he instructed.

The lieutenant looked at Petey one last time, shaking his head in shame. He quietly and deliberately said, "You make me sick." Looking at the officers, he instructed

"Pleasure without conscience
Knowledge without character
Life can change with a single drop."

them to, "Get these two out of my face."

As they were being led away, the lieutenant looked around at the drug lab. Why was it so clean he wondered? "Hey you, Meneto," he called out. Meneto turned and the lieutenant asked, "Why's this place so clean?"

"'Cuz it hasn't been used yet," Meneto responded.

So this is the official drug lab that those boys use?

Smiling, Meneto simply said, "I'm sure you got people that can tell you that."

Still on Top

Everyone was wondering where Mizz was cuz he hadn't shown up for warm-ups. The commentators played it up doing their best to add drama to the moment, and just like he had told Razah he would, Mizz made his grand entrance on to the court with just two minutes left before game time. The crowd went nuts. TV reporters compared it to when Michael Jordan played his first game back outta retirement. From the opening tipoff, Mizz was unstoppable. As many suspected, he proved that he was the best player not only on the court but across the nation. The other team had no answers on how to stop Mizz. When the fourth quarter ended, he had racked up fifty-five points, seventeen assists and fourteen rebounds, a career high and the best triple double of his young career. As fans poured onto the floor, their voices could be heard chanting his name, "Mizz! Mizz!! Mizz!!!" His team had won the state championship as all the experts expected.

Immediately, reporters swarmed Mizz to get a quick interview. Shouting to get his attention, various reporters were screaming his name. Once Mizz caught his breath, he faced the sea of cameras and microphones.

"Pleasure without conscience
Knowledge without character
Life can change with a single drop."

"You've won the championship as many expected you to after the season you've had. How do you feel?" asked one seasoned reporter.

Mizz paused to gather his thoughts. "First, I wanna thank God, then my family. Loyalty is key. I want to make one thing clear; someone very special to me recently told me that there is no 'I' in team. I know, I know, it's a cliché, but that's real talk. Especially with the journey we all have been through on and off the court. That's the truth," Mizz spoke humbly and from the heart.

At the award ceremony a few minutes later, the team was standing with the coaching staff on a raised platform. Everyone was smiling and waving to the crowd. Before awarding the championship trophy, the MVP trophy was awarded. There was no suspense as the league official announced, "The tournament MVP is awarded to … Mizzier Sanders." The crowd erupted as Mizz walked over to receive the trophy. He raised the trophy into the air while scanning the stands. He suddenly stopped when he saw her shining face, her smile glistening like a diamond in the sunlight. It was Michaela. Their eyes met. The moment was interrupted by the official's voice awarding the championship trophy and handing it to their coach.

Razah waited for the interviews and autograph signing to end so he could congratulate his best friend. "My G," he said hugging Mizz. "You did it. Like there was any doubt that you'd bring the chip here, first time in school history. We both on top of the world, G," Razah said proudly. "We gonna be on the cover of Sports Illustrated, for real. We came a long way from nothing to something, believe that, Bro," Razah was excited.

Mizz looked ponderous for a moment, considering

"Pleasure without conscience
Knowledge without character
Life can change with a single drop."

what Razah said. He agreed, "Word up, B. We been through it all and stuck together through it all. We stay humble but we are ready for anything Bro, word."

They paused for a moment. They each realized that separately they were a force, but together, they were unstoppable. It was one of those rare moments when true friends realized the importance of their friendship.

Changing the subject from this *Hallmark* moment, Mizz said with a smile, "Check it, B, I saw Michaela."

"Word? A'ight!" Razah, still unsure of Mizz and Michaela's status, said with a confused positiveness.

. Almost on cue, Michaela called Razah's phone. Razah handed Mizz the phone, "It's for you." He looked at Mizz and told him that he'd be right back. Mizz was confused about Razah's sudden departure until Razah nodded and smiled in Michaela's direction. He looked at the number and couldn't believe it. They hadn't spoken since their last encounter on the phone, which had ended badly.

"Hello," Yea'," said Mizz, "Hey girl," he said shyly.

"Hello Mizz. It was good seeing you tonight. You looked good," she said, referring to his game.

"Thanks. When I was accepting the MVP trophy I saw you in the stands. That was the best part of the whole night," he sincerely said.

Embarrassed, she said, "Thank you. I don't think that's entirely true." She sighed, "Mizz, let me keep this short 'cuz I know you want to spend time with your teammates and friends. I need to let you know that I'm going out of town with my parents, there's a family emergency. I'll be gone about a week. But, I will tell you what, we have the conference next week and we can chop it

"Pleasure without conscience
Knowledge without character
Life can change with a single drop."

up then and catch up wit' everything then. Real talk Mizz."

What he felt was genuine concern as he said, "I hope everything is well with your family. I will say a prayer for all of you. I'll be looking forward to you coming back. I agree, we do need to have a serious conversation. I've got some things I need to get off my chest. Michaela, just remember, you my girl."

"I should get going," Michaela said. "I miss you Mizz. I'll talk to you soon. Love you."
"I love you too," he told her.

Mizz, hung up the phone looking dumb happy, grinning from ear to ear.

He headed to the locker room to shower and get dressed. Afterward, he went looking for Razah. Even though the game had ended a while ago, there were still people milling about. He saw Razah near a concession stand talking to Leak. Mizz handed him the phone, cheesing and said, "Good looks Homie." They were watching one of the TVs off to the side hanging above from the rafter.

Leak said, "I cannot front, you are the dude, fam, ewh!! You was killing' B, word," as they dapped each other.

"Yeah, that's my G," Razah added. Looking at Mizz, he reported, "Check it, B, that dude Petey, he was twenty-six. Dumb old trying to get us got."

"Twenty-six? He told Chantress he was twenty-two! He dumb nutty for that. Where'd you get all that?" Mizz asked.

"Leak and I saw it on the TV. Breaking news and all. The kids here were going crazy hearing how old that fool was," Razah responded. "They all set. They hit for

"Pleasure without conscience
Knowledge without character
Life can change with a single drop."

what they got caught with buying, selling, intent to distribute, school zone and trespassing. Don't forget that stuff at Petey's house too. Smh, it's a Reynolds for them two. Wrap it up," Razah said while laughing, "You know what I mean?" he added with a wink.

"I told you forget them jokers, they got what they deserved, for real. I feel so relieved though. Real talk they both even stupider than I thought they were," Mizz said smiling.

"So what's good wit' shorty?" Razah asked referring to Michaela. He tried to hold out asking anything about the two of them but after seeing them tonight, he considered it a safe question.

"Ahh, we good. We gotta talk an' we will but she's got a family emergency. She's gonna be gone probably a week, so it'll have to wait," said Mizz.

"Sounds good. No worries, G, you two gonna get old together," encouraged Razah.

In the meantime, the boys headed over to the club to celebrate and chill wit the fam.

Mizz walked in the door first with Razah directly behind. As he turned to ask Razah why all the lights were off, all his fam and friends jumped out and yelled, "SURPRISE!!!" Mizz laughed and turned to look at Razah who only shrugged and smiled. Mizz looked around and saw his fam and true, true friends. He also noticed some very fine looking ladies mingling with the crew.

Leak approached Mizz and Razah from behind and put an arm around each of their shoulders, "Surprise my brothas, this is my lil' gift to you."

Leak answered with a wink. "It's all good. You guys deserve it. Hard work pays off." Mizz and Razah

"Pleasure without conscience
Knowledge without character
Life can change with a single drop."

mingled amongst everyone. Everyone was congratulating Mizz and offering their best wishes. After they observed the atmosphere and looked over the crowd, someone started chanting, "Speech, speech," and as the rest of the group joined in, Mizz raised his hands to quiet everyone. He didn't want to disappoint them so he decided to give them a few words of his appreciation.

"My friends, my fam, I'm glad and so very lucky to be sharing this time and opportunity with the people that care about me, love me, just as I care about and love you. My fam, you have been with me when I had nothing and now, we have a little something," he smiled as he paused, knowing that everyone knew they had more than a 'little something.' I'm proud we are together, safe and sound, feel me?" With that he was done.

Leak approached Mizz and looking at him he said, "Mizz, Homie, you always got some good and clever stuff to say. But I had a long day. I need to talk to you brother."

Mizz said, "Anything, what's up?"

Leak seemed to struggle, "I have been doing some self-evaluating, some hood soul searching since all of this went down."

"Real talk, why Bro?" Mizz questioned him.

"I know you always looked up to me while you were growing up," Leak began, "but after today I was just talking to myself. "It's like this," Leak sighed, "Dude like me, man... I love the game....I love the hustle!!! I feel like you and Razah, one of those ball players or somethin' .You know a brother got dough, I could leave the streets. But if I leave... the cars, the jewelry, the ladies, the hustle," balling his fists, "the streets still gonna love me man? I get love out here in Waterbury, Mizz." Sucking his teeth, "I done sold

"Pleasure without conscience
Knowledge without character
Life can change with a single drop."

coke and crack on these streets, dope, wet, dust, weed, heroin, meth, and pills. As long as fiends was filling it, a dude like me could hustle it. That's my thing, Mizz. Like your thing is ball... my thing is hustling."

Mizz responded, "Dang, Leak. A behavior that can't be taught, huh, Leak?"

"That's my gift in life." Leak paused for a moment while Mizz gave him his undivided attention. Then he shared, "But lil' Bro, that's my issue. I made my bed, I gotta lie in it. So for rite now I'm gonna relax and continue to enjoy life and especially my freedom. I just needed a minute to think. Now I'm a fall back and chill...good looking on hearing me out, love u Bro."

Mizz responded easily with, "Love you too, and no doubt, anything for you Leak!!"

"Appreciate you fam," Leak said with gratitude.
Mizz looked around and saw everyone enjoying themselves. He felt good knowing that he and Razah were able to be sharing this moment of joy, relishing in their accomplishments. Thanks to Razah and him, his fam would get to enjoy a better life, one that was afforded through their success. They could all enjoy the finer things in life.

New Life

Even though a week had passed, Mizz's fame had not subsided. At the convention, he was still posing for pictures, signing autographs and answering questions. He wasn't quite used to the notoriety but he certainly was beginning to enjoy it.

Even though he had spoken to Michaela on the phone over the past week, the conversations were more about her family emergency and light chitchat as neither

"Pleasure without conscience
Knowledge without character
Life can change with a single drop."

wanted to have the overdue deep conversation on the phone. He looked around trying to spy Michaela when finally he spotted her walking with Tess. As usual for these functions, Michaela was dressed to impress, wearing nothing but top label designers. She looked as if she had just stepped off the cover of a fashion magazine. Not wanting to miss his opportunity, he maneuvered his way through the crowd and headed over to them.

"Hey look, Michaela, it's Mr. Superstar. Can't nobody get close to Jordan," Tess said laughingly.

"Girl, you ain't lying. He definitely feelin' himself. He forgetting about us little people. You know how stars do," added Michaela. Now both girls were laughing.

"Ladies, ladies. You both need to stop, I'm standing right here and I can hear you," Mizz said jokingly. Whistling, he added, "Dang, you would think we was at a model shoot seeing how fine you two are looking. No need to ask how you been, I can see, DANG."

"Boy you crazy. I just wanted to say thanks for hooking me up wit' a drug dealer undercover cop! Nice Mizz, real nice. What I ever do to you? Hooking me up with ol' stank breath," Tess laughed, "that corny fake drug dealer. And I mean 'old' too. That boy was twenty-six!"

Mizz laughed, "Sorry girl. I didn't know he was a dealer. My bust, I also didn't know he had a dookie mouth either," he said laughing.

"It's all good babe. By the way, congrats on the chip, too," Tess said, still laughing about the whole Petey thing.

"Thank you girlfriend, felt great to win," he said. Turning to Michaela, "Girl, you know you need to stop. You know you my heart, so chill or is there something I

"Pleasure without conscience
Knowledge without character
Life can change with a single drop."

don't know?" he asked knowing that something was up but not sure what it was.

"Aww Mizz, you know I just joking baby, but we need to talk serious," she responded staring into his eyes.

"Of course, baby. We definitely will do that," he sincerely replied.

Sensing she was becoming the third wheel, Tess interjected, "I still can't believe that nutt Petey."

"I know right. Shame how you think you know people and you really don't, 'specially when they try and get in your circle," Mizz added.

"Mizz, I have a question. How you know he wasn't real? Babe, I'm from the street an' real recognize real and Petey was far from both, you digg?"

"I give you your props on that, for real, Mizz," Tess said. "You called him out from the start 'cuz he sure was a bum. I'm tellin' you, he was mad corny and wanted to be thorough wit' his ol' stink mouth." Tess then changed her tone to all sweet, "Anyways, where is your boy Mizz, chocolate?"

Word!! That's new news. "Tess, real talk, you ain't heard it from me, but my bro really feels you, y'know. I'm gonna set that up ASAP, feel me?" Mizz meant it too.

Michaela laughed, "You two are so funny but it's my turn to get it in playa. LOL, I've gotta give my speech. Tess, I'll holla at you later and Mizz, you an' me, don't forget that talk?"

"Ok, I be waiting on you. Good luck, girl," Mizz said as he gave her a quick wink.

"Thanks babe," she said. As she walked away, she was thinking that Mizz was being extra nice. She hoped he would be the same way when she told him what was

"Pleasure without conscience
Knowledge without character
Life can change with a single drop."

poppin, and didn't act up. She knew how he could be.

Michaela stood in the wing of the stage awaiting her introduction. She didn't think she was nervous but her stomach was bubbling. Michaela said to herself, 'I hope I don't have the BG's (bubble guts).' That could be more from her condition than her nerves. She waited patiently for her name to be called.

Razah eased into his seat next to Mizz and said, "What up?" Your wifey looks dumb good today!! "She does, right.

"Razahhhhhhh!" Mizz said mildly startled, "Why you late?"

"I was wit' shorty from the party. She is crazy, word! She got me open. I think I'm in love," Razah joked, as he leaned back tapping his heart with his hand.

"You sound mad nutty right now. I'm about to tell you something and you going to forget all about that chick dooke. Tess told me straight up that you amazing and chocolate, word," Mizz embellished a little.

"Yo cuz', word?" Razah excitedly asked. "You know I be dumb loving that girl. I want to get at that, word forever. You know what I mean?"

"Word, you ain't in love no more with the party girl?" Mizz laughed. "You mad nutty, clown!!"

"Party girl? What party girl?" Razah said pretending not to know what Mizz was talking about.

"True story. I can't believe she waited so long to say something Homie. Anyway, take it to the limit, word," advised Mizz.

"You know she's wifey material. Her pops own 7-Eleven's, slurpees, crazy chips and dip B, word," Razah said jokingly.

"Pleasure without conscience
Knowledge without character
Life can change with a single drop."

"You mad crazy," Mizz said grinning. Then the grin disappeared as Mizz got serious, "But for real, why Michaela telling me that we need to talk. I think she wanna quit me B, real talk."

"You're mad corny! She loves you boy. She didn't see you in a minute and she misses you a lot and she just wanna catch up and talk. Don't worry about it. You straight Homie, you good! Trust me dooke!" Razah was trying to ease his worries.

"Yeah I know, but before we got in here I was chopping it up with her in the lobby and I sensed she wasn't feeling me," Mizz expressed his concern.

"Yeah, you definitely wilding out. Listen G, we got all tied up in that Petey mess and with the b-ball tourney you were busy. Then she was gone for a week. Like I said, she just misses you, don't worry about it Homie, you good, trust me, She loves you," Razah said trying to ease Mizz's concerns again.

"I hope so. You right, you right," Mizz said, trying to sound convinced. "Oh, hold up, here she comes," he said to Razah as the emcee announced her name.

As Michaela crossed the stage making her way to the podium, Razah leaned over and whispered to Mizz, "Your wifey looking dumb good. Just had to tell you again."

Mesmerized, Mizz could only nod in agreement. Michaela stepped up to the microphone and did a quick little sound check before she began.

"Good evening everyone. First and foremost, I want to thank God, the Almighty, for waking me up and allowing me to be able to speak to you today. Also I wanna give a shout out to our president Mizzier for winning the most valuable player of the championship game and also

"Pleasure without conscience
Knowledge without character
Life can change with a single drop."

bringing home the first state championship in their school's history. Lastly, our president was voted the number 1 high school player in the world. Mizz, can you come up and say a few words?" The crowd roared as Mizz made his way up to the stage. "Michaela, thanks for that lovely introduction. It swept me off my feet. I wanna thank God first of all for giving me the strength and opportunity to make all of this possible. I wanna thank you, the fans, for your support and making it a positive journey for me to shine. I don't wanna take any more time from the lovely and beautiful Ms. Michaela, but again, thank you and I look forward to seeing you all again in the future." Michaela stepped back up to the podium stating, "Thank you and good luck."

Michaela's speech outlined having goals and how to achieve them, the importance of staying in school, the upcoming summer and the vitality of family, friends and loyalty. As she was finishing her closing remarks, she noticed Mizz getting up and heading toward the lobby. Upon thanking the audience, she headed off stage amidst thunderous applause. As she opened the stage door, she spotted Mizz standing outside, looking in. He waved to her and she went out to join him.

"Hey boy, trying to sneak out without talking to me," she charged.

"Of course not, girl you bugging," he replied. It's just really hot in there. Dang girl, you really worked that speech. You had my mind in a whole different place. Seriously, you made me proud to even know you, true story."

She blushed at his comment, "Thanks Mizz, all I do is try to touch peoples' hearts and minds and have them search their souls. Y'know, make them think."

"Pleasure without conscience
Knowledge without character
Life can change with a single drop."

"I feel you. Since you're into touching peoples' hearts and making them think, let me express what I'm thinking. I know things haven't been copacetic lately. We've had a lot of ups and downs recently. Please forgive my ignorance and my bull and whatever else I've done to make you not feel at ease," he said, pouring his heart out.

She laughed. "Wow, it's funny what you can say in a room full of hundreds of people that you can't say in front of one person. This past week I know we chatted a couple of times, but we weren't talking. Mizz, I never stopped thinking about you."

"Michaela, you're my heart. I want us to be close again," he said as he stepped a little closer.

"Really? Your timing is impeccable. You're the great Mizz, the number one everything. You get what you want, when and where you want it. Nothing is difficult for you," she snapped.

"Well, if getting you back isn't mission impossible, difficult is a walk in the park for me. I love you and there is nothing difficult about that," he said, still trying to smooth things over.

"Mizz, you always had game but I'm just not big on words these days. As they say, actions speak louder..." Michaela's voice trailed off.

"Ok, ok, I apologized once and I know I screwed up..." he began.

Michaela interrupted, "Dang right you screwed up. You hurt me, you played me and you did not consider my feelings. That day we talked on the phone, you acted like some dude who didn't even know me. Mizz how could you?"

"I know, I know and I'm dead serious. I miss you,

*"Pleasure without conscience
Knowledge without character
Life can change with a single drop."*

Michaela, and I never missed anyone before in my life and I miss you. I'm in love with you," his voice was almost pleading.

"Let me tell you something Mr. Mizz, everything is not always about you. Let me clarify, this isn't about your love. This isn't about your mind games, or your freaking 'G'. This is about you not being able to love me the way I deserve to be loved. That's what this is about!" she said trying to fight back the tears that were starting to well up.

"You think I'm just saying this to get cool points? What? I got nothing better to do but express myself to you," he said in frustration. He couldn't understand where he was going wrong.

"Ain't nobody say nothing 'bout cool points. Why you gotta make it about you again," she demanded.

"Why you acting like this?" Mizz asked genuinely confused about her reaction.

"What Mizz! Acting like what?" she snapped back.

"You're being all ghetto high post and acting like you don't know me," he lashed out.

She drew in a deep breath and gathered her thoughts, "I just finally realized Michaela has to lookout for Michaela 'cuz no one will lookout for her except her. You, I know you look out for yourself so I gotta do the same. So I gotta do me and you, Mr. Mizz, superstar, gotta do you. In other words, I have to take care of my business and I suggest you take care of yours."

Losing his temper, which he didn't want to do, he sternly said, "Look Michaela, I know you're feeling yourself right now. You getting scholarship offers and there's a lot of people wanting you to speak at their functions. You have amazing opportunities opening up for

"Pleasure without conscience
Knowledge without character
Life can change with a single drop."

you and I get that. You and I have fun together and we have great times. We are friends and companions as well as lovers."

"Mizz I don't want to argue with you. You could be right, but Mizz, for real, give me one reason why I should take you back, just one. One," she demanded, pointing her finger to emphasize 'one'. She glared at him awaiting an answer.

He stood there silent. He was so confused by her attitude that he couldn't decide what she would consider to be the right answer. Time seemed to stand still to him, but not to her, as she was not patient for a response.

"I thought so," she sneered. "You one good for nothing. Smh. You know that? You just as bad as that clown Petey, leading people on to think it all good and to find out you ain't who you're supposed to be. Sorry to bust your bubble Mizz, but I'm pregnant. Now I gotta get all nasty and ghetto, so you either going to stand up and be a man or be a deadbeat like the rest of these jokers around your hood 'cuz either way, I'm having this baby. Either you going to be a part of your baby's life or not?" She couldn't hold back the tears anymore. This isn't how she had wanted it to go.

"You're what?!?" Mizz wasn't sure he heard right.

"You heard me Mizz, I'm pregnant. So either you gonna stand up or you're not?" she demanded.

"For real? Michaela, why didn't you say that before?" he questioned. His face lit up like a light bulb being switched on. It was all making sense now.

"Remember when you were being a real wise guy? I wanted to talk to you and you wouldn't pay me any mind? I wanted to tell you then but you hurt me so badly with your

"Pleasure without conscience
Knowledge without character
Life can change with a single drop."

bad attitude. I decided to wait 'til I cooled down and think. There was no family emergency. I stayed with my aunt down in Baltimore so I could figure things out. That's when I decided I would have this baby with or without you and talk to you face to face about things."

"Oh Michaela, I'm so sorry," he replied with a heavy heart. "You are so right. I was a clown and now I totally understand where you're coming from. Of course, I laid down with you and that is my responsibility. I will take care of my seed wit' great respect. I love you Michaela. I will be the best father I can be. So how you feel about that?"

"Mizz, I'm scared," she said looking up at him, tears slowly rolling down her cheeks.

"I know baby, I know. I'm scared too. I also know that you and I can be the best parents ever," he said passionately as he wrapped his arms around her. She felt safe in his arms as they held the embrace for a moment.

She slowly stepped back and looked up at him again. The tears had stopped.

Michaela's tone changed, softened slightly, "Well, if it's a girl we going to name her Maliyah. I've decided that it's not going to be a boy, so I didn't think of anything." She smiled with a twinkle in her eye.

He smiled back. He was okay with all of this. This was the girl he loved and soon, he'd be a father.

Her smile disappeared as a look of concern washed over her face, "But, real talk Mizz, what are we going to do about money? I don't wanna struggle and I don't want our baby in that situation. I wanna know where our baby's next meal is coming from. Doctors, clothes, diapers…"

'Ahh, finally an easy one,' Mizz thought to himself. "I understand but trust me baby, money is not a problem.

"Pleasure without conscience
Knowledge without character
Life can change with a single drop."

We are straight for life. Trust me…for life," he emphasized. She looked at him puzzled. "Just don't ask questions," he added pulling her close to him again.

"I don't understand but I have to trust you," she said, realizing that dealing with this by herself over the past few weeks had made her exhausted.

"I have one question for you," he asked while gazing into her eyes, "Do you love me?"

"I told you, I'm scared. Please, don't hurt me again!" her eyes wide like that of an innocent child.

"Michaela, you are my life now. You, me and our baby. Our baby will have everything I never had. The most important thing our baby will have is love from both parents. This is not a game. Like you told me before, there is no "I" in team and we are a team. We are together, now and forever. I love you girl. You're the mother of our child. This is the best gift you can ever give me. I love you." He kissed her gently on her forehead.

Still not entirely convinced, she needed to hear the answers, "But, I wanna know if you and I don't work out, will you turn your back on your child? Will you leave her high and dry and be a dead beat? Will you just pay child support? I need to know these things so I can be prepared for everything, especially the worst."

"Michaela, no matter what happens between you and me, I will always be our baby's father. I will never leave her… or him… high and dry. I will never be a deadbeat dad and I will never be mailing you a check every week for child support. I will always be an active part of our child's life," he replied sincerely.

They stared into each other's eyes for a moment in silence. Michaela, after a moment considering what he said,

"Pleasure without conscience
Knowledge without character
Life can change with a single drop."

broke the silence, "Ok Mizz, I knew in my heart of hearts that you would do the right thing and be a man where our child was concerned. The answer to your question is yes, yes, I do love you. Baby, I want to make this work." She smiled a beautiful smile as she leaned in and kissed him. Things were better now. She wasn't going to face this alone. She had a superstar by her side to take care of her.

Their moment was interrupted as a voice called out, "Oh there you are Michaela, excuse me, oops sorry." It was the convention organizer. "I'm sorry, but they're ready for your Q&A session," she said apologetically realizing that she had interrupted a moment.

"Oh shoot," Michaela blurted, "I forgot about that. Oh no, how bad's my makeup?" fearing the worst from the tears.

Mizz turned her into the light, "No, you're fine, no streaks or anything."

'Thank goodness for waterproof mascara,' she thought to herself. Speaking to the organizer, Michaela told her, "I'll be right there. I just need to stop at the ladies' room."

"That's fine dear, I'll let them know you're on your way," the organizer responded, turning and heading back to the hall.

"I'm sorry," she said.

"No, it's fine. You go answer some questions and I'm going to look for Razah," he paused, "Is it ok to tell him?"

She smiled, "Of course, the baby is going to need a godfather anyway."

"More like Uncle Razah," Mizz joked. They both laughed at the thought.

"Pleasure without conscience
Knowledge without character
Life can change with a single drop."

Michaela and Mizz kissed one more time and each said, "I love you." She went back inside to find the nearest ladies' room.

Mizz stood there a moment reflecting upon what just happened. 'Wow. I'm going to be a father,' he thought to himself and he was truly happy with it. Now, he had to go find Razah and tell him the good news.

Mizz located Razah as he was chilling wit Tess. "Hey," he said as he approached them. "Umm, excuse me Tess, but I need to talk to Razah, it's kind of important," he excitedly said to her.

"Oh that's fine," she replied giving Mizz an all-knowing look. Of course, Michaela had already told Tess the baby news.

"Razah, we need to talk now," Mizz said tugging at Razah's arm.

Once outside Razah warned, "This better be important. I was on that, for real B."

"Yo, don't worry. It is important, Uncle Razah," Mizz said with a devilish grin.

"Uncle? What wrong wit' you? Too much of that convention punch? You sound nutty." Razah asked quizzically.

"Michaela just told me she's pregnant. I'm gonna be a dad," Mizz said proudly.

"Wow! Word? Say word," Razah was genuinely shocked. "And you said she wanted to quit you? Good thing you was right about the Petey situation 'cuz you sure read this one all wrong," Razah said laughing.

"Word, word," Mizz laughed too. "You are my man. You know what that means."

"Means I'm gonna be a godfather?" Razah wasn't

"Pleasure without conscience
Knowledge without character
Life can change with a single drop."

sure what Mizz was trying to say.

"Yeah, that too," Mizz started. "It also means that I'm not in the game. You remember what we talked about? Call an emergency meeting tomorrow. We were going to know when it's time to stop. Well, I'm done, I'm good. You good. We good. Between me and you, not counting the candy money, we have 100 million and wit' the candy money we have over 400 million between us and that's in a few month's time. We built an empire like we said we would. We knew the empire wouldn't last 'cuz nothing like that ever lasts. Razah, we don't have to be stupid. We on top and no one has a clue. Therefore, we need to stop while we are ahead. We will never spend this money in our lifetime, so we don't need more of it. Let's do something positive wit' it now. Real talk," Mizz explained, hoping Razah was on the same page.

"Ok, you right," Razah said nodding his head, fully aware that Mizz was right. They both knew this day would come.

"Again as Mizz emphasized, I need you to call a meeting for tomorrow night," Mizz instructed. "Tonight I'm going to spend time with my girl." Looking through the glass, Mizz spotted Tess. "Why don't you spend time with yours," he said, pointing Tess out to Razah.

Razah smiled, "Sounds like a plan, G."

The next evening everyone had arrived and was mingling amongst themselves. They were all wondering what was going on that an emergency meeting needed to be called. The Petey situation had been handled, but maybe there were new dangers.

Mizz was observing everyone. He noticed how they were wearing top of the line designer clothing, custom

"Pleasure without conscience
Knowledge without character
Life can change with a single drop."

made shoes, diamond rings, a royal amount of jewelry and fine leather gear probably imported from Italy. With pride he was thinking how he and Razah had done this. Their family, their friends, this group of struggling two-bit hustlers and them, together were able to build an empire, an empire where each of them could taste the good life.

His one true wish for this group was that after tonight's meeting none of them would go back to their old ways. He was hoping they would take the money they made and continue making something of themselves. Taking a deep breath he stood up to address them all. The low murmur in the room ceased as they all turned their attention to Mizz.

Mizz began speaking, "Thank you all for coming. I'm sorry for the late notice. I promise, I won't keep you long so you can get back to your families or whatever else you like to do. Let me say that I love each and every one of you. Together, because of our loyalties and our faith in one another, we made a lot of money."

The group exploded in applause and hollers as they agreed with Mizz, they did all make a lot of money.

Mizz continued after they quieted down, "It's with mixed emotions that I say this, but unfortunately, it's a wrap. We're done. It's all over, we all set wit this." The words hung in the air like a dense fog, everybody looking at one another with confused expressions upon their faces.

From the back of the room, Jesse spoke up, "What you talking 'bout Mizz? That Petey thing was just some bull. It was nothing but a speedbump. You handled it. There's no need to sweat it, Bro. We good, let's get that paper."

A few in the group expressed their agreement with

"Pleasure without conscience
Knowledge without character
Life can change with a single drop."

Jesse. While the others were still letting Mizz's words sink in. "Nah, for real, I'm serious. You are my fam and I'm telling you I'm done, I'm all set. Around this room, everyone you see is a millionaire at least ten times over. Our friend Petey provided us with a wake-up call. Word, if we keep going some of us will be caught and I don't want to see it. You know I have everyone's best interests in mind. To see any of you in trouble would mean that Razah and I failed. Neither of us can live with that." Razah shook his head in agreement.

Slowly Mizz could see their faces changing, from confusion and mild outrage to those of understanding and belief. They realized that Mizz had brought them into this situation for which they were eternally grateful. The words he spoke now were just as impassioned as they were when he presented the original ideas to them. They believed in him then, just as they would believe in him now. He truly was their great leader.

"We all have millions, more than we can ever spend in our lifetime, that's real talk. We had a heck of a run, no jail time and more importantly, no one dead. Yeah, we hustled, but we hustled legally and right. There is no need to go wrong now. There is no need to be greedy. The bottom line is for you to do what you want. I can't tell you what to do, word my fam, I can't be a part of it."

"As for me," he continued, "I received another wakeup call last night. Michaela told me she's pregnant. I'm going to be a father," he said beaming.

Applause and shouts of congratulations filled the room.

"Thank you, thank you," he said smiling and nodding. Then turning serious again, Mizz continued, "It

"Pleasure without conscience
Knowledge without character
Life can change with a single drop."

was a shock, for real. It made me realize that I want to see my child grow up. I can't do that if I'm dead or behind bars or some jealous fool caps me because of their greed. I can't risk that."

"So for me, it starts now. I have to do something constructive with my money. I have to build a future for my family, give my child the life I didn't have when I was growing up. I need to be that positive role model for my kid. I just don't wanna be known as Mizz the b-ball player. I wanna be known as my kid's dad and to be the best father a kid can have. I wanna be Mizz the hero and not Mizz the hustler. I don't want people to say, 'He was great on the court, but he's a loser in jail.' That's not me, fam. I hustled to live; I'm not living to hustle. I was fortunate to be able to make certain decisions and create my destiny. I want my kids to be able to do the same. And now," Mizz looked to Razah for support. Razah smiled and nodded as Mizz concluded, "it's time for you to create yours."

Epilogue

In the early morning hours, Mizz and Razah stood shoulder to shoulder watching in silence as the sun snuck up slowly on their city. The iconic skyline was flooded in streaming golden light as a curtain of haze draped itself against the clouds and skyscrapers as the sun's beams played along the sidewalk under their feet.

Anyone rushing by them would see two seemingly casual observers in the game of life, when in actuality; no two men were ever more serious players than these. While each was lost in his own thoughts, tight as they were and would prove to be for life, they confidently stared down the future together without so much as blinking. Between them,

"Pleasure without conscience
Knowledge without character
Life can change with a single drop."

they held one singular and binding thought: today, yes, they felt quite certain that today the sun, the city, and life itself, was shining on them, just for them, and it felt good.

THE END

"Pleasure without conscience
Knowledge without character
Life can change with a single drop."

Author's Note

What has this story taught us especially in the time, age and era that we live in? It has shown us that life is continuous. Its ignorance and intelligence, tragedy, deception, self-empowerment and self-destruction, the good times and the bad times, but what it all boils down to is what life decisions you make and what paths you take. In this game of life, nine out of ten times people choose greed, which then brings death and deception. In the blink of an eye, you can go from rags to riches. Loyalty and respect are the real keys to success. It is not money, power and respect. That ends up in even more money but also more problems. In the end, you control your own destiny. It is not your environment that controls the outcome of your life. No matter what you do or say, you still have to look at yourself in the mirror and face yourself and your decisions.

They say in this game that this is the life that you chose, no matter how long you been hustling, 5-10-15-20 years scrapping, struggling, scheming, lying, cheating, stealing, pimping, manipulating, begging, and sheistyness. When your run is done, what's left? Imprisonment? Death? Then what? A hole in the ground? You cannot take anything with you when you go. No cars, jewelry, money, nothing when you're six feet deep. Be real with yourself.

"Don't be a product of your environment. Be a product of your imagination." Michael Sanders

"Pleasure without conscience
Knowledge without character
Life can change with a single drop."

21239939R00154

Made in the USA
Middletown, DE
22 June 2015